Em

W9-BBR-913

1836

Encounter
the Light

Other Five Star titles
by Donna Fletcher Crow:

The Cambridge Chronicles:

Book One   A Gentle Calling
Book Two   Treasures of the Heart
Book Three   Where Love Begins

Encounter the Light

Donna Fletcher Crow

Five Star
Unity, Maine

Five Star Christian Fiction
Published in conjunction with Crossway Books,
a division of Good News Publishers.

Cover courtesy of Crossway Books.

July 1999
Standard Print Hardcover Edition.

Five Star Standard Print Christian Fiction Series.

The text of this edition is unabridged.

Set in 11 pt. Plantin by Al Chase.

Printed in the United States on permanent paper.

Library of Congress Cataloging in Publication Data

Crow, Donna Fletcher.
    Encounter the light / Donna Fletcher Crow.
      p.   cm.
    Includes bibliographical references (p. 253)
    ISBN 0-7862-1949-1 (hc : alk. paper)
    1. Great Britain — Social conditions — 19th century
Fiction. I. Title.
    [PS3553.R5872E47 1999]
    813´.54—dc21
                                                  99-25260

THANK YOU

To Dr. Randolph Lee, for consulting on corneal burns,

To Martin Craig for providing such a gracious tour of Newcastle and The Potteries.

THE CHARGE
OF THE LIGHT BRIGADE

Half a league, half a league,
Half a league onward,
All in the valley of Death
Rode the six hundred.
"Forward, the Light Brigade!
Charge for the guns!" he said:
Into the valley of Death
Rode the six hundred.

— Alfred, Lord Tennyson

One

This was the day. This day would live in history. The English would win their greatest victory of the Crimean War. And Lt. Richard Greyston would earn the glory he had yearned for all his life.

At least that was the plan. But now Greyston was required to sit—he and his fellow soldiers of the Light Brigade. Sit and eat eggs and biscuits and wait. As impatient as his master, the finely bred black stallion moved restlessly under Greyston, requiring Dick to adjust his position in the saddle.

Slowly, the chilly, misty autumn morning had turned into a day of extraordinary brilliance and clarity. Now as Greyston looked out on the long valley below the ridge of the Causeway Heights, the scene was lit more brilliantly than any London stage. The lines were sharply drawn—British, French, and Turks at the west end of the valley; Russians at the east.

Although it had been less than a year since Dick, bored to the screaming point by his reading at Cambridge, had persuaded his father to purchase him a commission in the 17th Lancers, he had already proven himself a ready and able officer at the Battle of Alma. And today would bring him the advancement that would secure his career.

Anticipation made his impatience all the sharper. The goal was there—at the far end of that long, narrow valley. The Russian redoubts. Once they were in English hands, the day would be won. And all those who participated would be heroes. Dick closed his eyes and heard the shouts, pictured the waving flags.

Suddenly real shouts sounded in the distance. His head jerked up, and he saw the Heavy Dragoons taking the field. Dick Greyston ground his teeth. He would win no glory sheltering on the side while this thin red line of Highlanders advanced on the enemy. It was all very well for the Scots to have their fun, but when was the Light Brigade to take up the sword? Did Lord Cardigan intend to keep them standing here forever like the wives, camp followers, and tourists on the heights above them?

Richard cracked a boiled egg against the hilt of his sword and peeled off the shell. Then, as his teeth bit into the firm, rich yolk, a miracle took place before his eyes. The vast horde of black-bear-hatted Russians bore down on the red-coated Dragoons. And the Highlanders held. A few hundred Scottish horsemen turned back the great gray mass of Russian cavalry. The watchers cheered wildly.

Now the order would come for the Lights. Greyston turned to look at his superior. Impotent rage showed on Captain Morris's face when the order to advance failed to come. The captain dug his spurs into his mount and jerked him round to face Lord Cardigan, commander of the Light Brigade. "Sir, permission to lead the 17th Lancers in pursuit?"

Greyston held his breath. This would be the moment. Securing the Dragoons' victory was an elementary tactic. Now. He gathered his reins and tensed his knees to spur Legend forward at the command.

"Permission denied." Cardigan's voice was controlled, his face red.

Richard dropped his reins in disbelief. What was Cardigan thinking? Stunned, Greyston watched while the Russian cavalry, which might have been swept from the fields of Balaclava—indeed from the entire Crimea—escaped. The soldiers muttered angrily to one another and cast dark glances at their commander. And before their very eyes, the Russians returned to the east end of the valley, taking possession of the embankments of English cannon along the way. The Dragoons' valiant victory was wasted.

Richard's expectations of glory withered in the October air. He took a biscuit out of his pack and handed it to the sergeant behind him. Jamie Coke nodded his carrot-red head.

Jamie took a fierce bite out of the hard biscuit. "I've had enough of this sitting around waiting for orders that never come. I'm going to take up the sporting life when I get back to England. Horse racing—that's the thing. Start a small stable with good stock. One winner can make you."

Richard nodded, but did not speak. They ate together in silent, raging frustration.

Growing warm in his blue tunic with its white-crossed front, Richard pulled off his hat to let the desert air blow through his blond hair. And then he sat up straighter on his horse. Something was happening. In a flurry of flying gravel Lord Raglan from his command post on the heights sent his aide-de-camp on a madcap plunge straight down the precipice. A few moments later the rider raced across the valley and arrived with his horse blown and sweating to thrust a sheet of paper toward Lord Lucan.

The desert breeze whipped the paper as Lucan read it through for the second time. Lord Lucan, cavalry commander, lowered the sheet. Sounds carried readily on the light, dry air, and Richard heard the anger in Lucan's voice as he turned on the courier. "Attack, sir? Attack what? What guns, sir?"

The mere aide-de-camp threw back his head and flung out his arm in a furious gesture as he cried in a loud voice, "There, my lord, is your enemy. There are the guns."

Richard could see Lucan's seething rage as he wheeled his

horse and relayed the orders to Lord Cardigan. Richard tossed away his final bite of egg and spurred Legend a few paces to the right to watch. The two commanders reputedly hated each other.

Cardigan brought down his sword in sharp military salute. "Certainly, sir, but allow me to point out to you that the Russians have a battery in the valley on our front and batteries and riflemen on both sides."

Lucan shrugged. "I know it. But Lord Raglan will have it. We have no choice but to obey."

Lord Cardigan saluted again and issued his orders. A single trumpet sounded. "The Brigade will advance. Walk, march, trot." Lord Cardigan's quiet voice showed no sign of excitement.

But Lt. Richard Greyston felt the surge of excitement around him. This was the moment for which all of the Light Brigade had waited. The 17th Lancers and the 13th Light Dragoons rode first. Nolan, who had carried the orders from Raglan, requested a place in line from his friend Captain Morris. The aide-de-camp fell in in front of Richard, who was now fourth in line.

The Brigade advanced with perfect precision. Lord Cardigan rode alone at the head, with the sun gleaming on the rich cherry and royal blue of his 11th Hussars uniform, splendid with fur, plumes, and gold lacings. He rode quietly at a trot, stiff and upright in the saddle, never once looking back.

As the Brigade moved forward down the long valley, a sudden hush fell over the battlefield. For a moment gunfire ceased. The silence was so profound that Richard could hear the jingle of bits and accoutrements from all six divisions of the Brigade. They were the finest light horsemen in Europe, drilled and disciplined to perfection. Bold by nature, they had been held in check for hours, burning to show what they could do. Now was their chance. Richard heard Coke behind him encouraging his horse.

Nothing existed for Richard except that moment. Frustrations of the past, dreams of the future vanished. And the high-spirited Legend needed no prodding.

They had advanced no more than fifty yards, however, when an extraordinary thing happened. Nolan suddenly shot from the line, his horse's hooves flinging turf in Legend's face. He galloped diagonally across the front.

Captain Morris shouted after his friend, "It won't do, Nolan! We've a long way to go. Hold steady!"

Nolan galloped madly ahead and crossed in front of Lord Cardigan—an unbelievable breach of military etiquette. Nolan turned in his saddle, shouted, and waved his sword as if he would address the Brigade—to turn them back—to countermand the orders he had carried.

At that moment the Russians opened fire. A shell fragment tore into Nolan's breast. It ripped open his fine blue uniform. The azure wool turned red as blood poured from the wound. The sword fell from his hand, but his right arm stayed erect. His body held rigid in the saddle. His horse wheeled and galloped back through the advancing Brigade. The gruesome specter was shoulder to shoulder with Richard when the stiff mouth suddenly opened. A strange and appalling cry burst forth. Richard felt his blood freeze at the unearthly howl. The horse ran on carrying the still-shrieking body.

Cardigan never looked around.

But Richard looked. To his right were the redoubts of English guns, which the Russians had captured. The Russians stood ready to meet the English attack. Surely at any moment Cardigan would give the order to wheel and attack. Surely this was their objective—to regain the captured English guns. But no order came. Cardigan rode straight on past the redoubts. It seemed that even the Russian infantry gave a gasp of surprise.

Richard looked ahead. He saw what apparently Nolan had seen and what, incredibly, Lord Cardigan did not see. Their small force of less than seven hundred men was trotting down the valley in perfect order into a three-sided battery of Russian cannon. They were to expose themselves to a cross-fire of the most deadly kind. And they had no possibility of replying. They were to charge a bank of loaded cannon armed only with swords.

Richard looked to each side. Cannon on the left. Cannon on the right. Cannon ahead. Backed by battalion upon battalion of Russian riflemen, battery upon battery of guns. There was no escape. No hope of victory. The only chance was to charge. To break through that wall of death before the cannon could be fired. Recharged. Fired again. And again. Instinctively Richard tensed to spur Legend.

But Cardigan restrained them. They were to advance with parade-ground perfection. "Steady, steady, the 17th Lancers," Cardigan called. They steadied while the guns boomed around them.

All Richard could see at the end of the valley toward which he rode was a white bank of smoke. From time to time great tongues of flame flashed through the smoke, marking the placement of the guns. Horses screamed. Men cried out. Then another flash. The Lancer to his left clutched his shoulder and pitched off his horse. Jamie Coke moved up to fill the space. A shell hit the plumed hat of the officer riding ahead. And not just the hat, but the head beneath. As each man or horse fell, the column swelled sideways to ride around him and then closed ranks again to resume their straight, steady lines.

Now they were in range of the guns at the end of the valley. Restraint was impossible. The line broke and plunged forward in a gallop. Mad to get to the enemy, Richard seethed. He vowed to take two Russians for each comrade who had fallen beside him. This was to be the sum of his glorious military career. But he would not sell his life cheaply.

Whistling bullets and crashing shells took their toll at every stride. Smoke stung Dick's nose. His eyes watered. Sweat poured down his face, momentarily blinding him. He leaned close to Legend's neck as the superb animal tore forward, the long black mane whipping in Dick's face. The cheers and battle yells of the charging troopers behind and ahead rang in his ears as loudly as the repeated roar of the guns. And then the cheers changed to death cries. Men and horses fell screaming.

Now Richard and those still advancing faced a new horror —riding over the bodies of their fallen comrades—and worst of all, those not yet dead. Richard swung sharply left, barely missing a fellow Lancer attempting to crawl to safety. The ground was so thickly strewn with wounded men it seemed there was no place to turn Legend. He swung to the right to avoid a billow of smoke. It was a terrible mistake. Through the haze the first Lancer Richard had made friends with on joining the regiment held the bloody stump of an arm out toward him as if imploring help. Then wild-eyed, the man crashed forward, streaking Richard and Legend with his blood.

Richard turned in his saddle at the sound of wildly thudding horse's hooves. Mad with fear, eyeballs protruding, a riderless, fear-crazed horse bore down on him, seeking leadership. Yet through all the cheers, the groans, the ping of bullets whizzing through the air, the whirr and crash of shells and earth-shaking thunder of galloping horses, Richard had encountered not one Russian to attack.

It seemed years—a lifetime. Yet it had been less than ten minutes since the advance had begun. Now they were within a few yards of the battery. Richard could see the face of a Russian gunner. "Close in! Close in!" Orders rang in his ears. Only a few more galloping strides, and he would be past the guns.

At that moment a mighty roar split the air. The ground shook so that Richard first thought it was an earthquake. Huge flashes of flame shot out from the mouth of the nearest gun. The smoke was so dense it covered the sun. All went black.

Two

Jennifer Neville smoothed the skirt of her gray tweed uniform and pulled herself wearily to her feet. She had already been nursing for nine hours that day—feeding soldiers too ill or too desperately wounded to feed themselves, carrying slops along miles of corridors, changing bandages soaked through and caked stiff with blood, and scrubbing walls and floors in a futile attempt to reduce the persistent stench. And still the sick and wounded continued to pour across the Black Sea from the battlefields of the Crimea to the old army barracks-become-hospital in Scutari. They must do what they could to make ready.

Jennifer and forty-some other nurses had arrived from London with Mary Stanley a few days ago. Florence Nightingale had been furious. Jenny could still see her delicate features held in control, as rigid as her words. "There is not enough room for the wounded. Where do you expect me to put more nurses? Nurses I did *not* request. My own forty are crowded into three tiny rooms. There is no decent food."

"But, dearest Flo, that is precisely why we're here," Mary Stanley gushed. "We know how dreadful it all is—what a heroine you are. We want to help."

"I barely have time and strength to train and direct the women already under my charge. I cannot take on a fresh batch."

But Mary Stanley, her head full of romantic notions of caressing the brows of wounded men and inspiring them to recovery, heard not a word. "Don't be silly, Flo, dear. We

17

won't bother you a bit. I shall take charge of my girls. I'm certain it can't require anything like the fuss you're making. My girls are all from the very best families."

"Precisely. I expressly refused to take any young, well-born women for this job." Florence Nightingale held her ground. "This is no place for anyone with tender sensibilities."

Mary Stanley laughed. "Flo, Flo, if I hadn't known you all my life, I would think you were jealous. Could it be you don't want to share the limelight?"

Florence's face was a study of control. "Very well. I shall choose nine of your ladies to add to my staff. No more."

Jennifer had been one of the nine chosen. Now she was determined to make good.

The plop of a small, soft body hitting the stone floor made her jump and shudder with horror. She had learned to stifle her screams, but she couldn't get used to the sound of rats falling off the walls. It was strange, really, because rats were a small matter amid all the filth and suffering she had seen in her few days here. The rats, however, seemed somehow to symbolize the unbelievable chaos and misery Florence Nightingale and her small band of women were battling.

A soft swish of tweed on stone announced Miss Nightingale's entrance, swift and assured, as were all her movements. After even longer hours and harder labor than Jennifer had performed, Florence still looked fresh. Her large gray eyes and delicate features were emphasized by the small, close-fitting cap she required as part of the nursing uniform. "I've just received word, Miss Neville. We have another boatload of patients arriving from Sebastopol. We have nowhere to put them. They must lie on the floor in the corridors."

Jennifer could only shake her head. They already had

more than four miles of patients lying almost touching one another—those with cholera and dysentery next to the amputees and head-injury cases.

Florence continued talking as she sorted through the supplies stored in a tall cupboard, all meticulously indexed. "I have sent to town for fabric." She handed Jennifer a basket of needles and thread. "We will stitch bags and stuff them with straw from the stables. At least that is clean."

"How many are we to expect?" Jennifer asked.

Florence sighed. "Three hundred—more perhaps."

Jennifer couldn't imagine what they would do. Already the wounded lay up to the very door of the nurse's quarters. But Florence Nightingale never wasted time fluttering. She proceeded in orderly fashion to instruct all available hands in the stitching of pallets. Jennifer chose a chair near a window overlooking the harbor and began sewing.

Light was dimming by the time the *Andes* pulled into harbor, but Jennifer could still see the pitiful parade begin across the flat quay. She watched it snake its way up the steep precipice toward the hospital. Some—the "lucky" ones —walked alone, supported by improvised crutches or leaning on comrades. Others were carried on stretchers by Turks. Even from her distance, Jennifer could see the red blotches soaking through the rough field dressings of most of the wounds. And she could feel the agony of the injured men being jolted over the uneven ground. She imagined she could hear their cries when all too frequently the porters dropped their stretchers and the soldiers fell into the dirt, only to be slung carelessly back onto their conveyances and trundled on up the hill.

Florence glanced out the window on one of her frequent passes to inspect the progress on the pallets. "Those wretched Turks! Why can't they be more careful? We are fighting for their country, and they handle our dying soldiers more roughly than firewood."

"And after such a turbulent journey across the sea." Mrs. Watson, one of the sturdy, middle-aged professional nurses brought to the Crimea by Florence, shook her motherly head. Jennifer looked at the white-capped billows tossing the ships anchored below them in the Bosphorus Strait.

A soft voice on the other side of Jennifer added, "They cram them aboard, three in the space for one, so tight that if one dies, the others must continue to lie with him until they dock. Father, help the poor lads." Her needle still in her hand, Sister Mary Margaret crossed herself.

Florence nodded. "Yes. Most arrive in such a state of agony they are more dead than alive. I suppose it's a miracle that any survive the trip." An anger she seldom allowed crept into her voice. "The matter is simply criminal. On the last landing two died while being carried up the hill. We lost twenty-four on the first day. It should not happen. They should get better here—not worse. So—"

She whirled with a rapid, graceful motion. "Mrs. Watson, Sister Mary, Miss Neville . . ." She named six more of their group. "Bring all the finished pallets and come with me." Florence picked up five bags, an armful almost as large as herself, and led the way out the door, leaving the rest of the women to finish the stitching.

They descended the narrow stairway leading from their quarters in the tower and followed Florence down a long corridor with sick and wounded men lying against the walls on both sides. The passageway left barely room to walk, so the nurses had to be careful not to brush the men with the floppy bundles they carried. Jennifer couldn't imagine where they were going to find room to bed the new arrivals. Their leader seemed to be heading toward the unused burnt-out wing of the barracks.

She was. "I have ordered the women from the washing house to do what they can to make the space usable," Florence said. "Of course, there is nothing we can do about the hole in the roof and the broken windows, but if the men do not have blankets, I shall buy them with my own money if I have to."

Jennifer was too out of breath to reply. She had discovered that even in the occupied part of the hospital many broken windows exposed the men to the December air, and many of the supplies had been purchased with Florence Nightingale's own funds. The normal military channels often failed to provide the bare necessities, or—more maddening—supplies were locked in storehouses, barricaded behind miles of red tape, while men died for their lack.

"There." Florence led them into a cavernous room with blackened walls that still smelled of charred wood, but the floor was cleared of rubble and scrubbed clean.

As she began arranging her mats in neat rows eighteen inches apart, Jennifer decided she preferred the sharply acrid charcoal smell to the putrid, sulphurous stench of the other rooms. They had not finished laying down their pallets when the first of the wounded arrived.

Miss Nightingale kept Jennifer and four other nurses to take care of the new arrivals while the others returned to the tower for more mats. Mrs. Watson took several of the soldiers' wives and camp followers, who had finished cleaning the room, to get fresh basins of water and clean rags so the nurses could wash the wounded soldiers. One of the first things Florence had done when she arrived in Scutari more than a month ago had been to set up wash houses so the men could have clean clothes and blankets and the women of the camp could be provided with jobs. Before that the men had been left in their blood-and-mud-caked uniforms just as they were carried from the field.

But the nurses could do nothing more than wash the soldiers and give them drinks. Florence Nightingale was absolutely adamant—no nurse was to administer anything to a patient without specific orders from a doctor. Nurses worked under doctors' orders. And there were no exceptions. Even when Florence had first arrived and the doctors had refused to allow the women into the wards for any purpose other than scrubbing the floors, she had curbed her impatience and obeyed. Only the desperate pressure of hundreds of wounded pouring in upon them from the Battle of Inkerman had made Dr. Menzies give way and shout, "Miss Nightingale, where are your nurses?"

Jennifer took a pan of water and knelt by the pallet nearest her. The soldier couldn't have been much more than fifteen years old, and his left arm had been shattered at the elbow. The hastily applied battlefield dressing would have fallen off long ago if it hadn't stuck to the dried blood. Jennifer forced herself to give the lad a brave smile as she began washing his face. "What's your name?"

"Colin, miss," he answered in a broad Midlands accent.

"Oh, my cousin was named Colin—about your age, too." Jenny bit her lip, hoping the soldier hadn't noticed her use of the past tense. She tried to engage her patients in conversation in hopes of taking their minds off the pain, but mentioning her cousin who was killed at Alma would be of little comfort.

She was washing her fifth patient when Dr. Pannier arrived, followed by two orderlies carrying boards to set up a trestle table. Colin was the first to be moved to the table. Jennifer turned all her attention to removing the blood-stiffened jacket of a soldier with a shoulder injury. She couldn't bear to watch or listen. She knew what would come next. The hospital was so short of space that amputations had to be performed in the wards in front of the very men who would be operated on next. And performed without anesthetic. Dr. Hall, principal medical officer of the army, had cautioned regimental surgeons against using chloroform, although it was rumored that the Scottish surgeon Munro used it regularly for field amputations with good results. But the question was irrelevant—no chloroform was available at Scutari.

Florence Nightingale had determined, however, to spare the men awaiting amputation at least the horror of watching those before them go under the surgeon's saw. She entered now carrying a set of screens, which she set up around the operating table. Jennifer was thankful that at least Colin could have this small privacy. She felt a tightness in her throat as she glanced around the room, remembering Miss Nightingale's words: *In a whole wing of the hospital the men do not average three limbs apiece.* It was clear from the blood-soaked rags in this room that the statistics would not be improved. Jennifer returned to her washing with determined energy. It was the one thing she could do to help the men, and the harder she worked, the less time she had to think.

By eight o'clock that night all the new arrivals were washed and resting with clean blankets on clean pallets. Some were even sleeping, some talking to their neighbors. Some were drinking mugs of arrowroot laced with generous portions of port wine—Florence Nightingale's own recipe —which the nurses were able to serve reasonably warm since Miss Nightingale had established two new kitchens in the barracks. None of the day's arrivals had died. It was a victory as hard-won as any on the battlefield.

"Time for quarters, Miss Neville." Florence approached

Jennifer, who was holding an empty milk pail and ladle after serving the last of her arrowroot.

Jennifer nodded. The rule was inviolable: no nurse was to be in the wards after eight o'clock. It would not be proper. Florence Nightingale always made the final night round herself. And Jennifer understood. Part of Florence's careful attention was motivated by her deep love for the soldiers—caring for each one as if he were her own son or brother. Part of it was Florence's determination to see personally that everything was done right as far as was possible. And part of it must have been the fact that after the hectic crises of each day, a quiet walk through the wards was restful and reassuring. Jennifer felt the need for that herself tonight. "Miss Nightingale, may I be permitted to accompany you on your rounds?"

"Wouldn't you rather rest? I've observed how hard you've worked today."

"No harder than you, Miss Nightingale. And I don't think I could settle to resting just yet. I believe I would find a walk soothing."

Florence smiled and nodded. "I should be glad of your company, Miss Neville."

They made their way back to the crowded tower quarters where the other nurses were writing letters, reading, and chatting. Florence took her whale oil lamp off a shelf and turned once again to the seemingly endless corridors of the barracks. "You are a good nurse, Miss Neville. What is your background? You aren't trained in nursing, are you?"

Jennifer's reply was delayed as Florence stopped to help a man with one arm arrange his blanket more comfortably. She spoke a few soft words to him, brushed his forehead with her hand, and then turned to adjust a stump rest for the man on the next pallet.

Jennifer smiled and shook her head. "Hardly. You know how impossible that would be. My family would never allow such a thing. Charity work in London—that was acceptable, of course. I assisted a bit at one of Lord Shaftesbury's ragged schools. That was how I met Mary Stanley." Jennifer could see by the shadow flicking across Florence's face that Mary Stanley was not a happy subject. She changed courses quickly. "I had a cousin killed in the battle of Alma, so my family agreed to my coming to the Crimea to try to help other young men—after those awful stories appeared in the *Times* about the suffering here." Jennifer fleetingly considered telling Florence Nightingale about her other reason for wanting to get away from London, but then thought better of it.

Florence stopped again to speak to a restless soldier. Several times their progress was interrupted by men who offered a quiet greeting or merely a smile or wave. Florence helped several men who were unable to drink unaided from the canteens resting by their pallets.

Then she picked up her lamp and resumed her walk, continuing their conversation in a hushed voice so as not to disturb the sleeping men. "I daresay. Mr. William Howard Russell is the greatest hero of the Crimea for his war dispatches informing the British public of the true state of matters here. I would not be here myself had he not made the truth known."

Jennifer had judged correctly. There was no need to tell Florence Nightingale about the persistent Mr. Merriott. To her a passion for doing good was explanation enough. Jenny sighed. If only she could be so single-minded.

They had now reached the end of the corridor and turned into one of the large wards. Already the walk seemed endless, and they had covered less than one-fourth of the hospital.

The passages that seemed merely long during the day went on forever in the hush of the night. The very shadows muffled the sounds of men turning on straw-stuffed mats, the quiet moans or sharp cries from fevered sleepers, and the ever-present rustle and squeak of rats.

In the high-ceilinged ward the noises seemed farther away yet, the silence profound. A few dim lights flickered from window sills and wall brackets. Even the sleeping men appeared to become more peaceful when the light of Florence Nightingale's lantern passed over them. She set the light down and bent over another patient. Jennifer admired her manner—her touch was so tender and kind. Then Florence picked up her lamp, and they resumed their progress.

It was in one of the upstairs corridors that Miss Nightingale paused before entering a ward. "These poor men have been here since a few days after I arrived. They are from the terrible battle of Balaclava." She shook her head. "One hears such horrible stories of military blunders. I don't know—when there is so much unavoidable pain and suffering in the world, that which is inflicted by sheer stupidity seems to me the most evil. I try not to waste my time on futile anger—and yet sometimes . . ." Florence led the way into the room.

Somehow the silence in this room was more dead than in any of the others, as if the men, having been here so long were resigned to their suffering being endless. Or perhaps Jennifer was just being fanciful. Perhaps they were simply able to sleep more soundly in quarters to which they had become accustomed. Or perhaps some of them were nearer to recovery. One could at least hope, although it seemed unlikely. Always there was the inexplicable mortality rate from hospital fever among patients past the danger of wound fever. Men nearly ready to be released were known to sicken and die suddenly, as if the hospital itself made them sick.

Florence Nightingale set her lamp down to help a man with no legs find a more comfortable position on his cot. This ward was furnished with actual army beds rather than the improvised straw pallets. Jennifer looked at the soldier in the next bed. He lay half-sitting, propped against the wall, his forehead and eyes swathed in bandages. He seemed to be sleeping, yet his right hand moved restlessly as if groping for something that wasn't there.

Without stopping to think that she should seek permission, Jennifer knelt and slipped her hand into his. The restless motion stopped instantly. The sleeping man sighed. But Jennifer looked up sharply. "Miss Nightingale, this man has fever. His hand is burning."

Jennifer felt desperate as she looked at his high cheekbones, well-formed mouth, and squared chin beneath the bandages. Not yet another sacrifice to hospital fever. *Please, Lord, not this one, too.* In just the few days she had been here she had seen too many apparently recovering men go this way. Even with all the horrors of battle, far more men died of fever and disease than of wounds.

She looked at her supervisor. "Have we nothing we can give him?" Jennifer felt the fine, long fingers that gripped hers. This one wouldn't die if she could help it.

Florence Nightingale shook her head. "I shall ask Dr. Menzies tomorrow if we can give him some loxa quinine and theriac drops. Until then you may bathe him with vinegar water and give him sips of cool liquid."

Jennifer nodded. She knew the rules—nothing to be administered without doctor's orders. She managed to remove the cap from his canteen with her free hand. The water inside felt tepid and smelled stale. If only she had something better for him.

Then she knew. She had not taken her own allotment of

wine that day. That would calm him. Florence agreed. Army ration wine would not be beyond the scope of her authority to administer. "I will complete my rounds and then return here for you." The light of the lamp moved on, leaving Jennifer in semidarkness.

Carefully she slipped her hand from the soldier's. "I'll be right back," she whispered to the ear left exposed by his bandages. Perhaps he heard. She hurried through the dim corridors filled with silent men to the kitchen Florence Nightingale had established in the nurses' tower.

In a few minutes she was back kneeling by the soldier. She removed the ragged blue jacket of his 17th Lancers' uniform —he did not need the added warmth now—and unbuttoned his shirt. She bathed his arms and chest with a rag dipped in cool vinegar water. She could feel his hot body cooling under her hands. Every few minutes she slipped a spoonful of wine between his chapped lips.

When he had taken it all, she held his hand again. This time his sleep was less restless, deeper and more natural. Could the fever have broken? She prayed that it had.

Her legs were beginning to cramp by the time Florence Nightingale returned, yet she didn't want to go. Reluctantly, she got to her feet and joined her supervisor. "There are so many—it seems hopeless." Jennifer sighed as they left the ward. "Yet if I can save just one, my time here will seem worthwhile." She paused to sort out her thoughts. "Miss Nightingale, our vicar says Christ died for the whole world, but that if there had been just one person, He would have done the same thing. I hope you won't think it sacrilegious of me—but I feel I'm following His example in a small way."

Florence gave a tired smile. "Yes. I know."

In the dark and quiet of the night, Jennifer felt freer to speak to this woman who was already becoming a legend in

London. "Miss Nightingale, how do you *know* if something is right—if it's what God wants you to do? You always seem so sure. We are told to obey our parents—and yet . . ."

Florence nodded. "And yet it's not always so simple, is it? Perhaps you have heard rumors of how sadly I disappointed my parents by not choosing the brilliant social marriage offered me. But it was an easy decision in my case."

"Easy?" *How could such a decision ever be easy?*

"I was not quite seventeen when God spoke to me." Florence slowed her step, as if reliving the moment. "I do not mean through the Scripture or with an inward impression as He most often speaks. I heard an actual voice speaking to me in human words. From that moment I knew God had called me to His service. I did not know what form that service was to take, but I knew He would show me. When the way opened for nursing, then I knew."

The two women ascended the steep stone stairs to their tower rooms without further talking. In the small space filled with twenty other women, Jennifer all but fell on her pallet. She felt as if every bone in her body ached from weariness. Yet she could not sleep. A dim light shone under the door. Florence Nightingale was still up writing letters and reports.

Jennifer prayed that her Lancer would still be alive in the morning. Then her thoughts returned to her conversation with Florence. If only God would speak as clearly to her. What was she to do about the Honorable Arthur Nigel Merriott? He was such a good man. He wanted her to marry him. Her family wanted her to marry him. Was she being wicked and prideful to hold back? Or was she merely feeling normal maidenly shyness?

She knew it was evil of her to think of the horrors of the Crimea lasting one day—even one hour—longer than necessary just so she wouldn't have to return to London and make that decision. And yet she dreaded the prospect of returning.

A soft plop followed by the sound of scampering feet just inches from her ear told her that a rat had narrowly missed falling on her face. Still she did not want to return to London.

Three

The next morning Jennifer sped through her duties. She and Sister Mary Margaret were assigned to take breakfast to the men in the corridor below the nurses' tower and to the ward above and help feed the men not capable of feeding themselves. Although the patients in neighboring beds were always willing to help, Jennifer preferred to do it herself. She could never explain her dislike of the practice of men with fever and dysentery feeding others. So this morning, in spite of her desire to hurry, she took time with each patient.

Then the slops must be carried out and dumped in the latrines in the yard and the floors scrubbed. Miss Nightingale was fanatically insistent upon cleanliness, although the professional nurses from London hospitals laughed at her finicky ways. "Newfangled ideas. Never did it like this at Saint Bart's, I can tell you. But what can you expect from one who's always lived in fine houses? She'll learn." In spite of her grumbles, though, Edith Watson stuck her brush into the soapy water and attacked the excrement on the floor with vigor. Rats squeaked as they fled from her splashing brush.

Jennifer finished her duties by midafternoon. She would not be required to assist a doctor in changing dressings for an hour yet. She tucked loose strands of her thick brown hair back into her cap and hurried to the ward where she had spent so much time last night. *Please let him be alive,* she prayed.

She had heard the nurses who had been there longer than herself refer to some of the beds as death traps. "That's one o'

31

them fatal beds." Mrs. Watson had nodded toward one they were scrubbing near a few days ago. "Every man put in it sickens and dies. Mark my words." Jenny noted that the sulphurous stench of the ward seemed stronger there. Or was it merely her imagination?

And she had recalled Mrs. Watson's words a few days later when she found the pallet empty. Remembering that, Jenny slowed her steps now as she approached the Balaclava ward. She nodded to Sister Mary Margaret and three other Catholic sisters who were just leaving their duties there, carrying scrub brushes and pails. Inside the door Jennifer's eyes ran down the row of cots along the wall facing the tall, arched windows. Had it been the fifth down? Or sixth? No, those men were amputees. Seventh? Eighth? Her heart lurched. Both cots were empty.

She felt a sob rise in her throat. Clamping her teeth shut, she suppressed the cry. Among so many, why should she care so much about that one? She forced herself to go forward. She was here. She might as well see if there was anyone else she could help. She felt the pencil and thick pad of paper she carried in her pocket. There was never enough time to write all the letters the men would have sent home for them. She recalled how much her cousin Colin's letters had meant to all her family. Before they ceased coming.

This was what she had originally thought she would do here. Mary Stanley had painted a romantic picture of holding the hands of brave men, soothing their fevered brows, and writing letters for them. Jennifer would never have come if she had had any notion her time would be filled eighteen hours a day with scrubbing, bandaging, and carrying slops. Nor would her parents, who allowed her to do only the most genteel charity work in London, have permitted her to come. But now she was here. The need was overwhelming, and

Jennifer was not a shirker.

At the end of the row was a man with both hands bandaged. "Would you like a drink? Or a letter written for you?" She forced a smile at the sandy-haired man in the red jacket of the Sutherland Highlanders. The papers had been full of the bravery of "the thin red line" just before she left London. Perhaps this man had been one of them.

"Aye, lassie. Joost a wee drink, if ye please."

The nurses were supposed to make the men feel better. But this man's gentle voice and kind smile made *her* feel better. By the time she had refilled his canteen from the bucket of drinking water by the far wall, she didn't have to force her smile.

And then she saw. Coming in the door was a tall, thin man in a Lancers' tunic. His head and eyes were bandaged, and he was being led slowly by a man with one arm. Stifling a silly impulse to run to him, she turned instead to refill the canteen of the man in the bed next to the Scotsman. She worked her way back up the row—straightening blankets, filling canteens, and giving encouraging greetings.

The Lancer was back in his cot when she got to him. "Good morning, Lieutenant." She was learning to decipher the ranks of the stripes on their sleeves. "Are you feeling better this morning?"

He held out a hand in the direction of her voice. "Much better. Thank you, nurse."

She took the hand. It was cooler. Not yet normal, but cooler. *Thank You, Lord.*

"Would you like me to write a letter for you?"

He nodded. "My sister Livvy. She sent me one by the last packet." He leaned over and began groping for the small box under his bed.

"I'll get it." Jenny fell to her knees. In a moment she had

the single, closely written sheet. "Shall I read it out to you?"

The wide mouth in the face beneath the heavy bandages smiled. "Please."

It was a cloudy day, so the room was dim despite the tall windows on the other side of the room. Jennifer held the letter up to the light.

My dearest brother,

You shall be happy to hear that we are back at Greystoke Pitchers and shall remain here for Christmas. Auntie GAL fusses over everything as usual. George and Olivia shall join us next week. May I be the first to send you intelligence of our great news—Olivia is in an interesting condition. Now that will give Great-aunt Lavinia something to fuss over. Papa is less patient with her than usual and spends most of his time at the pottery. Dearest Dick, we read such terrible, terrible accounts of the war. Surely the papers exaggerate. The British military can't possibly be so inept as they say. Such awful charges against Lord Lucan and Lord Cardigan—your very own officers. Please assure us that your wounds are recovering apace. Be assured that we are all well here. I would send Legend a carrot for Christmas if I knew how to go about such a thing.

Your loving sister,
Livvy

Jennifer lowered the small sheet of paper. For a moment the warm words full of familiar family references had transported her back to her own family in England. She had not realized that next week would be Christmas. For an instant she could smell the sharp scent of pine boughs in the parlor and the sweet tang of spicy puddings boiling in the kitchen. She could feel the welcome warmth of the fire when she came in from the cold, wet street with her arms full of bundles.

"Oh." She recalled herself to her duty. "Your sister sounds charming." She drew the pad of paper from her pocket. "What shall you say to her?" She glanced at the envelope she held. "Lt. Greyston. Is that right?"

He was a moment in answering, as if he, too, had been caught up in the reading. "Yes, that's it. Richard, actually. Lt. Richard Greyston, 17th Lancers, ma'am." He made an impatient gesture. "Oh, blast these bandages. Livvy isn't half so charming as you sound. Why can't I see you?"

Jennifer gave a small laugh. "Perhaps to save you disappointment, sir. I assure you I'm very ordinary. Brown hair and eyes with the usual allotment of eyes, nose, and mouth. Now what shall I write?"

"Oh, tell her I'm well enough and anxious to get back to my regiment, but the doctor's keeping me under wraps." Jenny's pencil scurried across the paper. "Say I'm glad they're all in Newcastle for Christmas." He paused. "Congratulations to George on producing an heir." He turned his head restlessly on the pillow as if searching for words. "And Legend thanks her for the thought," he finished in a rush. Then he added between clenched teeth, "Heaven knows I hope he does. If only I knew where . . ."

Jennifer touched his hand in a professional manner. "Lt. Greyston, I've tired you. Your fever is coming back up." She gave him a drink of the wine she had brought with her. "Has the doctor ordered drops for you?"

Richard shook his head.

"I shall see what can be done." She slipped Livvy's letter and the unfinished one back in his box. "I'm on duty now. I shall try to return tomorrow—or the next day—to finish your letter. In the meantime, keep to your bed. You are not yet strong enough to be gallivanting about the corridors." She certainly understood the men's preference for using the privy rather than slop buckets, but it was a vast distance to the yard, especially from the upper wards.

"Yes, miss." His voice was weak, but there was a note of humor underneath, as if he were mocking her for playing the nanny. Then the note turned to pleading. "But must you go? Am I not even to know your name?"

"Jennifer Neville. And, yes, I must go." She almost ran from the ward and along the corridors. Miss Nightingale was strict about her nurses reporting at the proper time.

With the retreating footsteps Richard's impatience and despair returned. He was alone again inside the darkness of his bandages. Never during the almost two months he had been here had he felt closer to reaching up and ripping them off.

Once when he had been there only a few days, he had started to tear at them, and Miss Nightingale had caught him at it. He had received a sharp lecture on patience and obeying doctor's orders. Then her voice had changed to gentleness. "I realize how wearying and long it is. Burns are very slow to heal, and there can be complications. It is important to leave the wraps on." And so, with his stiff military discipline, Richard had stifled his urge to reach out and rip and smash, to shout, to do *something*.

And the days had passed. He had joined the cheering when news went around the ward that the 4th Light Dragoons had achieved the impossible and silenced the guns at the end of that dreadful battlefield—so he supposed the charge of the Light Brigade would be counted a victory. Yet even as the cheers rang, all in that room remembered vividly the terrible cost.

Night after night the dreadful scene played out again like a magic lantern show on the screen of his bandages: smoke, fire, blood . . . and then it wasn't the heat of battle he was feeling, but the burning of fever. His skin burned, his throat burned. He tried to reach for his canteen—or was it his sword? He groped over the rough surface of Legend's hide—or was it a blanket?

And then one night an amazing thing happened. An incredibly small, soft, cool hand held his. And he ceased groping.

Now he turned his head from side to side as if the motion would make everything come clear. Jennifer Neville, she had said. That had been her hand. And she had given him a drink. And he had slept. But now she was gone. And it was dark.

Richard turned his face to his pillow and tried for perhaps the hundredth time to pray. But the wall was still there. The brick wall he had charged into when the cannon exploded in his face and all the world went dark. The wall that now encompassed his whole world and stopped his prayers.

It hadn't always been that way. He recalled the end of his second year at university when he and two other gownsmen had gone to the nearby village of Waterbeach to hear the boy preacher who was causing such a stir in Cambridgeshire. A large thatched-roofed barn had been turned into a chapel with whitewashed walls, but the crowd was too great to get inside. So the eighteen-year-old Charles Spurgeon had preached in the open air. Richard had recognized a wisdom in the preacher's simple words—far beyond his years. He couldn't recall the exact words, but he remembered hearing that salvation was all of grace: love and goodness and forgiveness and mercy and eternal life. Nothing of works or judgment or rules, but all of love and grace. And Richard had responded.

It turned out that they had arrived on an anniversary day

for the little congregation, so the preaching service was followed by a most singular event—a baptismal service in the river. Richard, who only a few hours before would have mocked at such unorthodox proceedings, now stood reverently among the vast crowd of people lining the banks of the Cam to observe the baptism of six new Christians.

He could have closed his eyes and thought himself by the River Jordan, but he preferred to remain sharply observant. The simplicity and sincerity of the occasion affected him deeply. When he returned after that to his own more formal worship, he did so with a heart renewed. Two months later he left Cambridge for the Lancers—and the Crimea.

And now all that seemed long ago. He had only one thought—how much longer must he lie here in the blackness? The doctor had come by once or twice. Dick supposed his bandages had been changed—he had a memory of sharp pain and probing fingers—but the words were always the same: "Wait. Burns heal slowly. Complicated by fever. Wait."

So he waited. But still the fears came. What if it wasn't just the head wound and burned skin? What if it was his sight? What would he do with his life if he were condemned to live in this dark forever?

And then it was dark again. Dark until the whole world exploded with sharp, swirling light. And he wasn't sure whether he heard the booming of cannon or only imagined it. But there was no questioning that he did not imagine the searing pain behind his eyes. At those times it required all his willpower to keep from crying out. And then he was glad for his bandages, because they absorbed the tears he could not hold back.

Four

The days sped by, muddling in Jennifer's memory like the endless line of wounded men on straw pallets in the miles of corridors. On Christmas Day the nuns said extra prayers, and the nurses spent their short off-duty time singing carols to the men. But celebrations were sparse. Another boatload arrived from Sebastopol. Now the chilling cold was beginning to take its effect. The beds, emptied as often by death as by recovery, were filled with pneumonia and frostbite cases. Men arrived without overcoats, blankets, or even canteens, because in earlier days of choking heat they had been ordered by their officers to abandon their packs when scaling the heights above Sebastopol, and the supplies were never recovered. Now they must sleep unprotected on the frozen ground, wearing only light cotton shirts.

At Florence Nightingale's request, 27,000 woollen shirts had been shipped from England. And they had arrived. But the aged purveyor said he could not unpack them until the Board of Survey inspected and released them. Miss Nightingale had simply purchased more shirts in Constantinople.

"Miss Nightingale, you have behaved in a most irregular and unmilitary manner," the old officer had complained. "After all, you could have had the government shirts in three or four weeks."

Jennifer ground her teeth at this further example of official ineptitude and turned to nurse men whose frozen feet had been amputated to prevent gangrene. There were 11,000 soldiers in the camp above Sebastopol—and 12,000 in the army hospitals. And boatload after boatload of sick continued to arrive at Scutari. Later, when they again requested the with-held shirts, it seemed they had been released to some doctor. The signature was unreadable. And the shirts never showed up in Scutari.

Florence Nightingale shook her head as they prepared to receive yet another group for whom there was no room and yet for whom they must make room. "This is calamity unpar-alleled in the history of calamity," she said, then turned to her work. Jennifer and the others followed her.

Somewhere in this endless stream of days and rounds of work, Jennifer had discovered herself adjusting to the pattern of it all—not just responding to orders because she had no other option or because she didn't feel ready to return to London and Arthur. She had really become a part of the work. And in the rare moments when she had leisure to con-template a future beyond the next round of duties, she knew she could never return to her former life of making social calls, doing embroidery, and taking food baskets to the poor. She might not continue with nursing, but she would not be idle.

Certainly there was no idleness at the Barracks Hospital, but there was so little success. With Miss Nightingale's better food for the men, better care of the wounded, and better cleanliness in the hospital, they should be saving more lives. But they were not. And of those who didn't die, many, like Richard Greyston, continued to waver in an uncertain state from one upsurge of fever to the next.

"If only we could make them well," Jennifer said as she helped Florence sort supplies a few weeks later. "It seems the men just come here to die. Something must be wrong. We're doing our best, but we're losing the fight."

Her supervisor nodded. "There's certainly something wrong here." Ever the careful record-keeper, she sorted again through her neatly marked bottles. "Oil of vitriol, emetic tartar, sol-volatile, white arsenic . . . Two bottles of each are missing. This cupboard is never to be unlocked by any but my own hand. Miss Neville, if you see anyone—anyone at all —around my supplies, you are to inform me immediately."

"Yes, of course, Miss Nightingale." They worked on, counting pots of calomel and spermaceti ointment, citron ointment and Boric acid for eye diseases. All were in order, so Jennifer spoke again. "If only so many didn't die under our care."

Florence's reply was businesslike. "Quite. Our death rate is 42 percent. That is unacceptable. Unthinkable. So I have informed our new prime minister, Lord Palmerston. He is an old friend of mine. I believe he will hear me. I have begged and pleaded with all the words at my command that he send out a sanitary commission. Have you noticed, Miss Neville, that this hospital reeks even outside?"

Jennifer moved from the ointments to number a box of rolled bandages—purchased, she knew, with Miss Nightingale's own money. She set it on the shelf. "I have noticed. Only I thought perhaps it was just me—my clothes must be permeated with the smell—my very skin, I think." She turned to another box. "But will Lord Palmerston respond?"

"He must. If he wishes to avoid complete catastrophe and save the British army, he must." She spoke the words calmly as she continued checking her records, but the determination in her voice chilled Jenny far more than the February air pouring through the broken window.

Jennifer finished her job at the supply cupboard and took a round of tea—which was in truth little more than sweetened hot water—to the men in three wards. Then she had a half-hour break. She thought fleetingly of how good it would feel to lie on her cot. Or how pleasant it would be to write a letter to her family. They had only heard from her once since Christmas.

Her mother wrote faithfully every week, amusing letters full of news of the London season and All Souls parish. Arthur wrote less frequently but more vigorously of the great good they should now be able to accomplish with Palmerston in office. The new prime minister was stepfather-in-law to the crusading Earl of Shaftesbury whom Arthur, a minor civil servant, idolized. It was clear from Arthur's account of his many activities that he had every intention of removing the "minor" from this description. His letters abounded with reports of committees to deal with public health and factory laws.

We have had a great triumph with the model lodging-houses. Shaftesbury presented the facts to Parliament. In a season when more than 14,000 have died from cholera, there has been not one case in the model lodging-houses in George Street. Yet in Church Lane, which is but a stone's throw away, the ravages are dreadful . . .

Jennifer dropped the letter with a sigh.

There were soldiers who needed her attention more than her family and friends did. Forcing a spring she did not feel into her step, she jerked open the door of her room. A stocky figure with a high, balding forehead pulled back sharply from the supply cupboard in the hall. She started to scold him and then realized who it was. "Oh, Dr. Pannier. Can I help you with something?"

"My supplies of poppy syrup and catechu tincture are quite exhausted, and we have a new outbreak of cholera. I had hoped Miss Nightingale might have at least some linseed tea in her supplies." The gravelly voice paused.

"Yes, of course. Shall I find her for you? She has the only key."

"No. Never mind. I'll deal with it myself."

Jennifer nodded at his dismissal and turned her steps toward the upper ward. She had returned to Lt. Greyston two days after writing his letter and addressed it to his sister in Newcastle-Under-Lyme. Since then she had had a few hurried visits with him—enough to assure herself he was still alive in spite of the recurring fever. She did not know much about his injury, beyond the fact that it was a burn from cannon fire. And she had learned little about him beyond the fact that his brother George was heir to Greystoke Pottery, which made the famous Royal Legend pattern of china, and that he worried much over what had become of his horse named for that pattern. And the fact that all he had ever wanted was a career in the army, and he couldn't wait to get back to his regiment.

Jennifer shook her head every time he expressed that desire. "I've heard enough about the charge of the Light Brigade that I can't believe any man who survived would want to go back. It was a miracle that even 249 of the 673 men survived. That cannon fire must have put you out of your head."

She plumped his pillow and straightened his blanket, for she had chosen to write a letter for him rather than to her own family. She would not admit that she was almost glad he had taken the fever, since it kept him off the battlefield. But then she felt guilty as her hand brushed his. He was very hot. His cheeks were flushed, and his skin felt dry. She was glad she had thought to bring him her portion of wine today. The water smelled as bad as the barracks walls. This place couldn't be healthy for a sick man. She propped him up and held the tin cup to his lips, determining to get her ration to him more regularly.

"I received a letter yesterday," he said when she returned his head to the pillow.

Jenny started to reach for his box, but he pulled the crumpled sheet from the pocket of his tunic and handed it to her. She smoothed the sheet. "Oh, it's from your sister again. She writes from London. She is there for the season with your aunt. . . ." Jennifer read the bright account of London's social life, resumed with full vigor now that the terrible epidemic of Asiatic cholera, which had swept the continent and the slums of London that winter, had ended.

It would be impossible to exaggerate the gratitude one feels everywhere at the abatement of the pestilence from which we have escaped. The death rate had risen to 3,000 a week at its worst—but only in the poorer sections of the city, of course.

Mama and I attended a service of thanksgiving before ordering new gowns for Lady Royalston's ball . . .

Jennifer folded the letter and moved quietly away. Lt. Greyston was asleep.

Three weeks later Florence Nightingale came into the tower rooms flushed with pleasure, waving a letter. "We have triumphed! Lord Palmerston has appointed his son-in-law Lord Shaftesbury to form a sanitary commission for the Crimea."

Perhaps only Jennifer, who had so often seen the light burning under the door far into the night and discussed their needs with Miss Nightingale, knew what persistence, repeated urgings, even demands, this victory had required. Palmerston, a long-time family friend of the Nightingales, could not refuse this indomitable woman.

Florence read from the paper she held: " 'Commissioners:

The utmost expedition must be used in starting your journey. . . . It is important that you be deeply impressed with the necessity of not resting content with an order, but that you see instantly, by yourselves or your agents, to the commencement of the work and to its superintendency day by day until it is finished.' So run their orders."

All the nurses in the room applauded the clear official call to action. "At last," Jennifer cried. "Do you think they might actually get rid of the rats?"

"And the smell?" Edith Watson sniffed.

The commissioners arrived less than two weeks later—two doctors of proven energy from the Board of Health, a civil engineer from London, and the borough engineer and three sanitary inspectors from Liverpool where a sanitary act had been in operation longer than anywhere else in the country.

The commission had been in Scutari for only a few days when Jennifer was hurrying to her quarters, trying to be on time for curfew. She stopped at the sound of angry voices coming from one of the small, improvised kitchens. ". . . I know your game. You won't get away with this. . . ."

A muffled growling voice replied with a string of curses.

Jennifer moved back into the shadows. Should she try to slip past the open door or go around the other way and risk discipline for breaking the rules?

Then one of the speakers erupted from the room at an angry lope. She did not recognize him, but his well-cut clothes identified him as one of the London commissioners. Jennifer stayed in her corner for another long moment, barely breathing. What could that mean? Then another dark figure, this one short and stocky, the dim light shining on his bald head, slipped down the hall without seeing her. *How odd.* Dr. Pannier had been arguing with a commissioner. Was there to be trouble just when they could hope for success?

The next day she was busy until afternoon accompanying Dr. Menzies on his rounds, administering a fever mixture of powdered nitre and carbonate of potash in antimonial wine and salving burns with Drover's powder of mercury and chalk when bandages were changed. It was late in the day after a round of emptying slops that Jennifer heard the news.

Edith Watson and Sister Mary Margaret were talking to two other nuns outside the nurses' quarters. "You mean he was shot? Dead? Dear God." Sister Mary crossed herself and then tugged at the rosary hanging from her belt. "Come." She turned to the two sisters. "We will pray for his soul."

Near a battlefield where hundreds of men were shot dead almost daily, what was so alarming about this newest case?

Mrs. Watson explained to Jennifer. "It's not a soldier. It's Dr. Gavin, one of the London doctors come with the commission."

"How did it happen?"

"Accident. His brother and some others were cleaning their guns and target practicing. Seems one of the guns discharged by mistake."

Jennifer shook her head. At least it was an accident. Murder or suicide would have been an unthinkable complication. And yet she worried. Was this entire venture doomed? All their hopes were pinned on the Sanitary Commission. Would this be yet another official failure to add to the annals of the Crimea?

But Florence Nightingale had fought too hard for this breakthrough to accept failure now. She would write to London for a replacement commissioner before she attended Dr. Gavin's funeral. And then the work would resume—full force.

A few days later a ship brought the building supplies the commissioners had had the foresight to realize they would need. This was followed by the quick arrival of the replacement commissioner. Then the coming of spring put new energy into all their work. Jenny's workload didn't decrease, but it seemed that she got through her duties faster, and sometimes she even found herself walking down the corridors singing.

If only she could transfer some of her new spirit to the men lying sick and in pain all around her. At least the warmer temperatures meant they should have received their last load of frostbite victims. But improved weather meant increased military action. And the ships continued to cross the Black Sea with their loads of wounded men.

Richard's fever continued. He became Jennifer's personal crusade. On the days when the fever was the worst, she raced through her work—never slighting it, but simply putting more energy into it—and then made her way as quickly as possible to his ward carrying the inevitable cup of wine and basin of vinegar water. And now she could open the windows in the ward and let out the fetid air. Sister Mary Margaret and the nuns had taken to spending any spare moments they could snatch to run outside and gather wild flowers. Jenny saw to it that the jar of flowers in Lt. Greyston's ward stood close enough for him to smell them since he could not see them.

Some days Richard was well enough to sit up and talk about his family, about his days at Cambridge, and about his ambitions for his career—how he looked forward to advancement, how he would care for the men under his command, and how he would work to avoid the blunders he had witnessed in the Crimea.

At times Jenny wondered if she should suggest that he consider other possibilities—a less active career—but she could not bring herself to think, much less to recommend, a career a sightless man could undertake.

And more than once he had interrupted her thoughts by saying, "I can't wait to get these bandages off. I want to see you, Miss Neville." So she never gave voice to her fears.

But there were many days when the fever was too bad for conversation—days when her patient slipped beyond the reach of fresh air, flowers, and vinegar water—when even the quinine drops Dr. Menzies had finally approved seemed to do little good. Then Jenny sat by Richard's cot and held onto him by the sheer force of her will. She demanded—of him? of herself? of God?—that he get well. He did not get well. But he did not die.

Then the commission announced their findings. Jennifer could hardly believe it, and yet nothing less appalling could have explained it all so completely. For five months Florence Nightingale and her angels, as they had become known, had been nursing in a veritable cesspool.

Beneath the buildings lay open sewers choked with filth. The plaster walls soaked it up. The decaying mass sent up something much worse than the putrid smell. It emitted poisonous gasses. The mystery of the death-trap beds was solved. They were near the doors of the privies where the deadly gasses were the worst.

And worse discoveries followed. The water supply was contaminated. It was mixed with sewage and the entire system filtered through the decaying body of a horse. The water storage tanks stood right next to the temporary privies set up for the needs of men suffering from diarrhea. Jennifer thanked God for every cup of wine she had given Richard instead of water.

The commissioners hired an army of Turkish workers. The morning after their findings were complete, the hospital was invaded by two hundred workers who began carrying off garbage, flushing the water system, and cleansing the privies. Inside they tore out the wooden shelves circling the wards and exterminated the thousands of rats harboring there. Then they lime-washed the walls.

Florence Nightingale voiced everyone's thoughts: "It is a miracle that anyone survived. The commission has saved the British army."

And many heads nodded at Jennifer's reply. "But without your insistence, Miss Nightingale, there would have been no commission."

Almost overnight the death rate dropped. Within two weeks they began releasing men for whom a short time before there had seemed little hope. And, best of all to Jennifer, for the first time since her night vigil by his bed, Richard's hand had felt cool when he held it out to greet her.

The morning had begun bright, but now the sun hid behind dark clouds. Jennifer paused at the window across from Richard's cot. She hoped it would rain. Rain on the spring green grass made her feel as if she were back in England. For a moment the longing for home rose, cramping her chest and throat, making it hard to breathe. She forced herself to take a deep breath of the air, blessedly free of stench, and turned to her duties, accompanied by hammering sounds from the workmen in the next ward and the shouts of the Turks carting off refuse from the yard below.

Suppressing her nervousness over the news the day promised, she began in her orderly fashion at one end of the room, smoothing bedding and filling canteens with the now-purified water. But with every movement at the doorway, she looked up. Was that Dr. Menzies? No, it was one of the workers come for some tools he had left there. She moved to the next bed, giving each man her attention, and yet never unaware of the still form of the waiting man on the bed in the middle of the next row. For she knew that, anxious as she was for Dr. Menzies's examination, her anticipation could be nothing compared to Richard's.

He had lain in the darkness of his bandages for months, waiting first for his wounds to heal, then for the fever to abate, so he could finally be evaluated and released. All he had talked of in the past days was his hope of finding Legend—if only he had survived the carnage. "I just hope whoever took him up after the battle has taken good care of him. I can't imagine going back to the Lancers on any horse but Legend."

Jennifer made no attempt to keep the impatience out of her voice. "Lt. Richard Greyston, can you find nothing more sensible to talk about? Haven't you suffered enough? Hasn't your family waited long enough?"

"What? Are you suggesting I should return home? Abandon my duty?"

She sighed. "Certainly you have a duty to do. But don't you even want to return to your family in England?"

He sounded surprised at her suggestion, as if the thought had not crossed his mind. "Before the war is over? Before we've beaten the Russians and taken Sebastopol? Before the victory is complete?" He shook his head. "When all that is accomplished, it will be time enough."

Even as she argued with him, Jennifer had to admire such commitment. This was his chosen career. He would consider nothing short of doing his full duty.

So the day had arrived. The day he was to return to the Lancers.

"Nurse!" Dr. Menzies bustled in with his abrupt manner. A small man with black hair and beard, he never wasted time and never showed fatigue. Jennifer had seen his black eyes snapping as brightly after hours of performing surgery as they did now. She hurried to assist, holding the bag of instruments and bandages for him.

Richard held out his hand. Jenny took it and gave it a reassuring squeeze. But they did not speak.

"Scissors." Jennifer placed them in the doctor's hand. "Now we shall see how you do." Dr. Menzies spoke to the top of Richard's head as he unwound the first layer of bandages.

Richard had only one question. "May I return to my regiment tomorrow, Doctor?"

"We shall see. Bring a basin and sponge, nurse." Jennifer turned to obey as another layer of bandages came off. Outside she was all cool efficiency. Inside she could hardly breathe. Would the healing now be complete? Would Lt. Richard Greyston now be returned to the battlefield to be shot at again?

The earlier dark clouds rolled away. Bright sun streamed in the window opposite them as Dr. Menzies began on the last bandage. Jennifer smiled at the sensation of warmth on the back of her head. It must be a good omen.

The bandage fell away. Richard looked up. Jennifer had a fleeting impression of blue-gray eyes surrounded by red puckered skin. But it was only fleeting.

Richard gave a cry of piercing pain and flung his hands over his face.

Dr. Menzies nodded. "Just as I feared. Photophobia from corneal burns." He took the roll of clean bandages that Jennifer held in suddenly numb fingers and rewrapped Richard's eyes with three quick circles around his head. The springy blond curls had grown back sporadically around the scars on Richard's head. Tender red skin showed above and below the white strip that covered the light blue eyes.

After his initial outcry, Richard sat in stony silence and rocklike stillness.

"Doctor—" If Richard wouldn't ask, Jennifer would. And yet she couldn't find the words.

Dr. Menzies shrugged his shoulders. "Who knows? Sometimes there is improvement. Sometimes not. In time he may be able to bear light enough to see. Or he may not. Go home, young man, and wait."

Richard was silent.

Jennifer wanted to reach out to him. There must be something she could say. Something she could do. But she could think of nothing.

"Clean up here, nurse." Dr. Menzies indicated the bandages he had flung on the floor. "Then I shall need you to assist in surgery." Jennifer must have been slow to respond because he added, "Immediately."

Jenny just managed to brush Richard's hand as she turned to follow the doctor's orders.

She was on duty for the next eight hours. It was time for quarters—just past, actually—when she finished her last task. The rules were incontrovertible. She would be severely reprimanded for being in the corridors after eight o'clock. Nurses had been sent home for little more than that. But she must speak to Richard.

It was a cold night. After that critical burst of sunlight that had given so much pain to Richard's light-sensitive eyes, the clouds had returned. Now the rain fell heavily. Jennifer threw her short gray uniform cape around her shoulders and ran down the tower stairs, not bothering to take a lamp with her.

The corridors were deserted. Now with the success of the Sanitary Commission, men were recovering so rapidly that almost all their patients had been moved into real beds in wards. But what did recovered mean? Were men missing arms or legs recovered? Were men whose scars had healed but who still cried out in their sleep recovered? Were blind men recovered? Richard. Would he ever recover?

Jennifer opened the door and slipped into the silent, darkened ward. Hurrying down the row, she counted the beds almost subconsciously. But there was no mistake when she arrived at the middle. She was too late. Lt. Richard Greyston was gone.

Five

Five months later, on a bright day in August, Jennifer stood on the deck of the *Hansard* with a light breeze blowing her skirts. Gulls wheeled and called overhead, and the white chalk cliffs of home welcomed her. She wanted to push back the bonnet confining her thick hair, but gently bred Englishwomen did not go bareheaded in public.

"What will you do now?" Louisa, one of the returning "lady" nurses, leaned against the rail beside Jennifer.

Jennifer gave her a startled look. "Why, go home, of course."

"Of course! But I mean, will you nurse in a hospital? Or take private patients?"

The question perplexed Jenny. She had given the matter so little consideration. During all the months of battling overwhelming disease and filth, she had concentrated so hard on helping her patients survive and on surviving herself that she had given almost no thought to what she would do when it was all over. Most of the time it seemed that the horror would never end.

But it did end. Although the war was not yet over, by the end of July when the Sanitary Commission finished their work, there were only 1,100 patients in the Barracks Hospital, and fewer than 100 of those were confined to their beds. Florence Nightingale had been able to extend her influence to hospitals in the Crimea itself, and the demands on her nursing staff were greatly reduced.

It was then that Jennifer had received one of her mother's

persistent letters begging her to return home.

My very dear dau.,

You know nothing can give your father and myself more gratification than that our only child should be engaged in so worthy an activity. Indeed it is incumbent upon all of us who name Him Lord that we never neglect our duty to visit the poor and give comfort to the sick. But, my dear, there are so many needy right here in London. Cannot you find your way clear to return to doing good in the bosom of your own family? I know that you will be pleased to learn that the excellent Mr. Merriott has undertaken the added task of factory inspection.

Your loving mother,
Amelia Neville

For once Jennifer actually had time to consider her mother's pleading. And she decided that perhaps her mother was right. But now she must confront the issue that Louisa's question raised. Jenny had known from her early days in Scutari that she didn't want to continue nursing. But she was more sure than ever that she did want to help people. She was a far different woman from the compliant girl who had sailed across the Channel in the opposite direction less than a year before. She had seen what energy and determination could do. She had learned how far her own strengths could reach, and she now had some concept of what must be accomplished. She couldn't imagine what those who knew her before in her proper sheltered life would think of her. Her life would never be the same.

But she also knew that shedding her old life would not be enough. She must take up a new one. The hospital had been a success. The army had been saved. Richard had lived. Now she must find new causes she could care about as passionately as those. But she had no idea what they would be.

"Perhaps I will return to my ragged school work." Her vague reply satisfied Louisa, who turned to talk to another of the returning nurses. But Jennifer wondered whether it satisfied herself. The schools, mostly begun by missionaries of the London City Mission and overseen by the Earl of Shaftesbury, were a wonderful work. They brought the light of knowledge and of the Gospel to half-naked children living in the unspeakable squalor of London's slums amid bad water, open drains, and crumbling overcrowded homes. Such thoughts brought back the horrors of the first months at the Scutari hospital to her, and for a moment she felt stifled with putrid air in spite of the fresh sea breeze around her.

She shook her head. When she had taken part in Mary Stanley's excited vision of going out to Turkey to "help dear Flo and inspire our brave soldiers," Jennifer had had no idea she was to undertake anything that would change her own life.

And apparently not all felt so changed. Louisa and Felicia Burkston-Hodder talked excitedly about their plans. "I, for one, have had quite enough of changing bandages and fetching and carrying." The ribbons of Felicia's bonnet whipped in the breeze.

Louisa brushed the tiered ruffled skirt of the new day dress she had ordered during their three-day stopover in Paris on the way home. "Oh, you mustn't say that. We must always carry with us the inspiration of having worked with Miss Nightingale to save our dear boys. And every woman knows there will always be nursing to do—for our families, for those on our estate—" She paused in some confusion. "—that is, for those with estates—and always charity work for others," she finished in a rush. It was clear that Louisa had little thought for anything but returning to her family in Surrey.

And Felicia evidenced even less doubt about the life she was returning to. "My last letter from Papa was to inform me that he has agreed to allow Mr. Murray Relyea to make his addresses to me. What do you think, Jennifer? I have a great fondness for St. Marylebone, but it is rather out of fashion now. Would it not be better to be married at St. George's Hanover Square?"

Jennifer was glad that Louisa answered for her, giving enthusiastic support to the superiority of St. George's. This was a topic that would have greatly interested her less than a year ago. Here was another evidence of how much she had changed in these few months. What would Mr. Arthur Nigel Merriott think of her now? Indeed, what would she think of him? And having changed so much, would she be expected to change again?

She was still worrying later when the train steamed into the Tooley Street Station in Southwark. It didn't take long for her to spot the familiar figure among all the others waiting on the platform—of stocky build, medium height, but looking rather taller in his high top hat and sober but well-tailored dark suit, Arthur Nigel Merriott had come to meet her. He handed her down from the door of her car and took her hand luggage from her. His thick sandy eyebrows shaded his brown eyes as his square muttonchop sideburns curled forward with a smile of greeting. "Your parents were so kind as to allow me to meet your train. Although why you didn't come by private coach, I don't understand. One might be required to sit by anyone on a train." He signaled a porter. "Where are your trunks, Jennifer?"

"No, Arthur, this is all." She had to say it three times before he realized that she had only the two small bags. "I have not been on a pleasure cruise to require a steamer trunk," she reminded him.

"Yes, my dear Jennifer, I am aware of that." He led the way from the platform at a brisk pace. "But now you can put all that behind you. Of course, I'm certain it couldn't have been all the *Times* made it out to be. But you must have seen some rather unpleasant things. I still don't understand why you took it into your head to go all the way out to Turkey when there is so much to be done here. But never mind that now."

He hailed a hansom cab, and they were soon trotting briskly northward—as briskly as the congested traffic on London Bridge would allow.

"Mother wrote in her last letter that you have been appointed to the Factory Inspection Commission."

Arthur never needed encouragement to talk about his work. One of the things Jennifer appreciated most about him was his willingness to discuss such matters with her. Certainly her father would never talk to her mother about such unsuitable topics as politics or his work in the bank, and he never gave her mother or herself anything but the society page of the newspaper to read.

Arthur, however, was far too passionate about his work to curb his enthusiasm, even in the face of society's demands that the weaker sex be spared sordid facts. "Oh, you have no idea what work there is to do. The two hours a day of schooling provided for factory children is more often directed by anyone available at the moment—whether or not they can read or write themselves—than by any proper schoolmaster. And even the youngest children are required to work fourteen hours a day or more. If England is to remain the leader of the industrial world—"

"But, Arthur, what has become of the Ten Hours Act? I'm certain I remember that it passed long before I left." Jennifer blinked in confusion. It seemed as if she had been gone ten years rather than ten months.

"Quite right, quite right you are. It passed in substance. But the factory owners have found a loophole. They work children in relays, often requiring six-year-olds to remain at the factory from six in the morning until ten at night, with a few spare hours in the middle, which are of little use for recreation or education. And there has been almost no reform in the potteries. Workers are the foundation of industry. We weaken that foundation by being careless with this resource."

The hooves of the cab horse rang briskly on the paving stones, mingling with the cries of costermongers hawking their wares amid the bustling throng of shoppers. Jennifer gazed at the banking houses of the city, the smart shops of New Oxford Street, and—once the congestion of Oxford Circle was behind them—beheld again the quiet elegance of Regent Street. She leaned back against the black leather upholstery of the cab with a sigh and felt herself relax as the familiar sights of Portland Place drew closer.

" '. . . Tribes who killed unwanted babies or sacrificed their children to Moloch were merciful compared with Englishmen of the nineteenth century.' " Arthur's impassioned voice suddenly penetrated Jennifer's consciousness.

"What did you say, Arthur?"

"I was quoting one of the earl's speeches for the Ten Hours Act—one of his finest, I believe. I've got it all by heart. 'For we, having sucked out every energy of body and soul, tossed them on the rubbish heap of the world—a mass of skin and bone, incapable of exertion, brutalized in their understandings, and disqualified for immortality.' And disqualified for further work, I should have added had I been making the speech."

The cab came to a stop before Number 7 Portland Place,

and Jennifer saw her mother coming out the door to meet her. With a stifled sob, Jennifer barely waited for the butler to open the cab door before she sprang down. "Mama, I had forgotten how beautiful you are!"

Mrs. Neville returned her daughter's embrace and gave her a quick kiss on the cheek before suggesting they go inside where they would be unobserved. But Jenny was right. At barely over forty, with only a few gray hairs highlighting the rich brown hair beneath her lace cap and dressed in a deep violet dress with a wide crinolined skirt, Amelia Neville retained much of the beauty that had made her the belle of her coming-out season a generation earlier.

They entered the parlor decorated in rich shades of deep green and plum, with its dark wood furniture heavily carved and upholstered in thickest velvety plush, its mantel, piano, and tables draped with silk-fringed scarves. To Jennifer it was as cool and quiet as the heart of a forest where the sun never truly penetrated. Nothing could have been further removed from the plains of northern Turkey. Jennifer sank thankfully into a chair overhung by a verdant potted palm and accepted a cup of tea from the tray brought in by Hinson, the butler. She was home.

Arthur passed the tray of cucumber and cress sandwiches. "You can have no notion, Jennifer, of how needed our factory inspections are. I have witnessed children with a whole alphabet of deformities brought on by the iniquitous demands of their labors." Arthur placed a cheese and hazelnut sandwich on his own saucer before sitting down. "The side alleys of our cities are thronged with the dirtiest—"

"It was so kind of you to fetch Jennifer from the station, Arthur, dear. I know your support must have meant a great deal to her after such a fatiguing journey." Mrs. Neville took a sip from her flowered china cup.

Arthur's thick sandy eyebrows underwent a strange pattern of contortions as Mrs. Neville's hint registered with him. "Ah, yes. I was delighted to be of service. But, of course, now that you're returned to us, Jennifer, my dear, we shall have plenty of time to discuss all these matters. Indeed, Ashley— er, that is, the Earl of Shaftesbury—is to make a public address on the topic soon. You will doubtless wish to hear him. Perhaps you would allow me to accompany you, Mrs. Neville?"

By the time Arthur left them after his third bow, Jennifer couldn't decide whether to scream or cry. "Dear Arthur— such energy, such dedication, such goodness. It's exhausting to contemplate. If there were a dozen like him in the city, I'm sure the worst rookery should be swept clean in a matter of months. I do admire him so much."

"Indeed, my dear. Arthur is the finest of men. He's assured to go far, especially with the earl's support. I'm certain his future wife—whoever she may be—will find herself Lady Merriott one day."

"Yes, Mama. That had not escaped my consideration." But Jennifer laughed as she said it. She had learned months ago at Scutari that laughter was often the best release for the feeling of having been run over by a steam engine.

"But you must not be too quick about taking up your charity work again. You look woefully drawn." Mrs. Neville examined her daughter's hands. "My goodness, you look as if you'd been scrubbing with the housemaids. It's no wonder Mary Stanley returned after only a month of nursing. Why didn't you come then, too? I'm sure if we'd known it would be anything so difficult, your father and I would never have permitted you to go out to Scutari at all. There are plenty of good works to be done right here in our own city."

"Yes, Mama." Jennifer pushed her teacup aside. Her head was beginning to ache.

"Fortunately, I have a fine new cucumber and rosewater cream from Fortnum's. You must use it faithfully. A lady can never take too much care of her skin. And we will begin our calls next week. Fortunately I had the foresight to refuse all invitations for this weekend. We will visit my dressmaker in the morning."

"Yes, Mama." Whether it was the rigors of the past months or the specter of returning to a never-ending round of afternoon calls and dinner parties, Jennifer's head felt as if it would split apart.

By the end of the following week, however, the cucumber and rosewater cream had done much to restore Jennifer's work-roughened hands, and her wardrobe had been brought up to date by three new gowns from the patterns of Swan & Edgar.

And yet she had done nothing to grasp the vigorous new life she had envisioned for herself on the deck of the *Hansard*. She, indeed, was much changed, as she had foreseen, but her family was not. And she was also very tired. It had been much easier to stifle her own desires and slip black into old routines.

But today would be different. Today Mrs. and Miss Neville would attend the Society for Doing Good in All Souls Parish. Jennifer felt an upsurge of fervor. Now she would begin her work. She would undertake a bold new cause whereby she could help improve London as decidedly as she had helped improve Scutari. The Barracks Hospital had been but a training ground.

"Come along, my dear, or we shall be late. Lady Eccleson doesn't like to be kept waiting in her own parlor." Mrs. Neville pulled on her gloves and picked up her parasol.

Jennifer knew that no matter how flushed with crusading spirit she might feel, she must be the obedient daughter in her father's home. She carefully tied the mint-green ribbons of her straw bonnet and lifted the full skirt of her new green walking dress as she hurried down the stairway to the marble-floored entry hall where her mother waited.

Mrs. Neville directed her carriage driver to take them to Manchester Square at the top of Duke Street. "And hurry," she added. Lady Eccleson ruled the compassionate societies of the parish with an efficient, never-wavering devotion to the bodies and souls of the "less fortunate." And one did not demonstrate true Christian concern for God and the poor by arriving late to one of her committee meetings.

Fortunately, Mrs. and Miss Neville were not late. Two seats in the parlor remained unoccupied, however. Lady Eccleson regarded the vacancies with a scowl and then turned to her guests. The coils of silver hair over each ear gleamed beneath a lace cap as white as the ropes of pearls adorning the neckline of her black dress. "My niece and her children always stay with me when they are in London. Charlotte and her daughter will join us shortly, I have no doubt. Now." She peered at the assembled committed through her lorgnette as if calling Parliament to order. "There is good to be done."

The Misses Bales, sitting across from Jennifer on a love seat, turned from their giggling and gossiping to present serious faces to the room. Well into middle age, the sisters still tortured their blonde hair into ringlets and wore the ruffled styles of their girlhood. Mrs. Biggar, just beyond Mrs. Neville, smoothed the skirt of her bright blue dress—a shade far too overpowering for her diminutive size—and looked, as if for support, to her husband. Col. Biggar's white hair and mustache shone in contrast to the dark wood of the carved oriental screen behind him. His stiff military bearing bespoke the glories of Waterloo and the rigors of India. As he adjusted his monocle, it was clear he was prepared to give equal service to this new call to arms.

"It has come to my attention that we must form a new committee." Lady Eccleson cleared her throat. "While we have been seeing to the needs of the poor and fallen in Whitechapel, Dockland, and Limehouse, Satan has crept in the back door and established a bulwark on the very doorstep of our own parish. I have written a letter to the vestry committee of All Souls to draw its attention to the drunkenness and growing number of houses of ill-repute springing up around us. I hardly need to point out that such behavior is not seemly in one of the most genteel parishes in London."

Lord Selbourne, a dark-visaged, square-jowled man at whose home in Portland Place many such committee meetings were held, agreed vigorously. "Indeed, the vestry has received a letter of complaint signed by 248 members speaking against these gross outrages upon decency and morality and continual disorders that give great scandal, offence, and disgust. A complaint has been filed with the Metropolitan Police." He paused and observed the nods of approval around the room. "Our concern must be twofold: to wipe away this plague spot from our very doorstep, while at the same time contending for the faith, without which all social progress will be barren and fleeting. We must declare war upon the sin, while demonstrating the love of God to the sinner."

"Hear, hear!" Col. Biggar seconded.

The Misses Bales applauded.

A lively discussion followed as to methods for organizing. They must study the problem, gain official attention for action, and form a visiting committee to take aid to the victims of such sin and crime.

"Yes! And we must petition the Public Health Committee for an inspector. When they have examined the drains and latrines as they did in Scutari—" Jennifer felt a sharp jab of her mother's elbow in her ribs. She looked up to see Lady Eccleson's complexion change from bright red to an alarming purple.

Jenny closed her eyes, wishing she could crawl under the silk-fringed shawl that provided modesty for the legs of Lady Eccleson's piano. One did not mention drains—and worse—in a lady's drawing room, even during a committee meeting.

Fortunately Lord Selbourne broke the silence before the Misses Joye and Grace Bales could begin a fit of giggles. "Ah, you have foreseen my concern precisely, Miss Neville. I will send a letter to Dr. Pannier, who has just been appointed to a position in the Health Department. I understand he worked in the Crimea, so he should be well aware of such situations. Now I propose that this committee go on record as supporting . . ."

Jennifer struggled to follow the discussion of plans for tearing down a slum and building a row of model houses like those Prince Albert had designed for the Great Exhibition. She put a finger to her right temple and pushed firmly. Her head was beginning to pound. She made no attempt to grasp the statistics, but a statement of Lord Selbourne's suddenly caught her attention. "When we have provided a source of clean drinking water, then the poor will pay more attention to our urgings that they drink from the fount of Living Water." The words brought into focus the element she had been struggling to identify—the missing element in so much of the discussion she had heard since she came home. It seemed that since the Earl of Shaftesbury's committees had published the blue books exposing the plight of the poor, all the world was caught up in the work of improving conditions. But how many took up the work because it was a popular cause or because they wanted to live in a cleaner city themselves? And how many were working because they saw the poor as children of God and wanted to share His love with them?

A verse ran through her aching head again and again: *Though I bestow all my goods to feed the poor, and though I give my body to be burned, and have not charity, it profiteth me nothing . . . nothing . . . nothing.* Yet she had no clear understanding of how to apply those words. They rang as a warning to her—a warning to understand her own motives for any work she should undertake.

She couldn't claim a spiritual call such as Florence Nightingale's. She hoped she could at least claim as noble a goal as the betterment of society. She hoped she wasn't looking for a cause simply because society expected it of her or because she needed something to do—an amusement or escape from boredom.

Just when she thought she couldn't sit there another moment without crying out, the debate buzzing around her was interrupted by the entrance of Lady Eccleson's tardy niece Caroline and her daughter Lavinia. Jennifer was surprised that the daughter was almost her own age, after Lady Eccleson's reference to her niece's "children." As Jennifer acknowledged the introductions, she was thinking she would like to get to know this Lavinia. But for now the disruption of the meeting offered her a chance to escape.

"Please excuse me for a few moments. Just a breath of fresh air to clear my head, if you wouldn't mind, Lady Eccleson," she begged.

The great lady regarded Jennifer with the full gaze of her piercing blue eyes. "You look exceedingly peaked, my dear. Nursing is no work for respectable young ladies, no matter how much your services may have been needed by our brave, young men. It won't do, you know—young women gallivanting off to the other side of the world. I should never have allowed my great-niece to do such a thing." She leveled a severe look in the young lady's direction and then directed a scowl at Mrs. Neville before turning back to Jennifer. "I cannot imagine what your parents were thinking of. My dear, fresh air is highly overrated. Do not go into the garden. A sudden chill wouldn't be the thing at all. There is a most comfortable sofa in the library. Branman will show you." Lady Eccleson pulled a tapestry bell rope behind her chair to summon her silently moving butler.

At the door of the library Jennifer declined the butler's offer of tea or smelling salts. She slipped quickly into the dark, cavernous coolness of the high-ceilinged, wood-paneled room with its deep Persian rug. The double doors clicked shut behind her, and she felt herself relax. She walked toward the sofa in the center of the room. Then she stopped.

She was not alone.

Six

It was several moments before Jennifer's eyes adjusted to the dimness enough to see the form sitting with deathlike stillness at a small writing desk against the far wall. She gasped. Why would anyone sit at a desk in a library with the shutters half-closed?

"Well?" His voice was irritable. The single word wasn't spoken loudly, but it sounded like a gunshot in the silence of the room.

"I'm—I'm sorry. I didn't mean to intrude." Jenny took a step backward and started to turn when he raised his head and leaned in the direction of her voice. Light from the half-shuttered window fell across his face. It couldn't be. Yet it was. "Lt. Greyston!"

Now she moved forward rapidly, expecting him to hold out his hand just as he always had in the Barracks Hospital. "How is this possible? I thought you lived in Newcastle."

He did not offer his hand. His voice was so bitter Jennifer doubted that, if she had not seen his face, she would have known him. "I do not 'live' anywhere. My body accompanies my mother and sister wherever it is bid, but that can hardly be called living. If I had been two inches closer to that exploding cannon, it could have done its work properly and taken the top off my head as it was meant to do."

Jennifer longed for a pillow to plump or a blanket to straighten, any movement to break the tension and give her time to think. Her impulse was to open the shutters, but she recalled vividly the searing pain the light pouring through the hospital windows had caused Richard. Then she spotted a book on the floor and moved to pick it up.

She had no idea what to say, but she did know two things: that she should not offer sympathy and that Richard must be rescued from his doldrums, as surely he had been rescued from the fever in Scutari. With the book returned to its shelf and her headache forgotten, Jenny took a chair near Richard, near enough that she could reach out and touch him, but she didn't.

She felt a restraining awkwardness in their new situation. Besides, she had already committed one serious error today by speaking without thinking.

"Well, isn't this amazing?"

He made no reply.

She smoothed the satin of her skirt and forged onward. "So you must be Lady Eccleson's great-nephew. I have just met your sister, but I had no notion that the Lavinia I was introduced to was the 'dearest Livvy' of your letters."

"Correct on all counts."

Jenny cleared her throat and shifted on her chair. Richard sat with his hands folded on the small table before him. He had not moved since she entered the room.

"Doubtless you are finding the adjustment extremely difficult." She tried again in her most matter-of-fact tone. "I have been home only a week, but in many ways it seems that I have returned to a different world."

When Richard didn't respond, she continued with perhaps more vigor than she felt. "I suppose the change is more in myself than in my family or in London . . ." Her voice trailed off as she thought. Then she leaned forward in her chair. "That is it, isn't it? They haven't changed at all. And I have changed so much."

"It's certain *I* have changed." His voice was thick with irony.

Again she fought against the dead silence in the room. "I apologize for interrupting you. Your thoughts must have been deeply engaged." She hated the stiffness separating them after the closeness of those hours spent holding his hand in the hospital. Why must there be these barriers now?

"I was not engaged at all. To be brutally honest, I was hiding out from Mama and Livvy who forever insist that I accompany them on their visits. It took me only one experience to discover that a costermonger or policeman would be more welcome in a drawing room than a blind man as soon as the novelty of entertaining a war hero has worn off. 'What *does* one say when he sloshes his tea, my dear?' "

Jenny forced a small laugh at his bitter humor. Then she noticed the odd papers on his desk with the little rows of bumps on them. "But what are those papers? I've never seen anything like them."

"It's my excuse for taking refuge in here. A French fellow named Louis Braille invented a method for the blind to read and write using a system of raised dots. Mama is most enthusiastic that I should learn it, and so she will excuse me from any other activity if I tell her I wish to read. It doesn't work as well on Livvy, however, for she is still convinced my sight will improve, and I'll have no need of such rigmarole."

"And what does your doctor say?"

"My 'doctor' includes half the sawbones on Harley Street to whom Mama has dragged me off. Although she is energetic at the present, Mama has long suffered sporadic bouts of invalidism. She is well acquainted with that community. We have yet to find one doctor with a cogent idea of what to do beyond rubbing my eyelids with citron and spermaceti ointment and hoping for the best."

Jennifer could think of no reply, so she asked, "What are you reading?"

"Nothing. This confounded system is so slow. Or rather I'm so slow at it. I have no patience for this. If I had such inclination, I would have remained quietly reading law at Cambridge instead of convincing Father to purchase my commission. My dear mother entertains notions of my returning to something like that, and I haven't the heart to dissuade her. After all, she is Lady Eccleson's niece—she will admit to nothing, even blindness, being more than an inconvenience. And surely one could form a committee to deal with even that. The trouble is, I have never been the least good at waiting. I always thought Milton's line 'they also serve who only stand and wait' the silliest sentiment in all literature. Now I know it so." He pushed his chair back abruptly and rose to his feet with a jerk. He began pacing a small area in front of the corner bookshelves.

Jennifer held her breath lest he crash into the furniture. Should she rescue the porcelain urn from the pedestal next to the chair on the far wall?

"Richard—"

He seemed to sense her uneasiness. "What? Are you fearing for the family porcelains? A priceless collection, as is appropriate for a pottery owner, Aunt Charlotte will tell you. Relax. I can see shapes well enough to identify objects. I can tell a cat from a dog, a horse from a cow, and a man from a woman quite readily. Useful knowledge to possess. The trouble is, I can only bear to look at anything if the room or weather is too dark for even a clear-sighted person to see well. So what it comes to is that I could see a meager amount if I could bear to see at all."

"So Livvy's optimism isn't entirely without foundation?"

"That depends on what one is being optimistic about. It's clear I'll never be of use to my regiment again."

"And therefore you can never be of use to anyone?" If

71

Jennifer had hoped to goad him into moderating his position, she had failed.

"It's hard to see how. I certainly have no desire to join the Inns of Court and qualify as a solicitor. And my brother George will take over the pottery one day." He flung his lanky form into a wing-backed chair. As if to demonstrate his imperfect vision, he hit the chair slightly sideways and knocked it into the bookshelf, but did not fail to find the seat. Ignoring the ruckus he made, he continued, "Since you went to such considerable trouble to save my life, I suppose I owe it to you to explain this the best I can. It is as if I had ridden Legend at a full gallop straight at a high stone wall, and we hit it full tilt. The world has simply come to a crashing halt." He paused. "And there it is."

Now the silence in the room grew deep, but not with the uneasiness Jennifer had feared before. She took her time, giving careful consideration to all Richard had said. Certainly she, too, had been plodding through her days ever since she had returned home. Richard was not the only one without a goal, a reason for getting up in the morning. Her mother would have her fill her calendar with social functions. Arthur would have her plunge into social causes for the good of England. But she had found no way for herself.

With Richard sitting across from her, she realized it was *he* who had sustained *her* through the worst days in the Barracks Hospital just by being there for her to care for. She had sped through chores that could easily have bogged her down, because she knew that if she finished in time, she could then go to Richard. She hadn't given a single thought to returning home with Mary Stanley or any of the other nurses, not because of the countless number of men who needed her, but because of one man who needed her.

She rose and walked to him, and this time she did not wait

for him to hold out his hand. She simply took it in both of hers. She felt the slight jerk and thought he was going to pull away. But he didn't.

"Richard, I am so glad to have found you again. I—"

"Miss Neville!" The double doors burst open with a crash, causing Jennifer to jump backwards. "Great-aunt Charlotte has sent me to fetch you. Tea is being served." Livvy Greyston stood in the lighted doorway, blinking at the darkened room. "Oh, I see you've met my brother. I don't suppose it's any good asking you to come to tea, is it, Dick?"

He shook his head, holding up a hand to shade his eyes against the light from the open doors.

"All right. I'll tell Branman to bring you a tray, shall I?"

"Oh, could I take mine here with your brother? We're old acquaintances, you see. I was one of Miss Nightingale's nurses at Scutari."

Livvy hesitated, but Richard was adamant. "That would never do, Miss Neville. You have been summoned to Lady Eccleson's tea table. 'Ours is not to reason why; ours is but to do or die.' "

Jennifer smiled, then murmured a farewell to Richard and obediently followed Livvy from the room. "So you are Livvy. I wrote several letters to you for Richard."

Livvy stopped and flung her arms around Jenny. "Oh! How marvelous! I can't wait to tell Mama. It will mean so much to her. Just think of you being there with Dick, and here we are together—it's like Providence. It must have been *meant.*" She took Jenny's hand and almost dragged her down the long, paneled hall hung with dark, gilt-framed portraits. "We've longed to know more of what happened in Turkey, but Dick won't talk about it."

As soon as they were settled in a corner of Lady Eccleson's parlor, Livvy began plying Jenny with questions. But Jenny felt a restraint. If Richard had not chosen to tell his family about it, she wasn't sure it was her place. So after a few comments about how heroic Florence Nightingale and the sanitary commissioners were, it was easy to encourage Livvy to return to what quickly proved to be her favorite topic of conversation—her brother.

"I think we were all surprised when Dick chose a military career. Of course he always played soldiers when he was young, and he was an absolutely mad rider—no fence was ever too high for him to jump. But he was so quiet and gentle too. The thought of him killing anything always seemed strange to me."

The perky features of Livvy's round face softened with memory. "I was sickly as a child. Dick would amuse me by the hour, reading stories he couldn't possibly have enjoyed. And he could always make me laugh. He would slip little asides into the stories. He was very sly, so I had to listen carefully, or I'd miss the fun. And then he would take me out in the pony cart when I know he would have rather been riding pell-mell over the fields."

Jenny listened with amazement. Here was a side of Richard she had not seen at all—or even thought to look for. Suddenly she began to wonder more about what he had been like as a child. All at once he was more of a person to her—not just a case to be cured by her skill.

"Mrs. Biggar, please take another of the egg mayonnaise sandwiches, but do avoid the smoked salmon. It is far too high for your constitution." As Lady Eccleson gave her peremptory order, another surprising thought came to Jennifer. Had Lady Eccleson known perfectly well that Richard was in the library?

Jennifer toyed with her cucumber sandwich. So what was she to do about Richard? The problem he faced now, and the challenge to her if she were to help him, made the demands of Scutari seem almost simple. If only the problem of redirecting one's life—of finding a purpose for living—could be overcome with the directive of a sanitation commission to flush a sewer system and lime-wash a few walls.

She did, however, have one glimmer of an idea. "Livvy, what about your brother's horse? I know he cared for him a great deal—he used to talk to me about him in the hospital. Did he ever find out whether Legend survived?"

Livvy set her cream horn back on her plate and licked a few traces of chantilly from her fingers. "That horse was a magnificent creature. Named for Royal Legend—our most popular pottery pattern—but then I expect Dick told you that. No, I don't think he's made any attempt to learn anything. Of course, we've only been in town a short time."

"Do you know where one would go to make such inquiries?"

Livvy considered. "Horse Guards, I should expect. Aren't all army records kept there? About men and regiments anyway—I don't know about horses. Why?"

"I was thinking of making inquiries myself. Would you like to go with me?"

Livvy, at least three years Jenny's junior, arranged her blonde hair in clusters of ringlets over each ear and wore a violet afternoon dress with each flounce trimmed in ruffles of lace. Now all the curls and ruffles bounced. "Oh, what a charming idea! I should like it above all things."

Sometime later in the dark library, Richard heard the rattle of carriage wheels on stone and knew his aunt's guests, including Miss Jennifer Neville, had departed. With a sweeping gesture he pushed the books and Braille-dotted papers from his table to the floor. But the effect on the thick carpet was unsatisfying. He had hoped for a gratifying thud or crash. He clenched his fist and slammed it against the solid oak of the desk. Then, fighting for control, he lowered his head to his tight fists. It was no good smashing things. He must channel the energy of his outrage. He must find a useful outlet for all he felt churning inside him.

And right now he must use that energy to fight down his fear—the fear of having to grope through another day, another week, a week that would grow to a month and then a year. He could not go on like this endlessly. He must make something out of the perpetual darkness he found himself locked in.

Perhaps he would get better—but perhaps not. He had to assume he wouldn't. He couldn't sit and wait for an outcome that could take months or years—or never come at all. He had to find a source of inner light to replace the external light denied him. He must walk by faith rather than by sight—as that preacher at Cambridge had said. But he had no idea how to go about it.

Seven

The expedition to Horse Guards was not as easily accomplished as Jennifer had hoped. Mrs. Neville would not hear of her daughter gallivanting about town unescorted, and Miss Greyston hardly constituted a proper escort. Jennifer's mother herself could not be expected to go off on such a hair-brained escapade, as her calendar was quite full. Besides, all matters of livestock were clearly men's business. "When Arthur has time to see to it, I'm certain he will deal with it in the most competent manner."

As Arthur had gone to Bristol on a factory inspection, it would be some time next week before he could go with them.

Jenny did not bear waiting with patience. "Mother, I am going to take up my charity work again," she announced.

"Certainly, my dear, you must accompany me next week. We shall distribute baskets of food to the deserving poor of the Norton Street settlement, as we discussed at Lady Eccleson's. That should be quite enough alongside your social obligations." Mrs. Neville regarded herself in the heavily beveled glass of her oval mirror. "What do you think, Jenny—should I have this gown trimmed in the ivory lace or the blue fringe?"

Jennifer advised the ivory lace and left her mother's room. Why could no one understand her desire to do more than deliver food baskets once a week? But then perhaps it wasn't so strange, since she wasn't sure how well she understood herself. As she walked down the polished corridor of their home in Portland Place, she recalled the fetid, body-filled corridor of the Scutari hospital and Miss Nightingale describing the voice she had heard from God asking her to do a special work for Him. Jennifer sighed. How simple it would be if she could hear such a voice. That would remove all her own doubts and give her courage to stand against her family and the social expectations hemming her in.

As it was, however, a vague desire to help people and a need to find an outlet for her energy was all she had to lead her forward. But forward to what? She wandered into the morning room, assured of being alone there so late in the afternoon. On a table by the sofa was the copy of the *Times* her father had read before leaving for work. As always, Mr. Neville had pulled out the society pages for her mother.

Jennifer picked up the rest of the paper and leafed through it. An advertisement caught her attention: "Special Sale Announced at Tattersall's. The finest in well-trained, well-bred military horses, both light and heavy. At auction, Saturday fortnight." She thought of Legend and the unlikelihood that they would be able to find him for Richard. Perhaps they could choose another horse.

Before she had time to dwell on that, however, another notice took her attention: "Ragged School opens in Westminster. Any lady or gentleman willing to assist as teacher on Sunday or Thursday evenings will be greatly welcomed." Jennifer carefully noted the address and went to get her bonnet and shawl. Mrs. Neville was busy with her dressmaker now and would then take a nap before dinner. Jennifer would not disturb her. The butler appeared moments after she pulled the red velvet cord. "Please secure me a cab, Hinson. And if my mother asks for me, tell her I've gone calling."

"Very good, miss." In a matter of minutes, he returned from the sheltered cab stand at Langham Place with a hansom cab. Jennifer gave the address to the driver. He flicked the reins passing over the roof, and soon they were trotting along Tothill Street.

Jennifer had thought that the horrors of Scutari had made her proof against any shock, but she was appalled at the slum that had grown up in Westminster, almost against the walls of the Abbey itself. Only two streets away on the banks of the Thames, the Palace of Westminster rose, elegant and golden, with its imposing towers and ornamental oriels, pinnacles, and turrets. But in between the two grand buildings, the rabbit warrens of poverty and filth made the Barracks Hospital seem almost clean by comparison. Children of all ages stood or sat in squalid groups at the entrances to narrow, fetid courts and alleys. Their wan faces and haggard eyes followed the progress of the traffic choking the winding cobbled streets. Gray laundry drooped on lines stretched overhead between crumbling buildings.

The cab stopped in front of a converted warehouse. A small sign over the door read "Westminster Mission and Ragged School." Hesitantly, Jennifer asked the cabby to wait for her.

She stopped just inside the door and surveyed the plain but well-scrubbed room.

"Welcome, miss. And how might we be helping you?"

Jenny smiled at a man with dark hair and beard salted liberally with gray.

"Hiram Walker, at your service." He sketched a slight bow. The fabric of his black suit showed shiny spots from long wear and many pressings, but Hiram Walker was as well-scrubbed as his mission.

"I'm Jennifer Neville. I've come about the school. I've had some experience teaching. Not much really, but I'd like to help."

"Splendid, splendid. What an answer to prayer. The fields

are white unto harvest, but the laborers are few indeed. Come, let me show you." Already he was in motion with the short, rapid steps of one who knows where he's going but doesn't want to rush his companion. Energy and enthusiasm for his work showed in the missionary's soft brown eyes as he led her through remodeled rooms that housed a soup kitchen and meeting room, a schoolroom filled with rows of wooden benches, and two small rooms where he lived. The soup kitchen was abuzz with women whose well-made dresses were covered with copious white aprons, doubtless borrowed from their own cooks. They stirred vast pots of steaming soup and pulled loaves of crusty brown bread from the oven.

"We feed upwards of a hundred poor every night," Mr. Walker explained, "and then follow with a service. Feed their bodies, then their souls—that's my motto. We give them lots of singing—that's the part they like best. And then go to the schoolroom and feed their minds. We have adults and children both. We try to teach all who want to learn."

Jennifer thought of the half-naked children crowding the doorways of the rookeries beyond the mission. Their clothes were too ragged for them to go to a regular school. This small, struggling mission was their only hope of a better life. "Thursday evenings, your advertisement said?"

Rev. Walker's brown eyes sparkled brightly above his beard. "Thursday evenings at seven o'clock. We use a most progressive method here. The beginners are taught their ABCs by one teacher; then they move on to the next, who teaches them to form words; from words a third teacher helps them form sentences. They are reading the Scriptures within the shortest space of time." He would have gone on to explain his ideas for teaching mathematics, but Jennifer was content to know that she could be of use teaching the alphabet to the newest entrants.

She returned to Portland Place with a perhaps unladylike bounce in her stride and a gleam of determination in her eyes. She felt more alive than any time since returning home. It was wonderful. In the space of three days she had discovered work to be done in two great causes—Richard and the ragged school.

Mrs. Neville, however, was not pleased. "Mr. Neville, you must forbid this." She turned to her husband after Jennifer's announcement at dinner that night. "I have heard much of the Tothill Street area. Thousands of people live together in squalor, crime, and wretchedness. They resist all efforts for their own betterment, and they are bitterly hostile to those who seek to do them good. Why, even policemen only go into the area in groups, and I'm told they often go armed with cutlasses."

Mr. Neville had not risen in the banking profession by making snap decisions. He savored his last spoonful of mutton and barley soup, then returned the spoon to its plate and wiped his mouth on his white linen napkin before answering. "It seems to me, wife, that you may be giving in to the hysterical reports in the popular press. Surely all young ladies should be encouraged to do appropriate charitable work." He rose to go to the sideboard where the roast joint of beef stood, crisp and golden brown on its platter. With a few precise cuts of the carving knife, he placed thick slices of beef on the plates Hinson presented to Mrs. and Miss Neville before offering the vegetables and gravy around.

Jennifer seized her opportunity. "That's right, Papa. Westminster is no worse than the Holborn area where I assisted before going to Scutari. And the mission appears very well-run and clean."

She had miscalculated, however, in mentioning Scutari, for her mother had heard of the conditions there. "I'm sure we should never have permitted your going out there if we'd had any idea. Mary Stanley spoke only of soothing the brows and easing the suffering of our brave young men."

Mr. Neville swallowed a bite of roast potato. "The girl seems to have come through the experience quite unscathed."

"I'm not so certain about that, husband. Not so certain at all." The lace lapettes on her cap bobbed up and down as Mrs. Neville regarded her daughter.

Jennifer herself wondered just how unscathed she was. Outwardly, now that her complexion had recovered and her wardrobe had been updated, she appeared little changed. But inside she knew she had grown up far more than any young woman who had remained safe in the comfortable world of London's upper middle class. And she was beginning to see how uncomfortable that could make her.

By Thursday afternoon the matter was still unsettled, and Jennifer was wondering just how far she could or should go in opposing her mother's wishes. Then Hinson announced the arrival of Mr. Arthur Nigel Merriott. "Arthur!" Jennifer flung her embroidery aside and hurried to greet him.

Mrs. Neville followed close behind her daughter, ordering that a tea tray be brought in. Between sips of tea and bites of rich, dark fruitcake, Arthur told them about his factory inspection.

". . . And although some factory owners are too shortsighted to see the truth," he gestured with a piece of cake, "I'm convinced that the new factory laws will be for the good of industry and the good of England. It's common sense. Healthier, happier workers will build a stronger, happier nation. Such laws are a protection against the kind of revolution they have had on the continent."

Mrs. Neville paled and flung her hand to her chest.

"Surely you aren't suggesting those horrid Chartists might actually get the upper hand. Arthur, you don't expect revolution *here?*"

"I think revolutionaries would find limited support here, ma'am, because we are seeing to reform through our laws."

The color returned to Mrs. Neville's cheeks as she refilled her teacup. Jennifer smiled. She could imagine Arthur making that very speech on the hustings as a candidate for Parliament. Already he spoke of the laws as if he had a hand in shaping them.

"By the way," Arthur continued, changing the subject, "I had an interesting experience on this trip. I went to Ashley Downs—you know, the orphanage George Muller runs outside Bristol? I delivered an offering from All Souls to the orphanage and took a meal with them while there." He shook his head. "It was most amazing really. That fellow Muller takes the phrase 'Give us this day our daily bread' quite literally. The larders rarely contain more than a day's supply of food. And yet the children tell me they have never gone hungry. Muller will never tell any person about their needs —only the Lord in prayer. Then when the need is filled, it's certain that it was by no human means."

"You sound skeptical, Arthur."

"It seems a bit helter-skelter, you must admit."

"But the Scriptures say we're to live by faith."

"Well, yes, faith for our salvation, of course. But a bit of vigorous energy on our part seems to be required for the rest of life. How would it be if the rest of us just went along doing good and expected the Lord to take care of us? What would happen to business, to industry, to the poor whose lot we're trying to improve?"

Here was Jennifer's opening. "Arthur, there's a ragged school in Westminster, and I'd really like to teach there."

After his defense of the need for personal action, he could hardly back down now.

"By all means, a noble idea. But in a very bad area. Mrs. Neville, perhaps it would ease your mind if I accompanied Jennifer."

And so it was that only a few hours later, Jenny sat in a corner of the mission schoolroom. With six barefoot, half-naked urchins around her, she began unlocking for them the mysteries of the strange markings and sounds that made up the English language. Each child had copied a wobbly large *B* and small *b* onto a slate and was happily experimenting with the plosive sound of the letter. Suddenly the proceedings were interrupted by the entrance of a tall, thin man with a mass of jet-black curly hair.

A small, ragged scrap of humanity followed behind the man in the well-pressed black suit, but it was the gentle smile on the man's rather large mouth and the kindness in his light blue deep-set eyes that took Jennifer's attention. Strangely, the children did not cower before so dignified a figure, but were instinctively drawn to him.

Mr. Walker, who had just concluded a service in the meeting room, bustled in. "My Lord, what an unexpected honor. I have so little to offer you—perhaps a cup of coffee?"

The newcomer smiled, making his prominent nose appear even sharper. "On the contrary, Walker, you have everything to offer me. No coffee, thank you. It is more than nourishment to me to see your fine work here. And your dedicated workers."

Walker took the hint and presented Jennifer to the Earl of Shaftesbury, the man who had done more than any other in England to promote the work of ragged schools. Jennifer was immediately warmed by his kind face, intelligent eyes, and rather wistful smile. Then the earl propelled the small lad from behind his leg. "I have brought a new student for you, Miss Neville. Although perhaps we might postpone his lessons for tonight in favor of his being given a bath."

The child's skin tones seemed to be of two colors: red and black. His hands, feet, elbows, and knees were such a bright blood red as to appear to be entirely without skin. Indeed, Jennifer gasped when she looked at his knees, thinking the kneecaps completely gone. The rest of his body, as most of it was exposed beneath his rags, was the deep black of ground-in soot. Tears sprang to Jennifer's eyes. Even from the battlefields of the Crimea, she had not seen a sorrier sight. She bent down to his level. "Welcome to our school. And what's your name?"

"Joshua, ma'am." The voice came out in a whisper.

"Mrs. Watson!" The mission director summoned from the kitchen a sturdy, capable-looking woman with her hair tucked under a close-fitting cap.

Jennifer gasped and then flew to the woman in greeting. "Mrs. Watson—my dear Edith! When did you return from Scutari?" It was obvious that small talk would have to wait, but Jennifer could think of no more comforting a personage to take charge of the pitiful Joshua than Edith Watson.

Joshua apparently thought so, too, because he placed his hand in hers to be led off to strong soap and warm water. "Calamine lotion. I have a fresh jug of it in here—just the thing for those knees and elbows." Joshua gave a little hopping skip to keep up with her vigorous walk.

The earl urged the class to continue with the lessons he had interrupted. He would hear them recite. None of the students could have been as nervous as Jennifer, but her small charges made appropriate A-A-A's and B-B-B's for the man who for ten years had led the Ragged School Union. In that time hundreds, even thousands, of vagabond boys and girls had been rescued from the stinking slums squatting behind London's fine thoroughfares.

Arthur returned for Jennifer before classes were dismissed, and so made up part of the group gathered around the Earl of Shaftesbury to hear Joshua's story. "Day before yesterday I happened to rise earlier than usual. Standing by the window at the back of my house in Upper Brook Street, I saw this small boy, his limbs twisted and his back bent beneath the bundle of rods and brushes he was obliged to carry for his employer, who cuffed him as they walked back from work. But I knew from the soot and blood covering him that this lad did more than carry brushes. He had been sent naked up the chimneys to dislodge the soot."

Jennifer leaned forward and listened with fascinated horror. She had been only a child herself when the man before her had led the fight in Parliament to pass the Climbing Boys Bill, but she remembered vaguely the uproar it had caused among the housewives who gathered in her mother's parlor. Clean chimneys were essential to their very lives. More than one London house burned every winter, and often the neighboring buildings as well, from soot in the chimney catching fire. It was a pity if children were made uncomfortable in the effort—but what were they to do? Surely Parliament didn't mean to let London burn.

Jennifer came back from those long-ago memories to the earl's voice continuing. "And I knew from looking into the matter when our bill was before Parliament that the child was prepared for his work by being rubbed all over with salt water in front of a hot fire to toughen his skin. Skin that broke and bled would be rubbed with brine again and again until it was hard."

He paused, and Arthur urged him on. "Tell them about setting the fires, My Lord."

Shaftesbury nodded. "Climbing boys often stick in the chimneys, whether from the narrowness of the passage or their own terror. The sweep will light a fire of straw under him to cause him to struggle violently enough to free himself. Of course, if he doesn't come unstuck, the child suffocates." There was great sadness in the earl's voice, as if he felt personal responsibility for all the children he had been unable to rescue.

"The trouble is, this work is done while all decent Londoners are asleep in their beds. And the sweeps keep their boys locked up on Sundays so no one will see them."

"But is there no alternative?" Jennifer was still puzzling over those conversations recalled from her childhood. "We must have clean chimneys. Is there some way to achieve that without so terrible a cost?"

The earl nodded, his jutting black brows shading his eyes. "New methods are being invented, better brushes developed, new chimneys built with fewer twists and turns that collect soot. We shall see the day a Climbing Boys Bill will pass Parliament *and be enforced,* but I fear that even with our best efforts, it is far off. In the meantime I have rescued this boy. It is so little to do when I would do so much." He paused. "I offered to buy his apprenticeship from his master, but he'd not hear of it. So we tracked down the lad's father. When he heard I was offering free education for his son, the man was most cooperative." Again Shaftesbury paused. "But there are so many who go unrescued. Sometimes I hear them crying out to me in my sleep."

"But, My Lord, you've achieved so much." Arthur's sandy muttonchops bristled with enthusiasm. "You've ended child labor in the coal mines, and our inspection team found matters much improved in the textile mills. I do not think it an overstatement, sir, to say, as I did only this afternoon, that you have saved English society from the revolutions that shook the continent. The work of your committees has given hope to the poor, and the work of missionaries keeps them peaceful."

Arthur's words seemed only to make the earl more morose. "My friend, you sound much like the Frenchman who remarked to me that 'the religion alone of your country has saved you from revolution.' But that is the very thing that saddens me. Is it all mere 'religion' we are practicing? Or is it vital personal faith? Is it for the good of English commerce or for the good of our eternal souls? Do we love cleanliness and order, or do we love God?

"I was brought up in the 'high-and-dry' religion that saw the Church of England primarily as a prop of the government and regarded Dissenters and Methodists as wicked. I fear there is still much of this at every level of society. Without a strong moral basis and personal faith among our people, no reforms can truly help the nation. No matter how much our compassionate societies achieve, what is done only for the sake of society or a popular cause will do little good in the end."

With that the Earl of Shaftesbury pulled himself to his full height and shook the hand of each worker, offering words of gratitude for their efforts. He put on his tall black hat, which made him seem more towering yet.

Long after his departure Jennifer still felt the warm clasp of his hand. She was strangely moved by his fervency. She had never heard anyone speak so deeply from the heart. Certainly, Florence Nightingale had come close, in her efforts to carry out her vision for nursing and good medical care. But the scope of this man's accomplishments and his determination to press forward to right all the wrongs he saw was simply breathtaking. She had heard that he had little personal fortune, and yet he invested much of his own money in the work. All this while being an exemplary father to his own large family.

But it was more than his energy and dedication that gripped her. If fervency for social change had been all, Arthur could be said to be a young Shaftesbury. But there was a vital difference. The key must be in the earl's last words—in the matter of personal faith. And yet how did one sort that out? The Scripture said faith without works was dead, and it seemed that all of polite society was caught up in good works. Did as little of it spring from true faith as the earl indicated? And if so, what hope was there?

Eight

Jennifer stood in the middle of her room a few days later. She ran the dark green satin ribbons of her new bonnet through her fingers, but made no motion to put the hat on, even though she knew the carriage had been summoned.

The truth was, she felt guilty. She had held no intention of abandoning Richard or her new friend Livvy, and she had thought of them much during the past days. The business of restructuring her life in London, however, was proving far more trying than she had imagined. The changes in her values and view of life were taking time to sort out. And some days she seemed further than ever from determining what direction the rest of her life was to take.

Stating her objective was simple. She desired to serve God and society, as was expected of all young ladies of her class. But once that was said, what did one then *do*?

She had always understood God as one of the pillars of society. One served on His committees as one did those of Lady Eccleson. It was a comforting concept. She meant no disrespect by it. But now she suspected that such a childlike picture would not do to build her life on.

"Jennifer, we shall be late." Amelia Neville's voice cut through her daughter's reverie.

Jenny gave one last look at the soft swirls of her rich brown hair in the looking glass before tying her bonnet securely under her chin. She hurried to meet her mother. Attending Lady Eccleson's drawing room might not be synonymous with service to God, but Jennifer would not care to be the person to tell her so.

The trees along Queen Anne Street shone a bright red and gold, and fallen leaves crunched beneath the carriage wheels. Jennifer smiled and breathed deeply. This was her favorite time of the year. Then the bright beauty of the scene brought a crimp to her heart. If only Richard could see it. He could look at the trees at night and discern their shapes, but he could not bear the pain of seeing them in their beauty. *Help him Lord, and help me to help him.* With that quick, informal sentence, she realized she had not prayed instinctively like that since leaving Scutari. Was that what the earl had meant by a personal relationship with God? Rather than relying on the prayers in the prayer book and those led by her father, could she develop a closeness with the Almighty that allowed her to speak to Him as if He were in the same room at all times?

At Lady Eccleson's they were greeted, not by the pale, silent Branman, but by an effusive Livvy. "Jenny, where have you been keeping yourself? I've been longing to talk to you. Oh, isn't it the most divine day! You can have no notion how this makes me long to be in my beloved Newcastle—the Brampton is a blaze of color right now. And children build leaf forts, and the squirrels scurry everywhere, and—" Her headlong rush had carried them to the parlor. She paused, took a deep breath, and entered with suitable decorum. "Aunt Charlotte, Mrs. and Miss Neville have arrived."

The purpose of the meeting was to discuss the plans of the Committee for Bettering the Condition of the Deserving Poor in All Souls Parish, but since this was an informal discussion rather than an official meeting, tea was served first. "Aunt Charlotte's cook makes the world's most divine tea cakes." Livvy licked the melted butter off her fingers. She had chosen seats in the farthest corner of the room so she could continue her narrative to Jenny somewhat unchecked. "I've been so anxious to tell you. Last week I sent one of the footmen around to Horse Guards to inquire about Legend."

If Jennifer's hands hadn't been filled with her teacup, she would have clapped them. "Oh, tell me."

"Well, unfortunately I didn't really learn anything, but the officer on duty said that I might call in person at my convenience for further inquiry. I thought we might go today. Mama is quite complaisant about my going out in Aunt Charlotte's carriage."

Jennifer was more than willing to go with Livvy rather than Arthur. "If only Richard could go with us. The air is so invigorating. And I'm certain he could obtain more information than we could."

Livvy sighed. "If only he would. He's been like a caged animal these past days. He goes for long rambles at night and then attempts to sleep much of the day. But the plan doesn't seem to be working well. He won't allow anyone to accompany him, but he returns with his clothes torn and dirty so that we know he has been bumping into things. Last Saturday he had a dreadful bruise on his forehead, and just yesterday his cheek was gashed and bleeding. Yet he is quite determined."

"But is there no way he can go out in the light?"

"He went to a new doctor two days ago. Dr. Halston gave him a pair of dark glasses. He thought they would help."

"And have they?"

"I'm not certain Dick has tried them out. I'm—" She paused as if choosing her words carefully, which was unusual for Livvy. "I'm not certain it's just his eyes."

"Then what?"

"I think it may be the scarring. I suppose it might be quite alarming to one unprepared, although I never think of it. But

Dick may dread facing the reaction of others as much as he dreads the pain of the light."

Jennifer set her teacup down with a clink. "Then we must see what may be done." She was no longer in an elegant drawing room, but back in the Barracks Hospital, ready to meet the emergency of a new case. Lady Eccleson dismissed the young ladies with a nod.

Livvy led up the stairs and down a corridor to Richard's room. She hesitated before knocking. "He might not be prepared to receive visitors."

"It would not be my first time to see him in bed." Jennifer straightened her back as she often had at Scutari before marching into a ward.

Livvy's knock was answered by a short bald man with a ruddy complexion. "Please tell my brother he has visitors, Kirkham." It was clear that Livvy would have swept on in, but the sturdy Kirkham would have none of it.

"I'll see if it's convenient for Lt. Greyston, ma'am," he replied in a stiff nasal voice and left the door open only an inch.

Livvy grinned. "You haven't met Kirkham, have you? He was Dick's batsman in the Crimea. Showed up on the doorstep almost weeping a few days ago. He had thought Dick dead. Says he can never forgive himself for not attending him in the hospital. Now he seems quite determined to make up for lost time. Guards Dick like a bulldog. How Dick manages to escape him on his evening rambles I can't imagine—except that as a well-trained military servant, Kirkham will take orders."

The stalwart Kirkham was back in a moment. "Hit's not convenient, ma'am." He bowed and started to close the door.

But Kirkham had reckoned without one of Florence Nightingale's angels. Through the narrow opening Jennifer had seen Richard in the next room, his back to the doorway, standing in statuelike stiffness. She put her calfskin-shod foot in the doorway and pushed gently but firmly with a gloved hand. "That is regrettable. It is not convenient for me to be turned away."

Richard did not turn toward her voice. But he did not walk away. His stillness was like one not breathing.

Jennifer swept across his sitting room and into the bedroom where he stood. She turned to face him so abruptly that the crinolined skirt of her dark green afternoon dress swung like a bell. Richard started to turn toward the wall, but she grasped his hand, as much from long habit as from any calculated plan.

The light in the room was moderate, considerably more revealing than that in the library had been on her first visit. Dick looked her direction through nearly closed eyes. Livvy had not overstated. Jagged, puckered lines ravaged his once-handsome face. But the burn scars covering the upper part of his face did not hurt her nearly so much as the pain and bitterness she saw on his tightly-clamped fine mouth.

"Well, sir, I am most gratified to see that your wounds have healed satisfactorily. And your vanity should be pleased that your hair has returned with vigor." She suppressed an unladylike urge to touch the springy golden curls, not because the gesture would be unladylike, but because she dared not let loose of his hand for fear he would move away from her.

"I am pleased to give satisfaction. I rather fear, however, that someone without your medical interest might be less gratified."

Jennifer ignored that. "Livvy and I have come to seek your escort. We are going to Horse Guards on an errand of interest to you."

"I am told the sun is very bright today."

"Indeed, it is an exceedingly lovely day—one of autumn gold, a poet might say. Therefore it is most fortunate that your physician has supplied you with shaded glasses."

"Kirkham will provide you escort. It is not convenient for me—"

"It is not convenient for me to be escorted by Kirkham." She thought she saw the slightest hint of a smile cross his lips.

The detached, ramrod stiffness held for several seconds and then crumbled with his brittle laugh. "Oh, dash it. Why weren't you at Balaclava to order Cardigan around? You might have spared us the trouble of charging those blasted guns." He raised his voice. "Kirkham, fetch my hat and bring the carriage around. It seems we're going out." He turned back to Jennifer. "Will it be 'convenient' for you to be driven by Kirkham?"

"It will be most convenient." She was certain he could hear the smile in her voice if he couldn't see it on her lips.

He turned to grope among the articles lying on a small table. When the glasses hit the floor along with several other objects, he swore under his breath. Jennifer's instinct was to dash forward to pick them up for him, but she checked herself just in time. He found them and turned toward her with them on.

For the first time Jenny had to restrain her impulse to gasp. 'Dark glasses' had been a misnomer. Dr. Halston had supplied his patient with black eye patches. Certainly they would keep out any painful light, but they would prevent Dick from seeing anything. Now she questioned her forwardness. Would he face further humiliation that would make future outings more difficult?

She had gone this far, however, and there was no graceful way of going back. She took his arm, not as one leads the sightless, but as any lady preparing to stroll in the park on the arm of a gentleman. "Excellent. Let us proceed." And she lifted her chin a good two inches higher—a trick that had bolstered her confidence down many a long, dark corridor in Scutari.

Livvy grasped Dick's other arm with both hands and gave a delighted squeal as she propelled them all forward, obviously taking no thought for the comfort of a man walking in total darkness. But her enthusiasm got them over any awkwardness Richard or Jennifer may have felt.

Kirkham had Lady Eccleson's closed carriage with the gold coronet on its shiny black doors waiting at the end of the walk. All the way down Oxford and Regent Streets and across The Mall Jennifer kept up a bright narrative describing the traffic and people filling the congested streets and the beauty of the autumn foliage. Beside her in the swaying carriage, Richard seemed to relax a bit.

But when the carriage rolled between the two red-coated cavalry officers of the Royal Horse Guards facing Whitehall, she felt him stiffen again. Lt. Greyston would not wish to appear pitiable before any of the men with whom he had served. Nor did he wish to hear the bad news they were certain to receive, for between Jennifer's travelogue, Livvy had chattered enthusiastically about the purpose of their mission. Now her nervousness led her to run on unchecked. "I hope you won't be too disappointed, Dick, if we learn the worst. Jenny and I have quite faced the fact that this is a dreadfully long shot, and you must, too, but wouldn't it be wonderful if Legend had been recovered? And if we learn the worst, then you'll know you must look for another horse. Wouldn't it be a fine thing to go riding in Hyde Park on a day like this? Not as fine as riding across the fields in the Midlands, of course, but quite fine. Do you ride, Jennifer? I've never heard you say. If we could acquire mounts, we could get up a party." Fortunately she never paused long enough for anyone to answer her.

Inside the cool stone halls of Horse Guards, Dick pulled his black patches off along with his tall black hat. Jennifer was glad the light was relatively dim in there, for she knew he would endure severe pain rather than appear in eye patches. She led him to the desk of a red-coated duty officer. "Sir, madam." The young man came sharply to his feet.

"Lt. Richard Greyston, formerly of the 17th Lancers." Dick halted halfway to a salute. "We've come to inquire about the fate of a horse at the Battle of Balaclava."

Jennifer was glad Richard was spared the look on the young man's face as he shook his head. "Awful mess that was, sir. More than five hundred horses killed. But then I expect you know all that." He glanced at Richard's scars. "We do have one fellow here who might be able to help you. If you'd care to take a seat." He gestured to a bench along the wall, and Jennifer moved toward it. Already she was gaining confidence in her ability to lead without propelling.

But this time her confidence had come too soon. Richard crashed into the bench with a blow that must have been painful to his shins and then miscalculated in sitting down and half sat on the narrow wooden arm. "Take your time. Feel with the backs of your legs before sitting." Jennifer made no attempt to keep the nannying tone out of her voice. She had learned in Scutari that it could often be her most useful tool when she wanted her words to be accepted as a matter of course.

They waited several minutes before the long stone corridor echoed with the clipped stride of booted feet. "Greyston, my dear fellow."

Richard rose and turned in the direction of the speaker but did not reply. The blue-coated man clasped Richard's outstretched hand with his left hand. Jennifer saw that his right arm hung stiffly at an awkward angle. "Don't tell me that this scar has so ruined my beauty you don't recognize your old captain."

Richard broke into the brightest smile Jennifer had yet seen from him. Truth to tell, she had seen very few. "Morris! I didn't dare hope. You were right ahead of me when the shell exploded."

"Took that in my arm." Morris jerked his head toward his right elbow. "Then Crusader went down, and I took a cutlass thrust in the head. Thought I was done for, but my wife was out there. She got me home for nursing a few days later." He paused and looked at Dick. "That shell didn't do much more for your beauty than the cutlass did for mine, did it? But we're beastly lucky to be here, even if desk duty is all I'm good for now." He gave Richard a hearty slap on the back. "What can I do for you?"

"Trying to trace what became of my horse. You remember Legend?"

Morris laughed. "That big black brute? How could I forget the ugliest horse in the 17th Lancers?" Then the captain turned serious. "I did see him briefly. I had crawled to a ditch at the bottom of the hill behind the guns. Thought I was done for, happy to find a peaceful spot to make my last. Then this battle-crazed horse thundered by, eyes bulging and nostrils flaring. Had the feeling he was following someone— probably an officer."

Morris suddenly seemed to recall Jennifer and Livvy's presence and turned to them. "You see how it is, ladies, when a horse trained for battle loses his rider, he won't run for safety. He'll look for leadership—run right toward the fiercest action. Riderless horses added a blasted lot to the confusion on the field."

He paused and seemed to stifle a small shiver. "Strange, isn't it, how you'll remember a detail in the midst of all that horror? But it seemed so awful to me, the poor creature's terror. Of course, I was certain you were done for. I don't remember feeling nearly so bad for you as I did for your horse. I must have fainted then. Last thing I remember for several days."

The men continued in conversation for some minutes, but Jennifer sat back against the hard slats of the bench. She had been so hopeful. Finding Legend would have been such a boost to Dick's morale. Instead, she had just led him into another disappointment.

On the way back to Manchester Square, Jenny tried to ease any letdown Richard might be feeling by telling about her new volunteer teaching, about meeting the Earl of Shaftesbury, and about Joshua, the rescued climbing boy.

Livvy listened with a puzzled look on her bright face. "How good you are, Jennifer. Of course I'm happy to take baskets to Aunt Charlotte's deserving poor, but don't you find spending too much time among them depressing? I must admit that I far prefer a lively party."

Richard, however, was quite interested. "I met the earl once when I was at Cambridge—before he was the earl. He was there to address the Student Society for Doing Good. Don't remember much about the speech, but I recall what they said about him, that even though Ashley—as he was known then—had gone to Oxford, he was as true an Evangelical as if he had gone to Cambridge and studied under Charles Simeon.

"I remember being surprised at how pleased he seemed by that introduction and even more surprised by how the audience cheered it. I'd had the impression that being called an Evangelical was something of an insult."

"I have heard Rev. Baring at All Souls referred to as an Evangelical, and he isn't at all wanting in intelligence or decorum." The strong urge to defend those of fervent faith startled even Jenny herself, as she hadn't thought through her own opinions on the subject yet. But she had met the earl and seen the sincerity of his faith in action. "As a matter of fact, Rev. Baring is a friend of Lord Shaftesbury. I expect that's why the earl is speaking on behalf of the Society for the Prevention of Cruelty to Children at All Souls next week." She turned suddenly and clasped Richard's arm. "Dick, you must come. I'll hear no argument. This is the very thing. And you, too, Livvy. Surely Lady Eccleson will be attending anyway."

"Oh, yes, Aunt Charlotte never misses any opportunity to promote a good cause." Livvy winced. "Her tirelessness quite exhausts me. But perhaps I shall accompany her since Mama has been unwell again."

Jenny looked at Dick, but he made no reply. "Fine. I shall see you there." She spoke with as much decision as if all had agreed. Even though the excursion to Horse Guards had come to nothing, she had made a start. Now she was determined to carry on full steam ahead to stir Richard to action.

Nine

In spite of the failure to locate Legend, the following week was one of Jennifer's happiest since her return to London. She was up early every morning and out the door often before her parents were down to breakfast. In a burst of determination she had put her name down for the British and Foreign Bible Society, the Open Air Mission, the Christian Evidence Society, and several others. But what she enjoyed most was her teaching on Thursdays. After only one night she felt a part of the school. She was determined to make a real difference in her students' lives. She smiled as she sailed through the door of the mission building that evening, intent on the task ahead of her.

"Would yer like yer shoes blacked, miss?"

Jenny stopped and blinked. The small creature standing before her in the distinctive uniform of the Shoeblack Brigade looked familiar, yet she was certain he wasn't one of the boys she had taught last week. Certainly she wouldn't have forgotten that shining silver-blond hair sticking straight out in every direction like mown barley after a wind storm.

" 's a penny, but I'll do it special fer ya."

"Of course, you may black my shoes. But no favors. I shall pay my fair share." Jenny crossed the worn wooden floor to a chair and placed her right foot on the boot support of his box. The shoeblack took out a rag and began vigorous work on her half-boot although it didn't really need polish. Between slaps of the cloth, he looked up with a shy smile. The blue-brown eyes under the long, pale lashes brought Jenny's memory into focus. "Joshua! Can that really be you?"

"Yes, ma'am, it's me, right and true."

Jennifer couldn't believe the transformation. She recalled the impact the newly formed Shoeblack Brigade had made on London during the Great Exhibition four years ago when twenty-five boys in their special uniforms had cleaned more than 100,000 pairs of shoes. And she was accustomed to the familiar sight of uniformed shoeblacks on London's streets, but she had never given any thought as to where they came from.

Now Mrs. Watson bustled in from supervising the volunteers in her soup kitchen. "It's good to see you, Miss Jennifer. Didn't our young Joshua here scrub up fine?"

Jenny laughed. "I can't believe he's the same boy, Edith."

"Got him a lodging with the brigade just over in Lambeth, Rev. Walker did."

"So the boys live together?"

Edith Watson nodded with as much satisfaction as if she personally saw to the work herself. "Fine organization, the brigades are. Take hundreds of street arabs from the worst slums, clean 'em up, put 'em in uniforms, loan 'em equipment. They keeps their earnings except for a few pennies they pays back to the brigade organizers." She bent over to address Joshua, who was intent on his work. "And you mark my words, young man, you make the most of this opportunity. There's many a lad out there in a fine position now who got his start as a shoeblack. You wouldn't be the first to impress his customers so much he got offered regular employment."

Jennifer placed her left foot on the stand, admiring the gleam on the toe of her freshly shined boot. "Just let us teach him to read and write and calculate his numbers before you're hiring him out to a trade, Mrs. Watson."

That night Jenny had a group of eight students to review the letters A and B and proceed to C and D. She was just concluding her lesson when Arthur returned to escort her home. She could see by his flushed countenance and abrupt manner that he was in a considerable hurry. "Where is your bonnet? You did bring a shawl, didn't you?"

As Jennifer turned to collect her things, she heard the eager question, "Would yer like yer shoes blacked? 's only a penny."

Arthur took a step back from the child. "No, no. No time for that." He fished in his pocket and withdrew a coin. "But here's a copper for you."

Joshua looked uncertain. "It's all right, Josh. When Mr. Merriott has more leisure, you can black his boots for him," Jenny said, allowing Arthur to steer her toward the door.

"What has you so agitated, Arthur?" she asked once she was seated in the cab he had kept waiting.

"I must get back to Whitehall. It seems that we win one war only to lose two. Parliament has abolished the Central Health Board just when Shaftesbury was ready to put into effect his plans for piping clean water into London from Frensham Commons and for closing the overcrowded burial grounds inside London and opening spacious cemeteries outside the built-up areas. I have even seen his plans for a great system of underground sewers to carry London's filth off to where it could do no harm instead of dumping it all into the Thames. Now none of it is likely to be done."

"Oh, Arthur, that's dreadful news." Jennifer thought of the miracles she had seen achieved from good sanitation. "What will happen now?"

Arthur shook his head. "We are left with a ponderous Health Department that is certain to accomplish little. And if this warm autumn weather persists, London will be visited by yet another scourge of cholera. You'll see that I am right in this."

Jennifer hadn't the least notion that he might be wrong.

Arthur walked her briskly to her door but refused her invitation to come in.

It was clear that Arthur's mind was fully engaged on his work. Halfway down the walk, however, he turned. "Please tell your mother I shall call at seven o'clock Saturday to escort you both to the earl's speech."

"That will be quite convenient, Arthur—if you can find time." Her mild irony was lost on his departing back.

Saturday evening was tangy with just a hint of approaching frost in the air. The day had been warm enough to do without coal fires, leaving the air relatively free of smoke and smog. With such an inducement from the weather, plus the arrival of her new pelisse wrap from her dressmaker, Mrs. Neville happily agreed to Arthur's suggestion that they walk the short distance down Portland Place to All Souls. Her pelisse was the height of fashion, copied directly from a Parisian doll. Made of a dark blue open-knit weave that gave the garment the look of heavy lace, the three-quarter-length wrap fell gracefully over her wide crinolined skirt. The silk of Amelia Neville's dress added its gentle swishing to that of Jennifer's gold and brown watered taffeta and the rustle of leaves underfoot as they walked.

Jennifer could sense Arthur's unspoken urging that they hurry. But he had no need to push her; she could be quite as intent as he. Indeed, as the sidewalk was too narrow for two crinolined skirts, she stepped ahead. The swish of her taffeta increased as she left Arthur and her mother several paces behind. She would show Mr. Arthur Nigel Merriott that he was not the only person who understood devotion to duty.

When they arrived at Langham Place at the top of Regent Street, a number of carriages filled the square. Greeting friends in every direction, they entered the colonnade of the circular portico beneath the distinctive needle-pointed spire. The building had been designed by John Nash in the architectural heyday of the Regency. Inside, Jennifer saw that even the gallery that ran around three sides of the sanctuary was filled to capacity. All the free pews on the main floor were filled as well. They were making their way to the Neville pew when they saw Lady Eccleson and Livvy.

Arthur was well acquainted with the older woman, but he bowed deeply at his first introduction to her niece's daughter. Livvy's round eyes sparkled, and her blonde curls bobbed. "Won't you join us? We have extra space in our pew."

And so they did, leaving the Neville pew open for others. The Reverend Charles Baring, rector of All Souls, introduced the speaker of the evening in his earnest, simple way.

The earl took his place at the heavy pulpit before the painting of Christ mocked by the soldiers. Although Shaftesbury's long face and sharp features could appear earnest to the point of severity, tonight he glowed with conviction as he delivered his message: ". . . I am particularly pleased when I am asked to speak in a church, for it is my heartfelt and earnest desire to see the Church of England —the church of our nation, and especially of the very poorest classes—dive into the recesses of human misery and bring out the wretched and ignorant sufferers to bask in the light and life and liberty of the Gospel."

Lady Eccleson nodded her approval. Arthur sat forward in his seat. But Jennifer could not share their absorption. She looked around her in irritation. Richard was not there. Where was he? She had told him to come. Why had he not done so?

The question had indeed been much debated in Richard's mind. The excursion to Horse Guards had meant more to him than he cared to admit. And certainly he must go out more if he would begin living again. But he shied from the prospect of appearing in public with fierce scars and startling eye patches. Gently bred young ladies might faint at such an alarming sight. And what it would cost his pride to be led about, he didn't care to consider.

Yet there was no denying his interest in hearing the great Shaftesbury speak, and he would like to please Livvy, who had continued to urge him in that direction. As to the matter of pleasing the determined Miss Jennifer Neville, he had mixed feelings. Certainly there was no one to whom he owed more. And yet that was the root of the problem. His feelings about Jennifer were one of the most complicated things in his life.

Lady Eccleson had decreed a light early supper. Richard adjusted his eye shades and, running one hand along the wall for guidance, left the comfort of the library for the dining room. For two weeks or more now he had eaten dinner with the family. Livvy was right. He couldn't spend the rest of his life eating in his own rooms. He was finding it easier all the time, especially as Kirkham stood at his elbow to serve him and see that everything was cut into manageable bites. Inwardly Richard fumed at being fed like a toddler, but he suppressed his rage, as he did at so many things in his life. Again he felt the desire to reach out and smash that stone wall he had run into. But the wall would not be smashed.

Instead he turned toward Livvy's voice and gave a vague reply to her question about his plans for the evening.

Lady Eccleson's response, however, was anything but vague. "Nonsense. Of course, you're going, Richard. You've moped here quite long enough. The speech will inspire you to turn your efforts to doing good. That's the answer, you know. It will take you out of yourself."

The entrance of Branman carrying a small white card on a silver platter saved Dick the effort of a reply. "A guest for Mr. Richard, ma'am." Apparently unsure what to do with the card, Branman presented it to his employer.

She peered at the card. "Richard, do you know a Capt. Morris? It seems he would pay you a call at this most inconvenient time."

Richard's hand flew to his eye patches, then stopped. Dr. Halston had been most explicit. If there was to be any chance of further healing he must not expose his raw nerves to additional weakening from strong light. He knew it to be a bright evening, and Aunt Charlotte's dining room windows faced the west. He must swallow his pride. He lowered his hand with the wry thought that at least the patches covered some of the scars. "Of course, I know Morris. Send him in, Branman."

"Do as you wish, Richard, but I'm sure you'll excuse Livvy and myself. We shall leave within the half hour."

"I should like to greet Capt. Morris again, Aunt Charlotte," Livvy said. "Perhaps he has brought you good news, Dick."

"Be that as it may, you must say good evening to your poor mama before we go out, Livvy. My dear Caroline has been most low upon her couch all day. It seems her new doctor is doing her very little good." Charlotte Eccleson swept from the room in a rustle of silk, which Dick for some reason pictured to be a dark peacock blue.

Livvy walked by him, smelling of orange-flower water, and she stopped to squeeze his hand. "Oh, Dick, I do hope it's good news."

The door was barely closed before Dick heard a heavy male tread following Branman's almost soundless step on the parquet hall floor. He took a deep breath and stood to face the door.

"Richard, my dear fellow—" Morris stopped suddenly. Dick held out his hand in the direction of the speaker. Morris took it in his left hand. "I had no idea. That is, at Horse Guards—"

"At Horse Guards I was being vain and foolish. The fact is that if I'm to have hope of ever seeing anything again, I must see nothing for now." He quickly changed subjects as he gestured toward a chair for his guest. "Good of you to call."

"Yes, short notice, I'm afraid. Thing is, I'm on my way to Tattersall's. Special sale of military horses. I find it hard to believe there are enough left to make a sale. Of course, they aren't necessarily from the Crimea, but I thought, well, there's just a chance . . . Should be some good horseflesh to look at—er, that is . . ."

Dick laughed. "I quite take your meaning. Good of you to think of me. Truth of the matter is, you've rescued me from one of Aunt Charlotte's compassionate meetings. Pull the bell, will you? We'll take Kirkham with us. Do you remember my batsman? Showed up on the doorstep one day. A real godsend."

Kirkham drove them down Park Lane to Grosvenor Place and pulled into the narrow, congested lane to London's celebrated horse mart. This special sale had drawn a great deal of attention. The small courtyard was filled with every sort of fashionable conveyance, all pulled by the smartest of horses. Richard hated the awkwardness of being led through a crowd that he once would have strode through like Prince Albert himself. But with Morris on one side and Kirkham on the other, they at least gained their seats above the sale ring with a minimum of bumping into people.

Once in the security of a seat, Dick could indulge in the excitement of the sound and smell of horses. By listening carefully, he concluded there were three animals now in the ring.

When their showmen rode them around individually, he could judge their speed and weight by hearing and feeling the thud of the hooves on the soft dirt. He had always before taken such sensations for granted. Now he felt each thud go through him as surely as if he were atop the horse himself. And it brought back all too vividly how it had felt to be astride Legend. Even in the showroom he could almost feel the wind in his face and see the green of park and field rushing by, alternating shade and sunshine, as he sped between trees.

And neither his captain nor his batsman had to tell him that none of the horses in the ring was his long-legged, high-spirited Legend. They sat through the showing of five lots. Occasionally Kirkham would go so far as to say, "Aye, now there's a fine 'un." And two or three times Morris offered a bid on an animal that took his eye, but he did not follow to the conclusion of the bidding. And no one suggested that there was an animal in the ring worthy of taking Legend's place.

At last Dick felt he could sit there no longer. "Let us walk through the sale stalls and be done with this." Neither of his companions offered an objection. Richard remembered the large barnlike room behind the sale ring—the floor paved with Moroccan tile, the stalls of dark Spanish mahogany, the beams overhead stained dark against the cream-colored plaster, the row of gas-lit chandeliers hanging the length of the room. He smelled the clean straw in each stall and the tangy scent of horsehair and leather. He needed only the lightest touch of Kirkham's hand on his elbow to guide him to the first stall.

With a gentle nicker the horse put his soft muzzle in the palm of Dick's hand. Dick reached up and scratched behind the forward-pricked ears, murmuring softly to him, "Hello, boy. Easy now, let's just feel your neck." Dick ran his hand down the powerful neck. The smooth coat was warm and silky. It felt so good under his hand. When he reached the withers where he could reliably judge the animal's height, Dick caught his breath. He knew that feel. This horse was exactly the right height. He felt even more slowly now, talking to the animal all the time, the gentle dip down the back, then up over the rounding rump. The silky tail. Still letting the horse hear the reassurance of his voice, Dick ran his hand down the near back leg—a long, strong-muscled leg—to the well-trimmed fetlock. He tugged slightly just above the hoof.

"Come on, boy. Let me feel your feet. Have they taken good care of you?" The horse lifted his foot to Dick's pressure. Supporting the hoof against his own knee, Dick examined the hoof and the firm frog inside it. He set the foot down gently and stood up, running his hand back up the leg with short patting strokes.

At last he turned slowly away. "A fine animal. I just hope Legend has been as well cared for, wherever he is."

"He's a superb beast, Greyston—probably the best here. And he is for sale . . ." Morris didn't finish his thought.

Dick nodded. "A fine one indeed. But not the right one."

They made their way on through the sale barn and turned left through the subscription room run by the Jockey Club. This room was a mecca for patrons of the turf, from noblemen to innkeepers. Here the betting throughout England was regulated, forms for races could be obtained, the results of all races posted, and one could place money on any horse running in any race—and collect the winnings if lucky.

Tonight there was a considerable stir in the room over the just-announced results of the Shrewsbury meet, which had come in by telegram. A horse named Windflyer owned by a Mr. John Parsons Coke had won at odds of seven to two. It seemed that the name Windflyer was on the tongue of every person they passed, either in praise or complaint, depending on which way the punter had placed his money.

They were nearly out of the room when Dick stopped. A man to his left was arguing loudly, apparently to someone at a pay window, demanding his winnings. Dick was certain he had heard that gravelly voice before. But where? "Morris, do you hear that man? Do you know him?"

They stood still and listened. "I tell you, man, John Parsons Coke is my partner. One thousand pounds of Windflyer's winnings are mine. And I want them—now. Do you want me to have you up before the Jockey Club?"

"No." Dick could feel Morris shaking his head. "I don't know him—short fellow, bald, well-dressed, more sober than most punters. Looks like a lawyer or banker."

The description brought no name to Dick's mind. "Not army? I think I heard that voice in Scutari."

Kirkham scoffed. "Not military. Not 'im. Too stout to do credit to a uniform. Shoulders slouched under the clever tailoring. 'e looks too soft."

"I don't recognize him, I'm sure," Morris said. "But the name Coke—there was a fellow in the Lancers by that name."

"Ah!" Richard was disgusted with himself. Why hadn't he remembered? "Sgt. Coke! Could be him. I remember he was interested in sport."

"Shall I ask the man at the window who he is?" Kirkham offered.

"No." Dick shrugged. "It's not important. Just seemed to jog a memory I was trying to place. Sounds are so much more important now. I'm trying to get them right."

Dick left Tattersall's with a slow step. He shouldn't have come. The sounds, the feel, the smells—they had all made him miss so much more acutely what he had lost. Perhaps he should have listened to Jenny.

Ten

Yes. Jennifer leaned forward in the high-sided pew. As soon as the earl came to the heart of his message, her former distraction over Richard's absence vanished.

Yes, she thought again. This was what she wanted to hear. What could she do? What could all these people do to 'dive into the recesses of human misery and bring out the wretched and ignorant sufferers'? Surely the Earl of Shaftesbury could give her the direction she needed.

"So many people have asked me," the speaker continued, " 'How has this come upon us? How can such conditions exist in the greatest country in the world, in the greatest city in the world?' And those are, indeed, fair questions. Understand, my friends, that in the space of one generation—our parents' generation—England moved from being an agricultural society to an industrial one. For the first time in history we now have more people living in our towns than on farms. And the only place for this great influx of humanity to find shelter is most often in the vermin-infested rookeries existing behind the main boulevards of our city. I have seen with my own eyes as many as twenty people of all ages and sexes crowded into one filthy room."

An uneasiness rippled through the audience. This was not what these good people wanted to hear. But the earl did not slacken his pace. "Many say to me, 'But we have had our parliamentary reform; we have passed laws to deal with all this.' And I say we have barely made a beginning. And that beginning will be lost if we do not press ahead. Eight years have passed since the passage of the Factory Act, and still I must fight for the freedom of children where loopholes in the law allow tyranny."

Jennifer thought of the little group of urchins that gathered around her at the ragged school. She thought of Joshua, covered in soot and blood. How many small children were even now being rubbed with brine before hot fires to prepare them for such unspeakable work? And that was only one example. Shaftesbury began to speak of others, sparing nothing for the women in his audience.

"Recently I went to a brick field. I saw at a distance what appeared to be eight or ten pillars of clay. As I approached, I was astonished to find that these were children, filthy with clay, who ran screaming at the sight of a gentleman. I followed them to their work. There I saw little children, three parts naked, tottering under the weight of the wet clay they carried—some of it on their heads and some on their shoulders—and little girls with huge masses of wet, cold, dripping clay pressed on their abdomens. I watched as they carried their loads to the kilns. There they had to enter places where the heat was so fierce that I was not myself able to remain more than two or three minutes."

Then Shaftesbury's narrative moved from the brick fields to the potteries. Jennifer stirred. This was what Richard must hear. Why had he not come tonight? She scowled at the empty space in Lady Eccleson's pew. If Richard had heeded her, he would understand the reform needed in the industry from which his family made their wealth.

". . . In the potteries of our great Midlands there are now 1,000 children between the ages of six and ten who are sweated for sixteen hours a day for as little as half a crown a week. I saw them lugging molds from potters' wheels to furnaces where the temperatures blaze constantly at 120°. These half-cooked unfortunates have no hope for a better life unless we undertake to do something about their condition."

Jenny thought over her schedule for the coming week. It was very full, but clearly she should include time for Lt. Greyston. He must be made to see his duty.

"I will confess to you, my friends, that there are times when I question the mysterious ways of Providence that leave these outcasts to their horrible destiny. And then I am reminded of Christ on the cross, who gave His own mother into the care of His disciple. I am His follower. You are His follower. He has given the care of His children into our hands, we who are to be His hands on earth. And so we must persevere, for however dark the view, however painful and revolting the labor, I see no scriptural reason for desisting. Sins against children are sins against the God who made them, against the Giver of all life.

"The sins of our fathers' omissions have been visited on us, and we must act. These, the least and the lowliest, are children of God. We must care for them as our brothers and sisters, beloved in the sight of the One who said, 'As ye have done it unto the least of these, my brothers, ye have done it unto me.' "

Her heart so full that she was hardly aware of those around her, Jennifer rose with the rest of the audience. Surely there was no evil, whether social or spiritual, that could not be cured with enough energy. Hadn't Florence Nightingale proved that at Scutari? Through willpower and incredibly hard work, she had accomplished miracles and saved the British army.

Now it was all so clear to Jennifer—teaching in the ragged schools, seeing Joshua's desperate condition, hearing tonight's speech—now she saw it all as part of a whole. She had found her calling. She would accomplish miracles and save the British working children.

It was late that night after Jenny had extinguished her candle and snuggled deep beneath her comforter, that the glow faded. Glowing visions of saving the suffering children of England were all very well. But what could she do? Rushing off with a head full of romantic notions could result in a worse fiasco than Mary Stanley's arrival in Scutari with a shipload of silly society girls who had thought nursing soldiers a means to provide interesting tea table conversation.

The earl's words had made Jennifer see that the work to be done was, if anything, less acceptable for tea table conversation than conditions in Scutari. And ladies of her class were not allowed to go beyond the bounds of tea table and drawing room. No, she had not found the answer, but rather more intense questions. She had a desire but no means of fulfilling it. And still that was only half of her problem. She had also tried to understand her motives for doing the work. But surely the work itself was enough. Saving the children was enough. There need be no larger meaning.

She thought of the motives of those she knew who worked the hardest: Florence Nightingale was answering a direct call from God; Arthur worked for the economic good of England —and his own career; Lady Eccleson worked tirelessly to eradicate squalor because she disliked living around it and because such work was her duty; Amelia Neville did her share because she felt it was right to do what society expected of one; the Earl of Shaftesbury was living out his own love for God and those created in His image.

Jennifer could claim no high spiritual calling. So what was her motive?

She awoke the next morning to the pealing of church bells and realized she had been dreaming of pulling filth-covered urchins from fields of slime, from blasting furnaces, and from rooms crowded with sick people. And then the dream had twisted, and it had been Dick she was rescuing, first from a field exploding with cannon fire and then from a dark alley crawling with rats. She shivered in an effort to clear her head of the images. Betsy, the round-cheeked upstairs maid, bustled in to bring her a cup of tea and open her curtains.

Blinking at the brightness of the morning light, she thought again of Dick. If only he had heard the earl's speech last night. Surely he would be as fired to action as she. Well, she would take the message to him. She felt ready to ride full charge at the cannons of poverty, filth, and ignorance that killed and maimed so many around her. And she would not be happy until Richard was filled with the same spirit.

Before she could take action, however, the Sabbath must be observed. Rev. Baring presented his parishioners with a fine sermon. The cook presented the family with a perfectly prepared roast joint. Jennifer spent the afternoon doing needlework and reading her Bible while her mother rested and her father ensconced himself in his library. That evening all the servants presented themselves, freshly scrubbed and pressed, in the morning room where Mr. Neville read a lesson from the Old Testament, one from the Gospels, and one from the Epistles, and led in a lengthy prayer. Mr. Neville then returned to his library, and the servants were free for the evening, as supper would be cold cuts and salad.

On Monday morning immediately after family prayers, Jennifer was off to a meeting of the British and Foreign Bible Society. She returned just in time to accompany her mother on a round of parish visits. So it was late in the afternoon before she could call at Manchester Square and request Branman to announce her to Lt. Greyston.

She was shown into the library. Dick sat at the same table

where she had first encountered him. This time the table was piled considerably higher with papers, and Kirkham sat at another table with a well-shaded lamp in the dim room.

Jennifer began pulling off her gloves as she sailed into the room. "Ah, Richard, I am most happy to see you so well employed. That is what I have come to speak to you about."

Richard stood and turned in her direction. He grinned. "Hello, Dick, how nice to see you. I was just passing and thought I would call." He sketched a bow and changed his voice. "Jenny, what a delightful surprise. Won't you sit down? Shall I send for some tea?" Now he changed to a brisk, businesslike tone. "There. That should dispense with the social amenities. Now please do continue on the matter of my employment."

Jennifer sat down in a hard-backed chair, and Kirkham turned out his lamp and left the room. "It is most unkind of you to mock me, sir. I have come to do you good."

"That is a relief. But then I did not suppose you had come to do me harm."

His irony was lost on her, however, as she plunged ahead. "I was most displeased with you, Richard. You did not attend the earl's speech." She looked at him still standing by his desk as if at attention. "I am sitting, Richard. You may sit."

"Ah, yes. As I do not require my eye patches in a dark room, I had perceived your position. I had thought, however, that if I am to face execution, I should prefer to meet it on my feet."

A gurgle of laughter escaped Jennifer's lips.

Richard smiled and sat. "There now, that's better. I assume it's the matter of pottery reform that you have come about."

Immediately Jennifer's intensity returned. "Richard, you can have no idea of the conditions. If you had heard the speech—"

"On the contrary, I have a very vivid idea. I have, in fact, heard the speech three times. Once from Aunt Charlotte, once from Livvy, and once from your friend Mr. Merriott, who called this morning to beg that I acquaint myself with the facts contained in these white papers he left with me." He gestured toward the table where Kirkham had been sitting. "If you wish to recount the speech for me a fourth time, however, I shall be glad to listen. You have a far more charming voice than any of your predecessors."

"Richard, this is excellent news! I had thought I would have to push and pull and shove to stir you to action. This is just what you need, and much good will come of your effort. I am delighted that others have done the work of informing you, and especially that dear Arthur thought to bring you the reports of the study commissions. Now you will soon be reaping the benefits of doing good for others." She paused for breath.

But he broke in before she could continue. Now, however, the drollness was replaced by hard-bitten sharpness. "How very fortunate that you won't be obliged to waste further time on this duty. You may mark 'stir Richard Greyston to action' off your list of good deeds to do today." He came to his feet. "Miss Neville, I am not one of your charities. You needn't try to reform, uplift, or do good to me. Allow me to wish you a good day."

Jennifer was so stunned that she almost crashed into Kirkham, who had just entered the room. Anger crossed her features. Fine. She would mark "stir Richard to action" off her list as he suggested. Perhaps she would even mark Richard off her list. She swept to the door.

Dick heard Kirkham's measured tread follow the swish of Jennifer's silk skirt out the door. The soft click of the door told him he was alone. He had responded to Jennifer with sardonic humor and abruptness, just as he had earlier responded to his other visitors urging him to take up the banner of reform. Such attitudes served as a useful defense, but they did not deal with the issue.

He had allowed Kirkham to read the parliamentary reports because it was easier to do so than to make excuses for not doing so. His life's goals had been denied him. He had to fill the time with something.

But the truth of the matter was—the truth he might have admitted to Jennifer had she approached him with a less high-handed attitude—that the past two days of listening to Kirkham's droning reading had made their impact. The earl's speech, thoroughly recounted, plus graphic case studies and statistical evidence amassed in the Shaftesbury reports had threatened to breach his wall.

Now he must decide whether to allow the assault to continue. It was clear that he must find a new direction for his life. So what about this direction that was being thrust upon him? Had Providence put the awareness of this need in his way? Or would taking up such work simply be following the line of least resistance? And how much a part of the consideration was the fact that Jennifer Neville was urging him in this direction? No answers presented themselves.

He hesitated at the next question. How much of his reluctance was due to fear? How much good could a blind man do? What if he should try and fail? He did not need another failure on his tally.

Kirkham returned to resume reading, but Richard waved him away. "Read it yourself and give me a summary. I do not wish to be disturbed."

But Richard had made little progress toward answering any of his questions when Lady Eccleson entered the library sometime later. "The tea is getting cold, Richard. I am not in the habit of being kept waiting in my own drawing room."

"Thank you, Aunt Charlotte, but I am not in the least hungry for tea. Kirkham is just set to cover the last of these parliamentary reports with me."

Richard heard the rustle of silk as she turned to his man. "Even one as ready to perform his duty as you are, Kirkham, must be glad enough of a tea break occasionally. I'm sure my nephew will excuse you."

"Thank you, My Lady. If the lieutenant would permit . . ."

Dick sensed conspiratorial grins between lady and servant.

"Dashed unfair of both of you to take advantage of a blind man like that. Should be ashamed." Dick pulled the shades over his eyes and strode to the door, knocking over a misplaced chair on the way.

He did not slacken his pace until well inside the parlor where he all but cannoned into Lady Eccleson's visitor. Tall though he was, Dick instinctively raised his head to greet the newcomer whose long, slim fingers gripped his hand so firmly. Lady Eccleson presented her nephew to the Earl of Shaftesbury.

"Your aunt tells me you are studying my white papers with considerable assiduity. I am heartily gratified. That is a formidable undertaking—one I fervently wish more would attempt."

"Not nearly so formidable as the work of preparing the papers must be, sir. Your research is astounding. I cannot understand how any thinking, caring person could fail to be moved to action." It was a moment before Dick realized the implication of his own words.

The earl guided Dick to the sofa with a hand on his elbow and sat beside him. "There are many who think I overstate, that I would move too fast to reform. There are few in positions of power who would choose to have their lifestyles changed."

"Yes, but on this matter of child labor in the potteries, the report raised several issues . . ."

Dick was well through his second scone and third cup of tea before he realized he hadn't given a single thought to fears of spilling or clattering. He had so vividly pictured in his mind the conditions the earl described—both the appalling ones now existing and his hopes for a better future—that Dick had for a time forgotten he couldn't actually see.

Eleven

October arrived unseasonably hot, and the heat held for two weeks and longer. The grass turned brown; Michaelmas daisies and autumn crocus were too parched to bloom. And Jennifer, with a determined lift of her chin, continued to push Lt. Richard Greyston out of her mind. Her efforts yielded mixed success.

When thoughts of Dick intruded, she would wonder if he was continuing with his study and if he had come to a decision about his life. And she attempted to pray for him. But she made no move to contact him. His dismissal still stung.

In her honest moments, Jenny had to admit that it was not just Dick's words that stung, but her own. The memory of her high-handedness left her chagrined. Such behavior was exactly what those opposed to women taking up professions warned against. Perhaps they were right. She must remember she was no longer in Scutari. Society drawing rooms were not army hospitals. No matter how often her mother reminded her, it seemed she still relapsed. Would she ever be able to fit her two worlds together?

She thought again of Richard, also unable to put his world together since returning from the Crimea. She reached for a piece of floral note paper. Then withdrew her hand. No. She would send no messages. If Lt. Greyston had no use for her help, there were plenty of others who did.

She began calling on the families of her ragged school students as well as continuing her work within the All Souls parish. She was determined to make a difference in the lives of these people.

But it was so overwhelming. The more she did, the more needs she saw, and the more she realized how impossible the job was. The crowded tenements on the edge of the slums where a dozen or more filthy lodgers crowded into one rat-infested room and children played in the gutters running with refuse were bad enough. Bad enough that even Jennifer realized she dare not go there alone, and so she always waited for another committee member or mission volunteer to go with her.

But even worse, she knew, were the rookeries in the darkest centers of these pockets of poverty. She had heard stories of small children starving to death on the streets and their bodies lying, decaying in the gutter because no one cared enough to seek a burial place. Jennifer had not seen such sights herself, but she could well believe that the stories were true. Her experience in the Crimea had taught her that no horror was impossible.

The third Thursday in October she went as usual to the ragged school. That night even her best students were restless and inattentive, and the slow ones were impossible. It was just as well that there were several absences, since she accomplished so little. She supposed they stayed away because of the discomfort of sitting in a close, stuffy room when even the dirty streets of a crowded tenement might have the hope of a small breeze blowing through them. But then one of her small charges clutched his stomach and ran from the room as fast as his bare feet would go.

"Hit's the autumn pest, miss." A grimy girl of about six or seven scratched her streaked blonde hair.

"You mean cholera?" Jenny held to the edge of her table for support. She remembered vividly the horrors of the vomiting and dysentery that swept through the army, leaving many dead within hours, weakening others to linger for weeks or longer in great pain before they finally died or eventually made a slow recovery. It seemed that there had been an outbreak of cholera in London every fall for almost as long as she could remember, and yet she had hoped that this year would be different.

Cleanliness, sobriety, and good ventilation were the best prevention of the plague, so it was little wonder that the pestilence flourished in Tothill. Yet with all that had been accomplished by the Public Health Board and other committees, she had dared to hope. Surely conditions had improved enough to ward off the pestilence this year. But now the Health Board had been disbanded and replaced by a vague government department. And now more must suffer and die, victims of official bungling.

At last Mr. Walker dismissed the older students, so she could let her younger ones go. Jennifer had turned to pick up her bonnet when Edith Watson bustled in from the kitchen. "Jenny, I've no right to be asking it of you—ye look as peaky as some I've served in the mission—but the cholera has struck the shoeblacks' home, and I'm going there now with a rhubarb purgative. I know you're right fond of little Josh."

Josh! Josh was in danger?

"Of course, I'll go with you, Edith." Then she paused. Her family had not consented to her coming home unescorted, but as Arthur was out of town again, Hinson would send Betsy in Mr. Neville's carriage for her tonight. "Just a minute." She turned to Rev. Walker. "When my maid arrives, please tell her where we have gone. She may collect me there."

As it was growing dark out, the minister insisted on securing a cab to take the women across the river to Lambeth. Fog swirled around the vehicle on the way and encircled the gas-lit lamps in a glowing golden ball, each one disappearing behind them as another appeared in front. Jennifer was glad for the cabby and Mrs. Watson, for certainly she had no idea where she was as they left the lighted streets and entered an alleyway behind a warehouse. Mrs. Watson descended from the cab and paid the driver. Jennifer followed with a basket of medicine over her arm.

The shoeblacks' home was clean and orderly, if sparsely furnished. The entire top floor was a dormitory filled with rows of iron beds. But here where all beds should still be empty, their inhabitants out polishing the shoes of fine gentlemen entering their clubs or theaters, a third of the beds were filled with curled-up balls of misery.

Even before she turned to the boys, Jennifer strode to the far end of the fetid room. It required considerable tugging and shoving, but at last the shutters came unstuck, and she was able to open the window. Swirls of damp fog rolled in, smelling vaguely of the river but far fresher than the air in the room that had been breathed and rebreathed by twenty boys.

Mrs. Watson began administering doses from brown bottles. She paused to hand one to Jennifer. "Three grains calomel, eight grains rhubarb in a little honey. They will need the doses repeated three times at intervals of four or five hours." She looked under the nearest bed and then nodded with satisfaction. "This will assist nature in throwing off the contents of the bowels, so make sure they's a bucket under every bed. Just like we had in the Crimea, eh?"

Jennifer took the bottle and spoon, thinking, *Indeed.* Only in a way this was worse than the Crimea because the sufferers were children and because the official bunglers were closer at hand.

Mrs. Watson continued her lecture, as they had now been joined by the administrator of the home in whose hands they would leave the nursing. "In the morning they can be given my special tea." Edith Watson pointed to another basket. "That there's quince seeds, which are of a very mucilaginous nature. Pour boiling water over them and give each boy as much as he'll drink." She paused in the midst of administering spoonfuls of her rhubarb mixture between fever-cracked lips to shake her head. "Whey would be better—nothing coats the stomach like whey. But in this weather it'd go off too fast, so we must do the best we can with what we have."

Jennifer's skirt brushed the scrubbed floor boards, and for a moment the sound recalled the hours she had spent battling this same disease in Scutari. Here also she had a special patient for whom to fight. Josh's barley-white hair shone against the gray covers of the next bed. Jenny forced a spoonful of the mixture between his teeth, but he was almost too weak to swallow. She thought of the horrors this small creature had endured as a chimney sweep. Had he been rescued from that and given the hope of education and employment only to die of cholera? She hadn't felt such outrage against the unfairness of the universe since her darkest days in the Barracks Hospital.

"Don't you have any vinegar-water?" A voice penetrated her consciousness as if from a distance. "I remember how good that felt when I was in a similar state. Or maybe it was just the touch of your hands."

"Dick!" Jenny turned so quickly at the sound of his voice that she almost spilled Mrs. Watson's carefully brewed elixir.

"What are you doing here? How did you—" She thrust her half-empty medicine bottle at an assistant from the home and took Dick's hand. "I can't believe it. I was just thinking about you."

"I was thinking about you, too, Jennifer. I went to your home to apologize for our last parting. Hinson was just ready to send Betsy to collect you. I came instead. You don't mind? Betsy's better qualifications for 'seeing' you home will count for little in this fog."

Unbelievably her throat tightened. What was the matter with her? She squeezed his hand. "I don't mind."

Mrs. Watson bustled by, wiping her hands on her white apron. "There now—that's the first dose. Next one in three hours," she instructed the administrator.

Dick raised his head like a horse to a scent. "I know that voice."

Jenny introduced them, and the motherly Mrs. Watson hugged Richard thoroughly with delight.

"Well." Richard caught his breath. "Are you ready to leave?"

They were. As the carriage clattered over the uneven streets, Jenny stole glances at the man beside her. His prominent nose was silhouetted against the pale light of the carriage window. She turned just a bit farther until she could see the shadowed shape of his high cheekbones, square chin, and firm mouth. Perhaps this was the first time she had really regarded him thus—not a patient, not a friend's brother, not a compassionate cause, but a man of strong feeling and strong determination. Strong enough to survive the horrors of the battle of Balaclava and the Scutari hospital and fight his way back from the despair of blindness and loss to . . . She stopped. To what? She had been so anxious to thrust him forward without being sure of her own direction. Had he seen the pitfalls more clearly than she?

He had apologized at the shoeblacks' home, and she hadn't answered him. What would she say when they were alone in the carriage?

In a few minutes they left Edith Watson at the mission, Jenny promising to return in the morning to help her with the nursing.

Then the carriage door closed again, leaving them in their small swaying, fog-wrapped cocoon.

"Richard."

"Jennifer."

They spoke at the same time and then turned to each other, laughing.

"Jenny."

"Dick."

They did it again. And laughed again.

"You first," he said.

"I just wanted to say I'm sorry. You were right." Her words sounded inadequate in the velvet darkness.

"Jenny." His hand moved uncertainly on the seat. As of old habit, she took it in hers and felt him hold tightly. "Jenny, through all those months of horror, you were my only light. I heard Florence Nightingale referred to as the Lady of the Lamp, but you were *my* lamp, a small flame in all the darkness. And then I came home to continuing days of endless darkness, and I had no lamp—until you reinvaded my life."

Jenny gave a small chuckle. "Only I wasn't a lamp. I was more like a raging bonfire. I see that now."

In the dim light she could just see his smile. "Where you wanted to charge ahead, I wanted to think. I had seen disaster enough from charging ahead without thinking."

"Yes." Jenny could think of nothing else to say.

"Jenny, ever since that night in the hospital, I've longed to see you. May I?"

Slowly she took off her bonnet and leaned forward, directing his hands to her face. His touch was so light on her hair. He stroked it with just two fingers of each hand, following the natural swirls from her center part down over each ear and up again to the simple bun in the back. "It's brown," she said. "Darker than a walnut and lighter . . ." She sought for just the right metaphor. "Lighter than the garden soil after a rain."

He moved on to the hairline that dipped to a little heart-shaped peak over her high forehead, then the heavy eyebrows arching over her wide-set eyes. "Eyebrows dark—almost black, eyes brown," she narrated. His fingertips found the little hollows in her cheeks and then moved on to her wide mouth. He must have felt her tense because he pulled away.

"I'm sorry, I didn't mean to do that," she said. "But I've always hated having such a large mouth."

He shook his head. "You're beautiful. Thank you."

Wordlessly they pulled apart. The experience had been far more intimate than he had intended. It left him shaken. In the past weeks he had been coming to terms with the darkness. He had made up his mind that in time he would get used to the physical groping. He had to, and one could do whatever one had to do.

But the spiritual groping—the sense of groping for his life had been driving him crazy. Until the afternoon he had spent in the Earl of Shaftesbury's company. Since then Kirkham had read countless white papers and the longer blue books to him. The visions brought to life by the earl were beginning to take shape as ideas and goals.

He did not need this new complication. If he were sighted and unscarred, he might determine to give the insufferable Mr. Arthur Nigel Merriott a run for his money. But as matters stood, the notion was ridiculous.

The carriage stopped before Number 7 Portland Place. The silence grew uncomfortable. He could not walk Jenny to the door without a word. He cleared his throat and spoke as if giving a report to one of his aunt's committee meetings. "I want you to know that partly at the urging of your Mr.

Merriott, who has been calling regularly at Aunt Charlotte's, I have undertaken to pursue the matter of reform at Greystoke Pottery. It is not mine, of course, nor will it ever be, but I shall exert what small moral influence I have on my family. I have written to both George and Father urging them to look into the matter of schooling and work hours for the children we employ and the housing conditions of our workers."

"Richard, that's wonderful! Oh, I can't wait to tell Arthur. He will be so pleased!"

He felt the reference to Arthur more deeply than he would admit. "I had hoped *you* would also be pleased."

"Of course I am."

"As soon as Mother is well enough to travel, we will be returning to Newcastle. She has already stayed in London far longer than she intended. Now that the cholera season is upon us, she is most anxious to be off. A new doctor is coming tomorrow. Perhaps he can do something."

Since Jennifer had nothing more to say, he took her to the door in silence. Her voice had sounded genuinely delighted, so why did he feel deflated?

The next morning Richard was just finishing his platter of kedgeree and creamed kidneys on toast to the sound of rain beating against the window when Livvy flew into the room. "Oh, Dick, I'm longing to be back in Newcastle. I'm sick of being cooped up in London. Just think how golden the trees will be there, and we can go out into the country and ride for miles over the fields." She stopped suddenly. "Oh, Dick, I'm sorry. I forgot. How dreadful for you. I—"

"No. Please don't apologize." He held up his hand. "I quite agree it will be excellent to be away from London. Has the new doctor come yet?"

"Dr. Pannier? He's in with Mama now." Livvy sighed. "I don't suppose he can do anything the others haven't though. We must convince her to go home anyway. I'm sure the air there would do her more good than any new doctor."

Dick pushed his plate back. "You may be right. I think I'll just have a word with him and see what he thinks about her condition for traveling."

Dick refused Kirkham's offer to go with him. He knew his way around the house very well, so long as no one left a footstool or basket out of place.

When Richard entered his mother's room, the doctor was just concluding his instructions to Violet, Caroline Greyston's tall, thin maid. ". . . that's dried dandelion root, your best ginger, and Columba root—all well bruised and boiled together in three pints of water—do you have that, my girl? A glassful every four hours. Do not be slack about it." He turned back to Caroline on the couch. "That should do very well for the liver complaint. Now as to the palpitations, I shall speak to you very directly. Such conditions are most often caused by luxurious living, indolence, and tight-lacing. This you must conquer with the application of sturdy resolution."

In the dim light of the invalid's room, Dick could see the exaggerated gestures that so suited the doctor's august bearing. Dick had an impression of soft, white skin and macassared hair beneath a high, balding forehead. But it was the voice that brought Dick to a full halt just inside his mother's room. As the deep, gravelly tones droned on, giving self-important orders, Dick became more certain. This was the voice that had sounded familiar to him at Tattersall's. And, he now knew, it was the voice of a doctor in the Barracks Hospital. So the speaker was a perfectly respectable professional man who also engaged in a respectable sport. Why should the voice irritate him so?

Dick stood just in front of the door, requiring that the doctor stop mid-sweep in an otherwise imposing exit. "Ah, Dr.—" Dick paused pointedly.

"Pannier. William Pannier, surgeon."

"Yes. I believe we met in Scutari. You were at the Barracks Hospital?"

Pannier cringed. "I was." Then he looked severely at Richard.

Dick had the strongest sensation of wanting to pull back.

The doctor leaned closer, however, peering at Richard. Then he drew himself up. "Bread and water poultices on those scars, young man. Applied thickly twice a day." And he continued his exit as if followed by a train of courtiers.

Dick crossed the room. "Mother, how are—"

"Whatever can you be thinking of, Caroline? I will not have that man in my house, much less attending my niece," Lady Eccleson demanded as she entered the room.

"Why do you say that, Charlotte? I confess I was not much pleased with his advice, but that is not unusual."

"I'm surprised at you, Caroline, especially as Pannier is a Staffordshire man. I should think you would have heard of him in Newcastle."

"Alas, there is never any news in Newcastle. One must come to London to hear of one's hometown."

"Humph. From my memory of Greystoke Pitchers, there was little to do there but gossip. If it has changed materially since I left, I should be amazed."

"Aunt Charlotte, if you know something of Dr. Pannier that would disqualify him from attending Mama, pray tell us." Livvy, who had been standing by the door for several moments, crossed the room and kissed her mother. Then she tossed her blonde curls. "And whatever you know, tell us. It sounds like delicious scandal."

Lady Eccleson sniffed. "Scandal indeed. I do not repeat scandal, young lady. But I do not care to have my house visited by a man who is reputed to have fathered fourteen illegitimate children; whose mother-in-law, from whom he inherited property, died within a fortnight of moving in with him; whose wife died after a single premium had been paid on a large insurance policy; and whose brother was called to heaven less than a year later also with a large policy in favor of Pannier."

"But surely—," Caroline Greyston began.

"Aunt Charlotte, how do you know these things?" Richard frowned. He had not cared for the man, but such accusations went beyond mere gossip.

"Lord Selbourne is well acquainted with the matter through some business interests of his in the city. He was telling Col. Biggar much of it at a recent committee meeting. Pannier's name came up as a member of the Public Health Department, and Selbourne's opinion was asked."

Dick considered. "To be fair, that sounds like a most suitable appointment. Service in the Barracks Hospital should teach one all there is to know of the need for sanitation."

"What a tragedy for the poor man to lose so many of his family members." Livvy bit her lip. "It is shocking that people should spread such gossip about a man who served England and her army so valiantly."

Richard turned to the matter he had come to discuss. "Be that as it may, Mama, if you are not pleased with his advice, there can be little reason to remain in London for more of it. Livvy is longing to return home. Do you think you would be strong enough to make the journey—say in a fortnight?"

Caroline sank deep into her pillows. "I should like that very much. But what of Dr. Halston, Richard? Surely you would not want to be without his care."

Richard snorted. "Halston knows two sentences. 'Wait,' and 'Live in the dark.' I can do both as easily in Newcastle. And apply Dr. Pannier's bread-and-water poultices as well —should I run mad enough to choose to do so."

"Oh, that's famous!" Livvy flung her arms first around her mother and then her brother. "Oh, I've been longing to return for ever such a time! Richard, you are the best of brothers!"

Richard had accomplished what he intended, and he had made his sister excessively happy. He could not understand why the prospect of leaving London did not make him happier.

Twelve

Each morning of the following week, Jennifer found herself growing increasingly impatient with her father's droning Bible reading. She longed to be about her work. So far only one of the shoeblacks had died of the cholera—testimony to the efficacy of Edith Watson's remedies and insistence on open windows and clean floors. The *Times* had reported nearly a thousand deaths already in the poorer parts of the city. The newspapers were calling for the newly formed Public Health Department to do something before the epidemic spread to the better quarters.

"O Lord, from whom all good things do come, grant to us Thy humble servants, that by Thy holy inspiration we may think those things that be good, and by Thy merciful guiding may perform the same . . ." Jenny agreed wholeheartedly with the sentiment of her father's prayer, but she was thankful when at long last it came to an end and she could *do* those good things.

Which today meant, as it had every day for almost two weeks now, taking a hansom cab to the Westminster Mission and helping Edith Watson nurse the cholera-stricken. Although Mrs. Neville didn't approve of such unfashionable clothing, Jennifer had taken to wearing again the gray tweed skirt and jacket Florence Nightingale had prescribed for her nurses in the Crimea. To Jenny their comfort and convenience far outweighed the risk of being identified as a member of the disreputable nursing profession. With determination she tucked her hair inside her white cap and drew her short gray cape around her shoulders.

At least it was raining this morning. The cooler air would bring welcome relief to her fever-ridden patients—and to those who worked in stuffy, fetid rooms to bring them comfort.

And this morning she was well-rewarded for her efforts. Josh was sitting up in his cot practicing his alphabet with one of the older boys. Jenny gave him a hug as she handed him his cup of quince seed tea. He grinned. "I'll be back ta school next week, Miss Neville."

"And ready to go on to the next group, it seems. You'll be reading before the year is out, Josh. There is a fine story in the Bible about a man named Joshua. You must learn to read it."

The blue-brown eyes shone.

Jenny moved on down the row, noting three beds emptied by boys who had recovered and returned to the streets with their shoeblack kits.

But most of the city could not report such success rates. A doctor who had served with Shaftesbury on the now-defunct Board of Health was asking in newspaper articles and public speeches that all sewers be flushed regularly. Public opinion was divided between those who supported this sanitary practice and those who opposed it on the grounds that it fouled the Thames—the city's main water supply. Some rash young doctor had even gone so far as to assert that cholera could be spread through infected water as well as infected air. But few were ready to accept such radical thinking.

Mrs. Watson brushed strands of gray-brown hair out of her face as she approached Jennifer. "I 'aven't the right to ask this of a gently bred young lady such as yourself, but I'd be right thankful for your help at another call."

Jenny put her cape on and picked up her basket. "Of course, Edith. What is it?"

"It's, as you might say, a house for fallen women."

Jenny laughed as she started down the narrow, twisting stairs from the boys' dormitory. "Edith, do you think I don't know of such things? Why, even my mother contributes to the Society for Rescuing Fallen Women, Especially those Descended from Respectable Families. Are you afraid some of these in need of our help aren't descended from respectable families?"

Edith sucked her lower lip before she replied. "It isn't so much that, miss. It's more like these 'aven't been rescued yet."

They were now on the rain-washed street. "Mrs. Watson, do you mean we are to nurse women who are still, er, practicing their—that is, their trade?"

"That's it. I knew I shouldn't 'ave asked you. You just take a cab on back to the mission and direct those as are there to start the soup pots."

"Don't be silly, Edith. I don't know anything about making soup. But I'm a good nurse. I'll come with you."

Edith Watson looked relieved. "If you're sure." She stepped across a puddle and passed a cripple selling matches. The rain, which should have been cleansing, made the gray stone buildings and garbage-choked street look all the dirtier as it streaked the soot-blackened walls. Children played in the gutter, splashing sticks in puddles and sailing paper boats. A rag and bone cart trundled by, spraying them with muddy water while its owner called out his wares. The lane, lined with pawnbrokers, sweatshops, and tenement buildings, curved higgledy-piggledy down the hill. Jenny was amazed that Edith could find her way in such a maze. "We're almost there, Miss Jenny. I wouldn't a asked you to walk, but there weren't no cabs in sight."

"It's all right, Edith. I'm warm enough." And physically she was, but Jenny's mind was chilled. This was worse than anything she had seen yet. It was unthinkable that anyone could live in these rotting tenements. The buildings were warped with damp, the walls patched and repatched, looking ready to fall down at any moment. Even with the rain, and now a chill wind had picked up as well, the doorways and sidewalks were crammed with people huddled together. Here and there someone was lying on the stone sidewalks. She wasn't even certain some of them were still alive. And through it all was the smell of human waste and the squeak of rats. Jenny lowered her eyes and hurried on.

Two more twists of the street brought them to the brothel. Inside, the gaudy hangings of soiled red velvet and cheap lace seemed even more obscene to Jennifer than the filth on the street. A fat woman with brightly rouged cheeks and orange hair directed Mrs. Watson toward an upstairs room. Jennifer had just started up the stairs behind her when a door on the landing opened, and a man in a dark suit erupted with such speed he almost bowled Jennifer over. "What is the meaning of this, Mrs. Wimple? I was not informed—" The gravelly voice stopped sharply at the sight of Jennifer in the uniform of a Crimean nurse.

Jennifer looked again at the man. "Dr. Pannier. We were told they were in need of nursing here, but if they have a doctor—"

Mrs. Watson turned, halfway up the next flight of stairs. "If you don't mind, Doctor, I'll just go ahead with my special elixir—same one as we used in Scutari, so I'm sure you'll approve."

Dr. Pannier didn't even reply. He just nodded and motioned for her to continue before he pulled his tall black hat well down over his head and pushed out the door.

Jennifer and Mrs. Watson administered their doses in record time to the six women suffering from cholera. Edith gave explicit instructions for their continuing care to the orange-haired woman in charge, and Jennifer all but ran down the stairs to the street. Sooty and garbage-choked as it was, she preferred the street to the heavy, over-perfumed atmosphere of the brothel. A cab was just setting down a flashily dressed young man when they came out, so they were able to ride back to the mission. "Imagine that fine Dr. Pannier coming to doctor those poor women," Mrs. Watson said once she was comfortably settled in the cab. "He never struck me as the sort to be abounding with charitable works. Just goes to show you can't tell a dog by its spots."

Jennifer nodded, but she was feeling too dispirited to talk. By the time they got back to the mission, she was considering going home. How lovely it would be to sit in a quiet, well-appointed room and read the latest installment of Mr. Dickens's new novel in *Household Words* while Betsy built up the fire on the grate and Hinson brought in a tray of tea and sandwiches. Yes. She would just look in on the mission work and then go home. Surely she had done her share for the day.

But inside there were three new volunteers to be trained, and Rev. Walker was busy leading the midday service before the soup was served. Mrs. Watson would take care of the two kitchen workers—would Jennifer be so kind as to guide the young lady who had come to see the ragged school?

Jennifer smiled at Miss Susannah Thompson and led her into the schoolroom. In a few minutes Jenny felt the beginnings of a warm regard for the lovely blonde girl dressed in a subdued blue afternoon walking dress. After showing her the schoolroom and explaining Mr. Walker's unorthodox but effective teaching methods, Jenny suggested they sit on one of the forms to continue their visit. She was too warm in her tweed uniform and felt a little light-headed, but she did want to get to know Susannah better. "And what has turned your mind to ragged school teaching, Miss Thompson?"

Susannah laughed. "Do I still look so frivolous? I daresay a few months ago such an idea would never have entered my mind. But that was before our new preacher came to Park Street Chapel."

"Oh?" Jenny knew little of nonconformist preachers or chapels.

"Yes, he came to us from Cambridge where—"

"From Cambridge? A nonconformist?"

Susannah nodded, and her curls bounced. "You are right—that would be most unusual. The Reverend Charles Spurgeon is from the town of Cambridge, not the university. You have heard of the famous Robert Hall? Mr. Spurgeon preached in Hall's church in Cambridge—St. Andrews Street Baptist. That was where one of our church board members heard him and recommended that he be invited to fill our pulpit. Already we have added five hundred new souls to our congregation. Charles is the best preacher and the finest man—oh!" Miss Thompson flung a small white hand over her mouth. "Oh, that is, I mean . . ."

It was more her blushing confusion than the fact that she had called the minister by his first name that made Jenny understand the true state of Miss Susannah Thompson's feelings. "I see. You mean that as your minister urges you to good works, you wouldn't wish to be found wanting."

Susannah's round blue eyes shone. "Oh, it's more than that. He doesn't really say much about good works. It's just that he preaches so forcefully about having the love of God in our hearts, and then he goes out and ministers to the less fortunate himself. So how could we do less?"

Jenny nodded. Susannah seemed to have found a key to questions she had been asking herself. And the accord Susannah Thompson and her Charles Spurgeon seemed to share over such matters made Jenny think of Arthur's long absences from her presence—and from her mind—and of her strained parting with Richard. It seemed that all society was agreed on the necessity to do good works, and yet something seemed to be missing—something that apparently Susannah had found.

Jennifer's old goals had been set by the standards of society and the position of her family in that society. But recently she was realizing that there was a power more potent than society. Of course, she had always acknowledged the existence and authority of God. Indeed, all of society was built on that foundational understanding. And she had gone to church regularly, participated in all the Christian observances, and most mornings attended carefully to her father's Bible reading at family prayers. But now she wondered if there could be something more.

Susannah was still talking in her soft, musical voice, but Jenny's mind continued to wander in a somewhat different direction. It had been almost two weeks since she and Richard had parted. She had seen nothing of him or of Livvy since then. They must have returned to Newcastle. But would Richard have gone without bidding her good-bye?

". . . and you can't imagine what an impact that had on the entire congregation." Jennifer brought her mind back to grasp the thread of Susannah's conversation. "Last year when the cholera was so dreadful, Mr. Spurgeon had been with us for only a few months—and he was already so popular —especially among the poor—that he was sent for by the sick and poor without intermission day and night . . ."

Jenny felt the room closing in on her. Her vision blurred, and Susannah's voice seemed to fade in and out. Jenny was interested in what the girl had to say. Why couldn't she concentrate? It must be the heat.

". . . When he was so exhausted he feared falling victim to the disease himself, he saw a scrap of paper wafered to a shop window. It said, 'Thou shall not be afraid for the pestilence that walketh in darkness,' and so he kept right on—Miss Neville! Oh, are you ill?"

Jenny started to lean on the bench and then realized the forms had no backs. She felt herself slipping. Just before she hit the bottom of her long slide, a strong arm circled her shoulders and lifted her up. She blinked and looked into a broad face framed by light brown hair. The golden-brown eyes looked at her with concern.

"Oh, Charles, you're just in time," Susannah cried. "Miss Neville, this is the Reverend Mr. Spurgeon I've been telling you about."

Jenny tried to reply, but the room was spinning. It could have been hours later, but probably no more than a few minutes that she was dimly aware of Arthur marching in, complaining vociferously about the pigheadedness of someone at some meeting he had been attending. "Are you ready to go, Jennifer?" He looked at her and stopped suddenly. "Jenny, what's the matter with you?"

Mrs. Watson thrust a basket of fever elixir and quince seed tea at Arthur. "Get her home. Open the windows. Call a doctor. When remedies are taken early, the cholera need not be fatal."

"Cholera?" Arthur drew back. *"Jennifer?"*

"You're right to be surprised, sir. It don't often take the upper classes. But like I said, it needn't be fatal. Now take this." She put the basket in Arthur's hands. "And do as I say."

Even through her blurred vision Jennifer could see Arthur's face pale, making his reddish sideburns stand out in sharp contrast.

"Er—" Arthur backed up another step, and his voice was tight. "It can take the upper orders all right. Shaftesbury's brother-in-law was a vigorous young officer—stationed at the Tower of London. One day last year during the height of the pestilence, he fell ill and was dead of cholera within hours." Arthur tugged at his collar as if it would choke him.

"I can see you are pressed to return to your meeting, sir. If you would be so good as to give me Miss Neville's address, Miss Thompson and I will be happy to see her home." It wasn't until Charles Spurgeon spoke that Jenny realized he was still holding her up. Apparently Arthur required little persuading to leave her in the care of her new friends. She was dimly aware of the cab ride and being put to bed, but the all-consuming facts of her consciousness were raging thirst and the nausea that wouldn't let her keep down the liquid she craved. And the unspeakable diarrhea.

At moments she tried to pray, but she didn't know whether to pray to live or to die. It seemed that any escape would be blessed, and yet when she was lucid enough to think, she realized that she did not want to leave life before she had found her reason for living. Her family, Arthur, her friends—perhaps even Richard—would miss her. Her absence would be felt at the ragged school and her other charities, but someone else would take her place. She had accomplished so little anyway. Was this all life was about? Making one's family and friends happy, doing what little one could to serve God and society, and then dying? Was that all?

She was aware of her mother placing a fresh vinegar-water cloth on her forehead. She tried to acknowledge how refreshing it felt. Everyone was so kind. And yet to what end? She had tried to live by the rules of God and society, and she had undoubtedly done more than most young women of her class, and yet how awful to think that that was all there was.

Of course, young women were told that they would find their fulfillment in their husbands and children. She had not experienced that, so she could not know. But the idea of marrying Arthur and bearing his children did not seem enough to carry on for. And then another bout of nausea made even breathing unbearable, let alone thinking.

Five days later Jenny was at last able to keep down a few spoonfuls of calves-foot jelly and half a cup of beef tea. That evening her doctor gave her a gratified grunt, and she supposed that meant she would live. But for what purpose, she was unsure. Perhaps it was just the result of her weakness, but the thought of returning to round after round of charity work —where for every child rescued, hundreds died, where for every child educated, thousands lived on in their hopelessness—seemed more than she could bear. Her brief look at only one rookery—and she knew there were hundreds more just like it in London alone—taught her that she could not go on in blind complaisance, believing in her own ability to end such horrors with energy and application.

Even the work of the Earl of Shaftesbury—with all his years in Parliament, his numerous committees, and the reform laws he had led to passage was as a few boulders of goodness standing before an avalanche of evil. Her eyes filled with scalding tears that ran to her pillow. She was overwhelmed with hopelessness.

The next morning Jenny sat up in bed and fed herself from the tray Betsy carried in. "Small portions carefully prepared and nicely presented—Miss Nightingale's precise prescription for the feeding of an invalid. Thank you, Betsy, I am much better."

She had just finished and leaned back to rest when her mother came in and kissed her. "What a joy to see you looking better, dear. We almost despaired for you."

"I feel better. Thank you, Mama."

"Enough better that Arthur could call this afternoon? He has been very assiduous in inquiring after your health and is anxious to see you when you're well."

Jenny nodded, remembering that Arthur had been none too happy to see her when she was unwell. But then there was much to be done in the endless work of gathering facts and writing papers so that Parliament could be urged onward to passing laws to protect those in need. Arthur's work was important. "I shall be glad to see him this afternoon, Mama."

It was a great event that afternoon when Jennifer, robed in her best blue dressing gown and supported by her mother and Betsy, made her way to the rose velvet couch in the parlor to receive her caller. Arthur greeted her and her mother most properly, asked after everyone's health, and commented on the weather, but it was clear his mind was on other matters. "And how is your work progressing, Arthur?"

He leaned forward in his chair, eyes intense as if glaring at an opponent. "You can have no notion of the perversity of some of our highest government officials. And the Public Health Department is beyond all. We had hoped that they could be induced to carry out Shaftesbury's plans to buy land for spacious cemeteries outside the built-up areas of London. The dead cannot be allowed to foul the atmosphere of the living. But they have turned down a most sensible plan to buy plots of ground in Brompton, Highgate, and Kensal Green."

Amelia Neville smoothed the wide skirt of her plum taffeta afternoon dress and murmured a conventional condolence, but Arthur hardly noticed. "And if I have to hear the newest Health Department member say one more time that the great unwashed do not wish to be scrubbed behind the ears in a perpetual Saturday night, I really don't think I shall be responsible for how I might respond. Even the *Times* has taken up the cry that 'Master John Bull does not want to be scrubbed and rubbed and small-tooth-combed until the tears run into his eyes and his teeth chatter.' Have you ever heard worse nonsense? And yet Pannier will quote it."

Jennifer sat up straighter on the couch. "Dr. Pannier? Is he the one blocking progress in the department?"

"He's one of them, the ringleader, I'd say. But with even the *Times* fighting reform, it's hard to choose a villain."

Jenny frowned. "But Pannier was a doctor at Scutari—he saw the effect of the Sanitary Commission there. And he was even making calls in the tenements the day we were there." She blinked as she tried to recall the circumstances. "Or maybe he wasn't there to doctor; he didn't seem to have any medicine with him. Maybe he was investigating for the Health Department. But if so, how could he not have seen . . ." She lay back on the cushions with a sigh. Her head was beginning to ache again.

"Oh, my dear, we are wearying you. I will just go see if that new tonic is brewed." Mrs. Neville left the room with a rustle of her skirts and closed the door carefully behind her.

Arthur slipped to one knee before her sofa with such alacrity that Jennifer's first thought was that he had fallen. She almost laughed when he grasped her hand. It seemed so abrupt after the conversation they had been having. But she forced herself to composure. She knew how steadfast Arthur was and how good his intentions were. Indeed, she was well aware of all Arthur's admirable qualities. She would even go so far as to say that good intentions and admirable qualities were the only sort that Arthur possessed.

"My dear Miss Neville—Jennifer, I have waited through all these worrying days of your illness to speak to you.

Jennifer, now you are strong enough, I must speak to you on a matter near my heart. A matter that touches both of us."

"Arthur, I—"

"Jennifer, you know how long I have admired you. You know how highly Mama and my sisters all regard you."

"Indeed, Arthur, I am most gratified by your good opinion. And you know my family thinks equally highly of you."

"Yes! That is exactly what I'm saying. And you must not think I do not still consider you with excellent regard."

"No, Arthur, you have been most attentive." She couldn't resist adding, "As you have been to all your duties."

"I should hope one could never say less of me, as of any Christian. But, Jennifer, you have been more than a duty to me. You have been my exemplar. The ideal of your beauty, your goodness, your purity has been a great inspiration."

Jennifer searched her mind frantically for a reply. How could she serve as inspiration and ideal for another person when she did not understand her own simplest motivations? Then the door swung open, rescuing her.

"A visitor for Miss Neville." Hinson's eyebrows rose at the sight of Arthur Nigel Merriott on his knees before Jennifer. "A Miss Susannah Thompson." He presented the small white card to Jenny as Arthur struggled to his feet with as much dignity as he could muster.

"Please show her in, Hinson. You will like Miss Thompson immensely, Arthur. I do."

Susannah almost skipped into the drawing room in a green dress and matching bonnet with a tippet of buff silk trimmed with rows of black braid, which set off perfectly her pale skin and blonde hair. Arthur made a stiff bow, offered an even stiffer excuse, and departed. Susannah drew off her gloves and handed them to Hinson with her parasol before turning back to Jennifer. "Oh, dear. Have I come at an awkward time?"

Jennifer held her hand out to her visitor. "Quite the contrary. You have come at the most opportune time imaginable. Please bring us some tea, Hinson." Suddenly she realized Susannah was exactly the person she needed to talk to. It was so easy to express to this young woman the questions that had plagued her for months. "Draw your chair closer, Susannah. I do so need to talk to you."

"Jennifer, are you still unwell? I was told you were ready to receive visitors."

"Oh, yes, I shall be quite myself soon. That is the problem. I'm not sure I want to go back to my old self. I thought I had all the answers, and I worked so hard. And all around me I see people who think they have all the answers, and they are working so hard. And yet the flood of filth and evil and disease seems to rise higher every day. It is such a losing battle. I cannot fight on, yet we will be overwhelmed if we don't. And still we fight and lose." She put her hand to her head. "Oh, I'm going in circles. Do I make sense?"

"Yes, unfortunately you do. I know we are called to be servants and to fight the good fight. But, yes, one does get so weary."

"Rev. Baring says Satan is a defeated enemy. So why does he always seem to be winning? Oh, I know it's most unladylike of me even to be thinking about such things. Perhaps it is because I am a woman that I cannot understand. Am I wrong to be asking about matters of good and evil? Am I wrong to equate filth and disease with evil?"

Susannah blinked her wide blue eyes. "Miss Neville, I am quite in awe of you. I have not known anyone to ask such questions. Perhaps Charles—er, Rev. Spurgeon—could help you. I wish I could, but I have never thought on such things. I just do what I can to relieve suffering where I find it. But, of course, the greatest work I can do will be in supporting my husband someday. That is our first duty—to be wives and mothers—isn't it? But as you say, there is much to be done."

The somber silence in the room was broken by Hinson bringing in the tea tray. As Jenny was feeling very tired, she asked Susannah to pour. So was that the answer? Must Jennifer accept that it was not within the scope of things for her to understand the nature of the fight against evil? She had decided that simply making a good marriage—that is, to someone with a substantial income—and doing a good job of managing his household would not be enough for her. Yet she knew that devoting her life to a career of charity work was equally insufficient. So the dictates of society must be right. It was her role to be a helpmeet to a husband who would be a mighty warrior. And certainly there was no warrior more valiant than Arthur. The next time he attempted to speak, she would accept him.

Thirteen

Two days later the calendar turned the corner from October to November, and a darker, more dismal rain than any London had experienced since July announced the approach of winter. Arthur had not been back since his aborted proposal attempt, but Jenny started every time she heard carriage wheels on the pavement beneath the parlor window. She had made her mind up to accept the inevitable answer to her searching. Surely all of society knew best. Surely her conflicts grew from her attempts to fly in the face of accepted standards. Happiness for one of her class lay in marrying a fine, upright man like Arthur, in running his home and rearing his children. She would contribute to the world through her charities and through supporting her husband in his work in the larger world.

When a woman like Florence Nightingale stepped outside those bounds, she did so at enormous cost. Miss Nightingale had refused two offers of marriage in order to pursue her calling. That was fine for one who had heard the voice of God directing her to her work. But Jennifer had heard no such voice.

She would submit to the obvious choice. And in submission she would find her happiness. She thought briefly of the overworked, uneducated, starving children she had determined to rescue. Would marriage to Arthur really help them? But it must be so. Everyone said that was how it was done. Still, she was in no hurry.

Today the morning post had brought *Household Words* with the newest installment of *Hard Times*, Mr. Dickens's novel about the human cost of industrialism, and Jennifer was comfortably ensconced in the parlor before a warm fire when she heard the sound she had been dreading. *No, surely not dreading*, she argued with her own thoughts. What a terrible thing to think about the coming of the man who was to be her husband. And yet she could find no other word to describe her feelings.

She stood and smoothed her hair and fluffed the lace lining holding out the bell-shaped sleeves of her moss rose day dress as Hinson's footsteps approached. "That is fine, Hinson, you may show him in." She cut the butler's introduction in the bud, and then hoped her efficiency wouldn't be mistaken for unmaidenly enthusiasm. She stood very still and lowered her eyes at the approach of a firm male tread.

"Jennifer?"

She all but cried out in surprise and then rushed across the floor to take the hand held out to the room. "Richard! I had no idea. I mean, I thought you long gone to Newcastle." She pulled him toward the sofa, turned off the gaslight, and sat next to him, all without letting go of his hand. Suddenly she realized the impropriety and withdrew hers.

"Mama and Livvy left on schedule. But I could not leave London until I was certain you were out of danger."

"Oh." She caught her breath. She had no idea he cared so much for her welfare. "Yes, I'm quite recovered now. But, Dick, that is very dear of you to be so thoughtful. I think of you often."

She pulled away. No that would not do. She had just determined she would accept Arthur. She should ring for tea. Her mother was out. She should summon Betsy to sit quietly in the corner with her sewing. At the very least she should open the parlor door, which Hinson had closed. She should . . .

She could bring herself to do nothing to disturb their

closeness. "It is so very good to see you, Dick." That brought back the memory of his "seeing" her. The feel of his fingertips on her face made her throat tighten.

Blinking, she turned back and looked fully at him. And she realized that he was wearing glasses, not the solid eye patches but round, thick lenses of dark blue. They looked as if cut from the bottoms of bottles. She grabbed his arm. "Dick, are you better? Your glasses—"

"The glasses indeed are better. And the weather is worse —which for me is better." He paused. "I cannot claim much improvement in my vision, however much I long for it. What I can see of the world is seen as through a dark glass running with heavy water."

Jennifer smiled to warm her voice as she glanced out the rain-streaked window. "Well, today that is how we all view the world." And suddenly she could think of nothing more to say. She could have gone on chattering about the weather, but she wanted to talk about something more important, whatever that might be.

Fortunately Richard was not so unprepared. "I have brought you a copy of Mr. Tennyson's latest poem." He pulled a folded paper from his inside breast pocket. "I think you will find it interesting."

She took the paper and read the title, " 'The Charge of the Light Brigade.' Oh, Richard, that's wonderful! England's Poet Laureate has commemorated your courage and valor." She skimmed a few lines.

> *"Forward, the Light Brigade! . . .*
> *Into the valley of Death*
> *Rode the six hundred."*

"Commemorates the blundering of our leaders, more

like." Richard's voice was tight. But Jenny hardly heard his interruption as the rhythm and force of the poem carried her on.

> *"Cannon to the right of them,*
>   *Cannon to the left of them,*
> *Cannon in front of them*
>   *Volley'd and thunder'd;*
> *Storm'd at with shot and shell,*
>   *Boldly they rode and well,*
> *Into the jaws of Death,*
> *Into the mouth of Hell*
>   *Rode the six hundred."*

She put the paper down, blinking to keep back the tears. "Richard, it's beautiful—and dreadful. I can't bear to think of you in the midst of that—that inferno. But it's important for people to understand what it was really like. Do you mind if I go on?"

He made no objection.

> *". . . While horse and hero fell,*
>   *They that had fought so well*
> *Came thro' the jaws of Death,*
>   *Back from the mouth of Hell,*
> *All that was left of them . . .*
>   *Noble six hundred!"*

The fury of the rain lashing the window was the only sound in the room, but Jennifer was hearing the boom of cannon, the scream of wounded horses and men. Then her inner vision shifted from the fire and fury of battle and reek of cannon smoke to the darkness and stench of the Barracks

153

Hospital with the squeak and plop of rats. She closed her eyes and reached for Richard's hand.

The noise of a coal shifting on the grate broke the silence and made it easier for Jenny to speak. "I've been thinking long on such things—the horrors of the war, the stupidity that caused so much suffering, all those deaths . . . and the horrors of our own slums right here in London, the suffering of the children. . . . Are such things a metaphor for evil to warn us against hell, or are they evil itself?"

"It seemed like hell at the time."

She squeezed his hand. "Yes, I'm sure no fury of the Devil could seem more horrible than charging those loaded cannon."

Richard was silent for another moment. Then he seemed to come back to the present. "Looking back on it, I think perhaps it was the result of evil—if one can call vanity, carelessness, and stupidity evil."

"I don't know, but I know we must fight it, whatever name we put on it." Suddenly she felt a new surge of energy. "Oh, thank you, Dick. Thank you for coming and for bringing that poem. I had become so discouraged, so overwhelmed with the hopelessness of it all. Just being with you seems to give me strength to carry on." She paused. "Even though I'm not sure of my direction."

He shook his head. "I'm glad if I've encouraged you. I'm afraid I've had little encouragement myself. Both Father and George have given short shrift to my letters urging reform in the pottery."

"Oh, Richard, that's wonderful! Not that they disregard you, of course—but that you've taken action."

"Well, I've tried—to little avail." He was quicker than Jenny to hear the step in the hall behind them and pulled his hand away.

Mrs. Neville entered the room. "Jennifer, why are you sitting in a dark room?" She stopped. "Oh, Lt. Greyston, how nice. I did not know you'd called. Why haven't you sent for tea, Jennifer?" She tugged the bell pull.

Dick rose. "Please don't bother. I must be going. I called with an invitation from my aunt for you and Miss Neville to join a party she is getting up to attend Mendelssohn's *Elijah* at Exeter Hall this Friday. I believe the Earl of Shaftesbury is to be among the company. If the excursion wouldn't be too tiring for Miss Neville."

Jennifer didn't wait for her mother's reply. "I should like that very much."

"Until Friday then." Richard nodded to the women.

"I'll see you to the door." Jenny started to get up.

Richard turned her direction. "I can do it." But Hinson's appearance at the door mooted the question.

Mrs. Neville turned up the gas light when Dick and the butler were gone. "Jennifer, I am surprised at you. You really must be more careful about receiving callers unchaperoned. Whatever would Mr. Merriott say if he found you here alone with another man?"

"I am confident Mr. Merriott would make the most proper chaperone imaginable, Mama."

Fourteen

By Thursday evening Jennifer was strong enough to return to her teaching, although Mrs. Neville insisted that Betsy go with her to assist. And when they arrived at the mission, Jenny was glad to have Betsy's service to offer as well as her own. All was in a state of chaos.

Mrs. Watson met them at the door. "Miss Jennifer, I'm happy to see you. We're all at sixes and sevens here. Three of my helpers failed to turn up, and I did want to have a tasty soup and loaf to serve tonight, it being our last time."

"Last time? What are you talking about?"

Edith Watson threw her hands in the air. "Oh, here's me forgetting myself, and you've been gone so long. First, let me tell you how happy I am to see you recovered. I knew fresh air and my elixir would do the trick. But so much has happened while you were away, and—" She gave a sharp cry and ran for the stove where clouds of steam and sizzling sounds issued from a kettle boiling over.

"Help her, Betsy," Jenny ordered and turned toward the room where several were gathering for the preaching service. She found Rev. Walker looking even more harried than Mrs. Watson. She got the story from him.

"It's true, I'm afraid. For all I was sure this was the Lord's work, it seems He must have other ideas. At least there's some that have another use for this building."

"You mean the mission is to lose the building?" Jennifer looked around at the converted warehouse. It was poorly furnished and as rundown as any property off Tothill Road, but it had been carefully cleaned and arranged at the cost of enormous effort. The work here was just beginning to flower. They had helped so many. The hungry who came here every night—where would they find food now? Those who sang so enthusiastically off-key and listened to Rev. Walker preach from the Word—where would they learn of God now? The children in the ragged school, many who were just beginning to learn to read—where would they be taught now? "But what has happened? Can nothing be done?"

Hiram Walker shook his head. "It's the rent. The landlord's doubled it. The agent came around yesterday. 'This is a very valuable piece of property,' says he. Seems the owner wants to put a more profitable business in here."

Jennifer shook her head. What could be more profitable than seeing to people's minds, bodies, and souls? But if this was to be her last session with her students, she would make it her best. If only she could give them something to take with them. Then she knew. Back in the kitchen Betsy and Mrs. Watson had set all to order. "Mrs. Watson, that large book you write your recipes and remedies in—could I have some of the blank pages from the back?"

The small slates each child worked on were Mr. Walker's own, to be kept in hopes of the Lord opening a door to a new school, but Jennifer could send each student home tonight with a piece of paper on which each had written the alphabet and a Bible verse. She thought it over. John 3:16 would be too long for most of them to copy. She would have to settle for "The Lord is my shepherd" for the younger ones. And their names. Each child would have his or her own name in writing. That way at least the ambitious ones would have something to practice—if only with a stick in the mud. She was determined that no child should leave without the project completed, even those who had only been coming a few weeks.

She was still at work long past the usual dismissal time when Arthur strode impatiently into the room. Joshua was the first to see him. He came smartly to his feet. "Miss, I finished me writin'. Please, may I black the gen'leman's boots, seein' as 'ow hit's the last time?"

Jenny surveyed his paper. The page was smudged, the letters squiggly, but the lesson was complete. "Of course, Josh. You've done well. Now don't forget to keep practicing. You've learned so much in such a short time." She bit her lip. It was a tragedy that it all had to end.

Josh drew out his shoeblack kit, and Arthur was obliged to submit his foot. After all, he had paid for the service long ago.

"Oh, don't worry, miss. I won't quit until I can read like a gen'leman. That's what I'm goin' ta be—a gen'leman. 'e said so."

"That's fine, Josh. Who said so?"

"'im what give me a job. I'd be off ternight even if the school weren't closin'. You know how you said to tend good to my reg'lar customers 'cause I might get employed?"

"Josh! That's wonderful! What are you going to do?"

He didn't take his eyes off his work on Arthur's gleaming boot. "Not sure, miss. Somethin' to do wi' horses—up north. My gen'leman lives in London now, but 'e has business interests up north, and I'm ta 'elp look out for 'em."

"My, that sounds impressive. I certainly wish you the best, Josh."

Joshua hadn't put quite the last lick and polish to the boot before Arthur withdrew it and helped Jenny into her thick woollen pagoda-sleeved mantle for the ride home. Jennifer was glad for Betsy's presence in the cab. Arthur could hardly renew his proposal of marriage in front of her maid. As usual, he required little encouragement to talk about his work. "I think even Shaftesbury has despaired of the Public Health

Department. They are completely bogged down in red tape. We are returning to factory inspection. It seems that's where the most good can be done now. Even owners who believe that poverty and unemployment are necessary to stimulate the economy can be persuaded to stay on the right side of the Ten Hours Act."

"So you'll be off again, will you?"

"Yes. That's what I wanted to tell you. Sorry to miss Lady Eccleson's party to the concert. Should be a fine affair, but there is so much I must do before I leave in the morning. Birmingham—Sheffield. Horrid long train ride. Always get covered with soot. But part of the job. And I shall stop in Newcastle. Shall I carry greetings to Miss Greyston for you?"

"Oh, yes. Please do." Such attention to civility was surprising from Arthur.

When the cabby pulled up at Portland Place, Betsy jumped out and hurried around to the servants' door. Arthur took Jennifer up the walk and paused on the porch. "I shall not come in tonight. I would not wish to impose on your mother at such a late hour. But I must assure you that I have not abandoned that which is closest to my heart. When I return from Sheffield, we shall speak further. I must explain everything to you." He raised her hand to his lips.

Friday was cold and dismal. Black clouds hung low in the sky, seemingly coming down to meet the dark fog that curled up from the river. Jennifer was glad for the warmth of her new flounced green plush dress trimmed with fringe and its matching mantle. She ran her fingertips over the deep, soft velour and smiled. That would feel good to a man who couldn't see the richness of this particular shade of green. And she dabbed an additional drop of rosewater behind her ears. If Richard couldn't see the carefully arranged curls, she would give him something else to enjoy.

Each pair of the four massive Corinthian columns fronting Exeter Hall in the Strand bore large notice boards announcing the performance. The great lamp hanging from the center of the porch over the front door cast a golden pool in the fog, but it barely lit the way for those exiting from cabs and carriages. The Nevilles' carriage arrived just behind the Earl of Shaftesbury's and Lady Eccleson's, so the entire party entered the great upper hall together. Shaftesbury's wife, the countess, had not come to the concert due to their son's illness. Consequently the earl escorted Lady Eccleson, with Mr. and Mrs. Neville following close behind them. Jennifer turned gladly to take Richard's arm.

Upstairs, the tall windows that lined both sides of the Great Hall were dark, but the long chandeliers hanging from the vaulted ceiling glowed warmly. Jennifer tightened her grip on Dick's arm, fearing the brightness for him, but he did not slacken his pace.

The hall, which seated 3,000, was filled nearly to capacity for this great oratorio by Queen Victoria's favorite composer. The choir tonight was only slightly smaller than the 270 voices of the original production. A hum of expectancy filled the air as the orchestra tuned up.

Dick was unusually quiet, even for him, only nodding to Jennifer's small talk. Then he turned to her and said, "Jennifer, there is a matter on which I would speak to you. Perhaps at the interval."

"Yes, fine." She answered automatically, giving it little thought. Her mind was not on the event. She was still thinking about the question that was plaguing her again. What was she to do about Arthur? She was no longer sure about accepting his proposal. Now there was no war to run off to. There wasn't even the school to teach in. What was she to do with herself?

From the opening chords of the oratorio, however, when the prophet Elijah dramatically called down punishment on the people for deserting the true God, Jennifer forgot her own problems, Richard's request, and everything around her. She became absorbed in the gripping portrayal of God's dealings with a nation that had forgotten Him.

Then, as Elijah fought the wickedness around him, Jennifer found herself thinking, not of the superb performance nor of the nation of Israel of which they were singing, but of her own nation; not of Old Testament times, but of today. Wasn't the wickedness the same? The need of the people the same? Wasn't God the same?

"Baal, we cry to thee," the priests sang over and over. And Elijah replied, "O hear me, Lord, and answer me! . . . and shew this people that Thou art the Lord God, and let their hearts again be turned!"

Jennifer wondered if the hearts of those of her own nation who worshiped the Baal of money and industrial progress could be turned.

"Woe unto them who forsake Him! Destruction shall fall upon them."

The Crimea, the London slums, the children abused in mills and factories—destruction *had* come upon them. Why was everyone too blind to see it?

"Open the heavens and send us relief! Hear from heav'n, and forgive the sin."

Then, at length in the narrative, the Lord heard and sent rain upon the land. Jennifer's cheeks were wet as the hall rang with the cry, "Thanks be to God! He laveth the thirsty land. Thanks be to God, thanks be to God!"

Applause thundered around her at the interval, but

Jennifer couldn't move. She sat there with her eyes closed, her heart aching for God's rains to pour down upon her own thirsty land.

The gas lights brightened overhead, and the audience began moving. But Jennifer could not move. She looked at the earl sitting to her right.

The dark eyes in the long, bony face smiled at her. Without a word he handed her a clean white linen handkerchief. She blotted her damp cheeks and handed it back to him with a smile of gratitude. She began almost in the middle of a sentence, as if Shaftesbury had been privy to all her thoughts. "The land is so dry, so thirsty: poverty, greed, disease, ignorance. Is there even a cloud the size of a man's hand?"

The earl nodded gravely. "I know, my dear. I often ask myself that, and in my discouragement, I often answer that this time we've gone too far. This time there will be no restoration of the land. And then I see a small cloud—smaller than a man's hand, perhaps, but an encouragement. As example, some time ago when I attended chapel at my old school, Harrow, 120 boys took Communion. I was amazed. When I was a student there, not a single boy would even have dreamed of attending Holy Communion. I believe this foreshadows a great change coming over England."

Jenny nodded, hoping he would go on in his gentle, yet compelling voice. He did. "And though there is much, overwhelmingly much, to do, we must not lose sight of what God has enabled us to accomplish. Think of the coal mines. Ten years ago I saw girls, almost naked, chained to heavy carts drawing coal up dark, narrow passages underground; children of five years or younger incarcerated without light to work trap doors in rat-infested tunnels; children standing all day ankle-deep in water at the pumps—all this for twelve or fourteen hours a day, six days a week. It required years of struggle, but at last Parliament was made to see the right. Women and children have been freed from such slavery in the coal mines." He paused, then added with great sadness in his voice, "But, of course, it is only a beginning—so much remains undone."

Jenny looked at him hopefully. "So you truly believe that if we work hard enough, we shall win?"

Shaftesbury looked shocked. "Miss Neville, of course not."

"Then why—"

"We must do what we can. It is the call of every Christian, but we will never win by human effort."

Jennifer sank back against her seat. "That is what I feared." She had come tonight hoping to find an answer to all that troubled her. The oratorio had seemed such a promise of hope. The earl's words had been so encouraging, but here was the bare-faced reality of it: *We will never win.*

Shaftesbury wasn't finished, however. "Winning is not our job. We are merely chopping wood and stacking brush— as Elijah did on his altar. That is all that is humanly possible. It is for God Himself to strike fire to the brushwood we pile up. Elijah did not strike the fire that consumed his offering. This is a dry and thirsty land. We are spiritually parched. The land must have spiritual revival."

Jenny frowned. "But there are churches everywhere. All Souls is packed every Sunday . . ."

"Indeed, Charles Baring is one of the finest preachers in all the land—and there are many like him. Their pile of brushwood will soon be as high as the spires of their churches. But they cannot strike the light themselves. We must pray God to send the torchbearers. England needs an Elijah."

Jenny blinked. "Torchbearers?"

"Think, Miss Neville. How long has it been since this country has seen true revival?"

Jenny shook her head. She had no idea.

"You are right. Certainly not in your memory. Nor in mine. And yet it is for every generation to pass the torch, to light the fires against evil. But where are our torchbearers—our Wesleys, our Whitefields, our Rowland Hills? We have many good, even excellent preachers. But that is not enough. We must pray that the Lord will send a great one—an Elijah, a torchbearer that will turn thousands of hearts to Him."

The words were inspiring and discouraging at the same time. "And all we can do is pray?"

The earl nodded. "That is as the Scripture says, 'to pray the Lord of the harvest that He will send workers.' Pray, and keep stacking your brushwood, Miss Neville, so that when the torchbearer comes, he may light a great bonfire."

The chorus reentered, the 125-member orchestra took its place, and Jennifer turned from the intensity of her conversation with a start of guilt. Richard. He had said he wished to speak to her, and she had abandoned him. "Richard, I'm sorry," she began. His mouth was set in a firm line as if resisting pain; the scars beneath the blond waves drew tight across his forehead. In the darkness of the room she touched his arm as the chorus sang. He did not pull away, but neither did he respond.

Throughout the second part of the oratorio, Jenny wrestled with her divided attention: the beauty and power of the music, her ache to reach out to Richard, her struggle to understand all Shaftesbury had said to her. Now she was more confused than ever.

"He, watching over Israel, slumbers not, nor sleeps . . ." Was God watching over England? Was He watching over her?

The chorus sang, "O come, everyone that thirsteth."

164

Jenny felt as thirsty as the drought-ridden land. All her hard work had accomplished so little, and now the mission wasn't even there for her to continue her work. She had failed Richard in so small a matter as providing companionship for the evening. And Shaftesbury had confirmed her fears as to how little human effort could accomplish—even though he saw reason to labor on. She simply hadn't the stamina to struggle more. Susannah Thompson was right. She must simply marry Arthur and do as society expected of her. But with that thought, it was as if a great black abyss opened in front of her, threatening to engulf her. She felt as much in darkness as Richard sitting isolated behind his dark glasses.

Finally the ending chorus rang through the room: "And then, then shall your light break forth as the light of morning breaketh . . . and the glory of the Lord ever shall reward you. . . . Lord, our Creator, how excellent Thy name is in all the nations."

Light break forth as the light of morning . . . light break forth . . . light . . . The phrase rang and reverberated in Jenny's mind as the walls echoed and reechoed the great chorus. She turned and looked at Richard.

And it was as if the light broke through her darkness and shined on her heart. The answer had been there all along. It was so simple. So obvious. She loved Richard.

The moment stood still as if the world had quit spinning. She couldn't breathe. The light the chorus sang about was so bright she thought all in the room must be blinded. But she wasn't blinded. At last she could see. All her other questions remained unanswered, but this one thing she knew—she was in love with Richard.

"Thou fillest heaven with glory. Amen."

While the applause thundered around her, Jennifer turned to Richard. Surely he knew. Surely everyone in the great hall knew. A lightning bolt had passed through the building, but she was the only one who had seen it. Dick rose with the others, nodded her direction, and with his fingertips brushing the tops of the row of seats in front of theirs, he made his way out. The crowd pressed from every side. She held his arm, but there was no chance to talk, and he seemed more distant than at any time since she had managed to broach his wall on first coming to London. She understood her true feelings for him, but she had failed him.

Outside the hall he turned to her as the Neville carriage pulled up. "Miss Neville, I had hoped to speak to you at more length. I have determined to go north. I must make what effort I can to convince Father and George that conditions in our pottery must be reformed. I have spoken with Arthur Merriott. He is certain he can help me. I shall travel with him."

"With Arthur? But he is leaving in the morning. You will leave so soon? Before we can talk?"

"I am disappointed on that matter, but perhaps it is for the best."

"Jennifer, dear, are you coming? We mustn't hold up the carriages." Amelia Neville's voice cut through the fog in Jennifer's mind. Jenny felt as if she were drowning in fog, unable to reach Richard with the shining revelation she had experienced. He handed her into the carriage and closed the door.

Fifteen

Jennifer was in no way prepared for the desolation she felt when Richard was gone. She had expected to miss her friend—this friend that she could only wish were so much more—but she had not realized that a city the size of London could seem barren with the absenting of just one person.

She passed compliantly through all the required Christmas festivities, a smile fixed on her face, her person appearing well-groomed and graceful. But her heart and mind were focused northward to the Midlands where England's pottery furnaces belched out clouds of black smoke as the kilns produced the world's finest white porcelain.

Daily Jenny insisted to herself that such a state of affairs was intolerable. She could not go on being such an imbecile as to think constantly of one who did not think of her. And she had no intention of becoming a pale, poetic maiden pining away for a lost love. She busied herself with parish visits—a festive activity, indeed, with many holiday food baskets distributed to the poor. And her greatest pleasure was the Christmas party for the shoeblacks at the mission, although she missed Josh's shining white head and cheeky pertness—another piece of her heart that had gone northward.

But now the holidays were over, and the most distracting task she could find was sorting linens. So it was that, holding three sheets marked for mending, she smiled with eager anticipation when Hinson entered to announce a visitor. The name on the small ivory calling card the butler presented on his silver platter read, "Miss Susannah Thompson."

"Oh, by all means, show her in," Jenny instructed.

She turned to welcome her acquaintance, who entered with pink cheeks and a bright smile.

"Do forgive my intrusion, Miss Neville, but I had not seen you for such a long time, and I had to assure myself that you were completely recovered from the cholera."

"My dear Susannah, I am perfectly well. And delighted to see you." She requested a tea tray of Hinson before sitting beside Susannah on the sofa. "And what of you? You appear quite blooming."

Susannah put a hand to her cheek. "Oh dear, Mama says it is not the thing to go about with one's feelings showing so. But I am so very happy I simply cannot hide it."

"That seems a most reasonable thing to me, Susannah. There is little enough joy in the world. Do not let anyone temper yours. Tell me what is happening."

"Well, as the chapel couldn't come close to accommodating the numbers who longed to hear Mr. Spurgeon preach, the board has undertaken its enlarging. They completely knocked out the east end and are extending it vastly. It's quite amazing. As a matter of fact . . . ." Here the young lady paused, her blushes increased, and her smile widened.

She opened her reticule and pulled out a thick vellum card. "I hope you won't think it too informal of me to give this to you in person rather than sending it by post, but I would be so happy if you could attend the dedication of our new chapel." She handed the card to Jennifer. "You will see that it is to be something rather special." She dropped her eyes.

Jennifer took the card and then gasped with genuine delight, "Oh, Susannah, you're engaged? To Mr. Spurgeon! I'm so happy for you. And the wedding will be at the dedication? How wonderful! My dear Susannah, I should love to attend."

At that moment Hinson entered with the tea tray. The rest

of the afternoon sped by, Susannah regaling Jenny with stories—of the fishwife who announced she would have nothing to do with religion, but who then became devout after hearing Charles Spurgeon preach . . . of the Thames boatman's family who never missed a service since Charles had gone to the river, caulking knife and materials in hand, to demonstrate his own method for waterproofing a boat . . . of the notorious drunk . . .

Jennifer nodded often, recalling how the young preacher had helped her when *she* needed it. She was sure he was as fine as Susannah said, yet Jenny couldn't help but think of the newspapers' continual complaints against the Reverend Charles Spurgeon: He was perhaps the most unpolished preacher ever to appear in a London pulpit. He had no university degree. His sermons were filled with examples from common things. His services created a traffic hazard—with streets around the chapel constantly blocked by crowds.

"I know what an exceedingly fine man he is, Susannah. But . . ." Jennifer stopped. She would say nothing to dim her friend's joy.

"Oh, those odious papers. So many people simply do not understand. But, Miss Neville, you must judge for yourself. Will you come Sunday to hear Charles preach? We are holding services in Exeter Hall while repairs are made to the chapel. May I call for you Sunday afternoon? I know *you* will appreciate a fine sermon, such as my dear Charles always preaches."

Jennifer agreed more to please Susannah than for any great pleasure she expected from hearing a second Sunday sermon. But when the girl embraced her with such open delight, she knew she had made the right choice. If she could not be happy herself, she could at least please others.

As their carriage approached Exeter Hall the next Sunday,

however, Jennifer had doubts—not about the service but about its setting. Returning to the scene of her last night with Richard would do little to help her forget the void his departure had left. If she harbored reluctance, however, she must be one of a small minority. It appeared that even this great hall would not accommodate all who had come to hear the preacher. The Strand was lined solidly with people.

Susannah led the way to the preacher's private entrance, so they were comfortably seated before the service began. And in nearly the same row where Jenny had sat beside Richard to hear the *Elijah*. The great organ pealed, and the congregation stood to sing a hymn unfamiliar to Jennifer. But just the sound of the organ, the feel of it vibrating the seats, was enough to bring back painful memories. If only she had made time for Richard. What had he wanted to talk about?

Jennifer looked around her. Should she make an excuse and leave? In such mental turmoil, she would get little out of the message. It was a pity to occupy a seat when so many had been turned away. What would Susannah think?

Then Charles Spurgeon began to speak, and all other thoughts left Jennifer's mind. The preacher put on no more airs in the pulpit than he had when helping a cholera-dazed Jennifer home from the Tothill Road mission. He affected none of the ways of the popular schools of oratory, but spoke directly without raising his voice—a method that allowed the light behind his words to shine the more clearly. It was evident that Charles Spurgeon had an inspiration beyond that given to ordinary men. His boyish appearance made hearing the sermon all the more novel. The speaker exuded a confidence in himself that was born of a confidence in God, allowing him to speak as one having authority.

In a voice as clear as a soprano's, without any reservation, he declared what he sincerely believed. "The world is lost.

There is none other Savior to redeem it but the one who died on Calvary." He explained that one could find the Savior only through sincere repentance, which naturally bore the fruit of good works.

The crowded room became warm. The preacher in his wool suit and a huge black satin stock tied high under his chin began glowing with perspiration. He pulled a blue handkerchief, bright with white spots, from his pocket and mopped his forehead. But even such a homely gesture did not detract from the force of his words.

"There is only one answer: By grace are ye saved. Because God is gracious, sinful men are forgiven, converted, purified, and saved. It is not because of anything in them, or that ever can be in them, that they are saved. Rather it is because of the boundless love, goodness, pity, compassion, mercy, and grace of God. Tarry a moment then at the well-head. Behold the pure water of life as it proceeds out of the throne of God and of the Lamb!"

As Jennifer followed the preacher's words and pictured herself drinking of the water of God's grace, a sudden realization crept over her. She saw that it was all of God. Nothing of her own works. She had been eager to do God's works, but she must relax in His grace first. The works were the fruit of grace. They did not produce grace.

"Faith," Spurgeon continued, "is the work of God's grace in us. We must hold to the faith that God's good work will come to fruition. Hold to God's grace and to His promise that 'the vision is yet for an appointed time . . . though it tarry, wait for it, because it will surely come. It will not tarry.' "

Jennifer dropped her head. *How could I not have seen this long ago, Father? The answer was there all along. You were there all along. Was it that I always lived so surrounded by the truth that I didn't realize its uniqueness?*

Oh, Lord, forgive my failures. Forgive my rejection of Your grace as I tried to go ahead in my own effort. I've been so discouraged because I thought I had to do all this in my own strength. Now I see. All You ask is that I obey You. It's Your battle, not mine.

Only You can do Your work, God. Work through me with Your strength.

Now she could see how God had been guiding her. This was a continuation of the insight she had received at the *Elijah*—that one must do his best to prepare the way for a vast renewal of society. But first one's own heart must be in tune with the Creator of all. Creation could not be restored until the hearts of individual believers were right.

That was the key. Always Jenny had believed with her head. Now she believed with her heart, too. The coldness and distance that she had so often felt melted away, leaving only warmth.

Sixteen

Greystoke Pitchers was a large white Georgian house standing at the top of a rising green lawn on Brampton Hill above The Walks. When he had left home for London three months ago, Richard had seen the round, full-leafed outline of the trees lining The Walks and surrounding the house. Now, as the carriage from the station drew up the curving street, he could make out the bare, dark branches streaking the sky. He told himself the outlines were somewhat clearer, the pain of looking at them less severe. And certainly, the latter, at least, was true. But whether that was simply the effect of Dr. Halston's German glasses and the cloudy day, or whether he could claim actual improvement, he didn't know. Certainly, the weight inside him was no lighter. Not after the confidence Arthur had revealed to him during their travel north.

Before the carriage had come to a complete stop, Dick felt the door beside him being jerked open. "Dick! Oh, I thought you would never come. I've been longing to see you—" Livvy stopped mid-sentence. "Arthur—Mr. Merriott. What a pleasant surprise. I had no idea you were traveling with my brother."

Livvy immediately returned to her most ladylike demeanor. "Won't you come in? Mama will be most happy to see you. Although Papa and George . . ." Her voice trailed off.

Dick had barely set foot in the ceramic-tiled entry hall before he heard his father and brother bellowing at each other from the library at the top of the stairs. "Oh, dear," Livvy said. "I had hoped they would have run down by now. It's the new jolley, you see. It's stirred everything up."

"Livvy, you take Mr. Merriott to Mama and Aunt Lavinia. Tell them I will join them later. I've come to tackle Father and George about the pottery. Apparently the fat is already in the fire, so I may as well wade in right now." He automatically handed his hat to the butler. "Cannock, show my man Kirkham where to put my bags. Mr. Merriott will have the room next to mine. You'll know where to put Kirkham."

Without waiting for anyone to reply, Dick grasped the smooth, well-worn wood of the stair rail and made his way upstairs. The padded runner on the stairs was thicker than he remembered. He fumbled on the first three steps until he judged the distance precisely. Then he found his stride and bounded the rest of the way up, as he had since his earliest days.

He paused outside the library door to assess the battle. The situation was certainly not new—some of his earliest memories were of Father and George arguing. They never seemed to tire of it. As Dick got older, he noted that after a particularly prolonged bout, it was not unusual for his mother to suffer an attack of her complaint and require a removal to London for the attentions of a Harley Street physician. Father and George, however, seemed to thrive on controversy.

Today, as Livvy had indicated, operations of the pottery had sparked the battle. "May I remind you, you young puppy, just whose pottery this is?" Francis Greyston thundered at his son.

George's lazy drawl never failed to irritate his father. Dick could picture his brother sprawled in the leather chair before the fireplace, both legs extended with his favorite dog under his knees. "The last I knew, Father, it was still the rightful property of Aunt Lavinia. Unless you have contrived to do her in in the last quarter of an hour, in which case it has passed to me."

"Don't be a smart alec. Females do not manage property, no matter whose name might be on some piece of paper. I am the rightful manager of all the property of this family, and I say these newfangled machines of yours are an unneeded expense and will cause trouble with our workers." The senior Greyston slammed his fist against his writing table for emphasis.

"The workers be . . ." A growl from George's dog drowned out his words. "They simply need a firmer hand. Raise their quotas. If they choose to waste time protesting against the machines, they may work longer hours, or you can sack them. You are too soft, Father."

"Soft? Soft am I? I'll show you soft, you young whippersnapper."

Dick judged the altercation had reached its climax and would now degenerate into name-calling, so this was as good a time as any to make his presence known. He yanked open the tall double doors and stood on the threshold, feet apart, hands on hips. "Father. George. How pleasant to find such a cheerful homecoming. I needn't ask if you're well. I can hear you're both in excellent voice."

With a minimum of fumbling, Dick took a straight-backed chair and faced it away from the fireplace. "Thank you, I'd love to sit and join you. Livvy tells me you've installed a new jolley at the pottery. I assume that's the cause of this lively discussion."

Jollies and jiggers were the latest inventions to improve the output of pottery and bone china. Both had revolving molds in which a profile shaped the clay, replacing the old process of hand-shaping. The jolley for hollowware, the jigger for flatware—both were hated by the workers for stealing their jobs.

"The new jolley is an absolute sparkler." For once George abandoned his laconic drawl. "It turns out perfect cups and bowls every throw—in half the time it takes a potter to do it by hand. I say let 'em complain. Anyone who doesn't want to work can quit. We can increase production with fewer workers—and pay them less."

"No! That's exactly the wrong approach." Dick was surprised at the vehemence of his own voice. "Keep them all on. Shorten working hours—that's the key. Your workers will be happier and do better work."

"Nonsense!"

"Happy? Who cares if they're happy?"

Dick smiled. Nothing but his intervention could have put George and his father on the same side. "I shall forebear to point out that they are fellow human beings. As good businessmen, you'll be more interested to know that Minton and Wedgewood have both increased production and profits with their factory reforms."

Francis slammed his fist onto the table again. "Do you throw Minton and Wedgewood in my face, puppy? They both have far larger establishments than Greystoke and can afford to hire the best artisans. What do you know of their reforms?"

"I have read—"

He was interrupted by a hoot from George. "Read? And since when do blind men read? It's little wonder you have your information wrong, brother. Why don't you go play soldier, and let Father and me run our business?"

"I may be blind, George—enough to prevent my playing soldier, as you put it. But I have had my eyes opened to things you apparently can't see. Yes, others have read the reports to me, but I have my facts straight. I know the suffering caused to children required to work fourteen hours a day lugging saggars to the kilns. I know of the lung poisoning inflicted on women who breathe the raw clay dust for twelve hours a day and are not paid enough to afford decent food. They 'die a little faster every day,' the white paper said."

Francis and George both took breath to roar at him, and even Bennett growled again from under George's legs. But Dick was spared further onslaught by the rapping of an ebony stick on the dark oak doors. Great-aunt Lavinia, elder sister of Great-aunt Charlotte and matriarch of the family, stood in the doorway. Dick made out her tall, thin, black-clad outline and snapped to his feet. "Great-aunt Lavinia." He bowed in her direction. George and Francis came to their feet more slowly.

Lavinia tapped her stick for attention. "We have endured enough of your caterwauling. Richard, I am surprised at you. You always had better manners than to engage in these slanging matches—and before you greeted your ancient aunt. You may take me in to dinner, sir."

"With pleasure, Auntie GAL." Dick grinned, knowing his use of their childhood name for her never failed to soften her.

"I'll have none of your impudence now." Her voice was severe, but Dick heard the softer note at the end. He crossed to her, but misjudged the placement of the low table beside the sofa and took a sharp blow on the shin. His face flushed as he heard George snigger behind him.

In the dining room his mother was warmly welcoming, Livvy was still dancing her excitement over the arrival of her brother and his friend, and even Arthur seemed less intense than usual.

But the cheerfulness and the well-served dinner did little to raise Dick's spirits. It wasn't the difficulty of trying to convince his father and George to improve the conditions of their workers—he had expected that. Indeed, that was the very reason for his coming. Nor was it the new proof of the awkwardness of his disability—he had had plenty of that already. It was Arthur Merriott's confidence to him on the train, imparted in a burst of companionship, that he expected to announce his engagement before the end of this parliamentary session. And then when the next election was called, he should be well-placed to stand for Parliament. Richard wished Arthur well in his political career. But Jennifer . . . he had not realized before that his feelings for her were quite so deep.

"I said, Richard, did you have a pleasant journey?" His mother's voice penetrated his consciousness.

"Oh, yes, thank you. Quite amazing to accomplish in three hours what formerly took six or more."

"Railways." Great-aunt Lavinia gave a disapproving sniff. "Noise. Soot. Smoke. If the devil traveled, he should travel by railway."

"Well, I'm exceedingly glad you're here however you've come." Livvy's voice reflected her pleasure. "And just in time, too. The Shrewsbury Cup is running Saturday next. We must make up a party for it. Will you be going, Olivia?" She turned to George's wife seated on the other side of Arthur.

"I think not. I had quite enough of horse racing in Yorkshire." The tall, broad-shouldered woman in russet dress shook her blonde head firmly. The former Olivia Thirkell was the only daughter of a wealthy farmer from the Yorkshire Dales—of sufficiently rugged stock that even George's blustering failed to intimidate her.

Livvy shrugged. "Windflyer is the favorite, of course. All the county's talking about him." Since no one had thought to lower the lights in the dining room, and Dick would not ask that it be done in front of George, he was required to sit with his eyes closed behind his dark glasses. The sound of his sister's happiness pleased him, but the name Windflyer tickled his memory. There was some controversy attached to the horse—something about his winning an earlier race against large odds . . . Oh, yes, the voice at Tattersall's that had turned out to belong to Dr. Pannier collecting his winnings. The horse's name had been Windflyer.

"I should like to go, Livvy. It would be pleasant to be around horses again," Dick said.

"Yes, and it will give us a chance to show our county to Mr. Merriott." Again the smile sounded in Livvy's voice. But it faded when Arthur explained that he must be on his way in the morning to meet two other commissioners to undertake a factory inspection in Sheffield.

"However, we will also be working in Stafford later." He turned to Caroline Greyston. "With your permission I will call on our return."

She turned to Great-aunt Lavinia sitting at the foot of the table. "It is my aunt's home, sir, but I am certain—"

"Always happy to have young people about." Lavinia nodded her silver head under its black-ribboned lace cap. "Keeps one young. If they're cheerful, that is. Bickering will drive us all to an early grave." She looked meaningfully at George. But he was concentrating on his third serving of meat and potatoes.

Olivia stepped into the uncomfortable silence to inform her listeners about the antics of their little Francis George III, and dinner continued through to the ending Bavarian cream followed by tart fall apples and a rich, tangy Stilton.

Later when Dick was alone in his room, he walked around slowly, touching each item to familiarize himself with its placement. Bumps and bruises were simply part of his life now, but he would keep them to a minimum.

At last he sat in the overstuffed plush chair by the window. It was not the external bumps that concerned him. He knew his work was cut out for him if he were to accomplish anything at the pottery. It would be a long, hard struggle, but he was prepared to make the stand. He began a careful mental outline of all that needed to be accomplished and how he would approach each challenge.

Richard had been depressed and angry all day, but now as he focused on the task before him, his former discouragement fell away. Gradually he became aware of a vigor he had not known for months. At last the wall was down; the road was open before him. A steep, twisting road full of boulders and potholes, but there was a road to follow, a cause to fight for, a job to do, and, hopefully, accomplishment at the end. It felt so good he wanted to spread his arms and shout.

But at his next thought his newfound elation died, leaving him flatter than before. He had momentarily forgotten Jennifer. At least he had been warned. She had mentioned receiving letters from Arthur even in Scutari. He had known the blow was coming. And he had been given no reason to expect otherwise. He simply had not realized how much he would care.

Squaring his shoulders, he determined to face that when the time came. In the meantime, however, he could not leave Livvy to the same painful fate. He had heard the note of happiness and caring in her voice tonight when she spoke to Arthur. He must warn her.

A knock at the door brought Kirkham from the adjoining room to answer it. "Is my brother abed yet, Kirkham?" Livvy rushed in without waiting for an answer. "Oh, Dick, I just had to come again to tell you how lovely it is to have you back!"

"Livvy." He crossed to her and put his hands on her shoulders. "I am glad you came. I was just thinking of you. There is something I must tell you. I fear this will be painful to you.

But I will speak now to prevent worse pain later."

"Dick, what is it? You sound so solemn."

"I feel solemn." He took a breath and rushed ahead. "Arthur Merriott told me this afternoon that he and Jennifer Neville are to be wed early in the coming year."

Livvy went stiff under his hands. She was silent for a long moment and then pulled away. "No. That's all wrong. I don't believe it. You misheard him."

"No, Livvy. I cannot tell you how much I wish I had. But he was very definite, very certain. All timed to have him properly wifed before the next general election."

"No. It is wrong. Wrong." She walked from the room.

"Something is wrong, Betsy." Jennifer dropped the letter from Edith Watson that Betsy had just brought. "Mrs. Watson has visited the brigade. The shoeblacks are to lose their home. The landlord has refused to renew their lease for a reasonable rate. First the mission, now the shoeblacks. How can slum property be that valuable?" Jenny thought for several moments. "Bring my blue woollen mantle, Betsy. I should like to see this property that is suddenly worth so much rent."

As the hansom drove the familiar route toward the now-abandoned Westminster Mission, Jennifer thought that it was strange how one could feel happier and yet more burdened at the same time. Ever since her talk with the Earl of Shaftesbury at the concert, the meaning of his words and the conviction of their truth had been growing on her. And then a full understanding had blossomed under Spurgeon's preaching. She realized that their land must be redeemed spiritually before it could achieve lasting reform.

Faith simply wasn't a part of most people's lives. That must change if the nation was to change. The hearts of the

181

people and the homes where the children were nurtured —those were the building blocks of the nation. Good laws and a sound economy could help create a healthy atmosphere, but the key to true reform was spiritual revival. And there was nothing she could do but pray to that end. The fact was dispiriting and yet freeing.

The hansom lurched over a rough paving stone, and Jennifer looked up from her meditations with a jolt. If she had not been there so many times before, she would not have believed that they were at the correct address. The windows of the former mission were hung with gaudy lace curtains. Even in midday a lamp with a rose glass chimney glowed in the center pane. And the heavily painted woman in the low-cut striped satin dress who lounged by the door was no candidate for ragged school training. Jenny gasped for air.

"Shall I tell the cabby to drive on, miss?" Betsy asked.

Jennifer nodded. But just as they moved back into the stream of carts, carriages, and cabs, she glimpsed a stocky male figure in a black cape. "Stop," she called to the driver and thumped the top of the cab. "Wait here," she ordered Betsy as she gathered the full skirt of her brown merino dress and jumped out.

She was certain the man was Dr. Pannier. If the Health Department was investigating the brothel, maybe there was a chance it would be closed down and the mission could reacquire the property. Or if he was making a professional call, perhaps he would need a nurse. She approached the woman by the door. *Poor thing—she must be freezing, standing about in such a flimsy dress on a chill, gray morning.* "Excuse me, er— miss. But the man who just went in—I believe he's a doctor."

The woman shrugged. "So wot? We get all kinds 'ere. They're all the same."

Jennifer was shocked when she saw the girl up close. She

could hardly have been more than seventeen or eighteen, and pretty under her paint. Probably a parlor maid who, willingly or unwillingly, attracted the attentions of the master or son of the house and was dismissed without a reference when he was no longer amused. Jenny longed to do something for her. "Do you have a family in the country? There is a society for returning girls to their families. They would help you."

The face before her drew into hard lines. For a moment Jenny thought the girl was going to spit in her face. Then she broke into a harsh laugh. "Do-gooding busybody, are ye? Wot do the likes o' you know about it? I got no family anywhere. An' if I did, who'd want me back?"

Jennifer wanted to explain, but the girl cut her off. "Git on wi' ye now. Yer type's bad fer business."

As Jenny turned, the door opened behind her, and a strident female voice shouted, "It's no use comin' around 'ere. My girls are 'ard workers, and my accounts are honest. Call a copper if yer don't believe me."

The door slammed. The man who had just exited pulled his hat low over his forehead and the collar of his cloak over his cheeks and hurried away. Jenny's heart sank. If even the Health Department could do nothing, there was little chance of the school reopening. As her cab rolled on toward the bridge, Jennifer had a good idea of what she would find at the Brigade Home—a brothel, a sweatshop, a pawnbroker— some slum business that took advantage of the poor and put money in the pocket of the landlord or owner.

But surely somebody could do something. Pannier must be aided in his battle. Jennifer knew only one person who might be able to help him. The Earl of Shaftesbury. She glanced at the Houses of Parliament standing golden and grand to her right. She had no idea how to go about getting a message to anyone in there. If only Arthur were still in town.

Perhaps someone from church? Then she smiled. Of course. Lady Eccleson could contact the earl, and he would pay attention to whatever she told him. Jennifer rapped on the top of the cab again and gave the cabby the number in Manchester Square.

Lady Eccleson received her wearing a lace-trimmed lavender morning dress. Soon the grand lady was serving small cups of sweet coffee from the tray Branman set before his mistress. The lace lappets of her cap nodded over each shoulder as Charlotte Eccleson bobbed her head in agreement with Jenny's conclusions. "My dear, I am certain you are quite right. Shaftesbury must be told of these newest developments. Now that Lady Shaftesbury's stepfather is prime minister, there are no doors he cannot open."

"Oh, thank you, Lady Eccleson. I thought you'd know what to do."

"Quite. I always do." The lady set her cup aside. "But there is another matter that concerns me greatly." She peered sharply at Jennifer. "You, my dear, do not look well." She drew her lorgnette from the end of its ribbon for a thorough inspection of her subject. Jennifer tried not to shrink under the scrutiny. At last the glasses lowered. "Skin sallow. Dark circles under your eyes. Too thin. You are decidedly moped. The London air is most unhealthy this time of year. I cannot imagine what your mother is thinking of, but I shall have to take matters into my own hands, or you will suffer a relapse of the fever."

"I assure you, Lady Eccleson, I feel quite well."

"Nonsense. You are very peaked. You need to get away from these heavy fogs, or you shall take a pleurisy. I never stay in town through the winter. Don't know how anybody survives it. You shall go to Newcastle with me. I shall tell your parents. We'll leave Thursday."

Jennifer opened her mouth to protest. She couldn't possibly be ready to travel in three days. "Lady Eccleson, I—" Then she remembered. Richard was in Newcastle. She had suppressed the full force of the feelings she had discovered at the concert, making herself think of other things. But had Richard's great-aunt seen what she refused to acknowledge herself? Did the strain of such repression show in her face?

And then one overwhelming thought blotted out all others. Lady Eccleson would take her to Richard. Nothing else mattered. "—I thank you."

Seventeen

"And how do you expect us to compete with the continent if we give our workers shorter hours? Your eyes were not the only part of your head that cannon damaged!" An angry male voice thundered over Jenny's head.

Lady Eccleson pulled her buff kid gloves off one finger at a time, her eyes twinkling. "How lovely to be back to the peace of Greystoke Pitchers. I don't believe you have had the pleasure of meeting my great-nephew George, have you, Miss Neville?"

Richard's voice followed George's, coming down to them from the room at the top of the stairs. "With the greater output produced from using the jigger and the jolley, of course. Even a blind man can see that."

"Jiggers and jolleys can go to Jericho," a heavier voice rumbled over the others. "But I'll hear no more of this model village scheme unless you mean to pay for it from your own pocket. Have you any idea—" Thudding blows of a fist on a table accompanied each word.

"That is my dear Caroline's husband, Francis. Such a gentle soul." Lady Eccleson handed her gloves and traveling cape to Cannock.

Jennifer gave her hostess a wry smile and then turned at the sound of silk skirts on the tile floor. A woman smaller and more wrinkled than Lady Eccleson but sharing her proud carriage and twinkling blue eyes entered just ahead of Livvy. "Ah, my sister Lavinia." Charlotte Eccleson embraced her elder sister. "Vina, this is Miss Neville, about whom I wrote to you."

Jenny acknowledged the introduction while the argument rolled on above their heads. Livvy darted across the tile floor and hugged her great-aunt. "Oh, I'm so glad you've come, Aunt Charlotte. You can make them stop." She nodded her head toward the stairs. "It's all we've heard for days and days. Dick is determined the pottery should be reformed, and Papa and George will have none of it. They say the most dreadful things to each other."

The elder Lavinia's eyes twinkled. "Don't you dare stop them, Charlotte. I find their conversation most instructive. Since females are to know nothing of business, if men didn't shout at one another, I'd know little of the conditions on my own property."

The door at the top of the stairs opened and slammed shut. Jennifer did not have to look up to recognize the sound of the feet that felt their way to the first step, then descended rapidly, accompanied by the sliding of a hand down the guide rail. Suddenly she froze. She had been so wrapped up in her own delight over seeing Richard again, it had not occurred to her to worry about how he would feel on encountering her. Had Lady Eccleson informed him she would be bringing a guest? Livvy hadn't seemed surprised—or terribly pleased—to see her. She took a step back when the footsteps reached the ceramic tile.

"I heard the carriage arrive, Aunt Charlotte. Forgive my delay in coming to greet you. We were—ah, discussing a matter of business."

Charlotte kissed the air near her nephew's cheek. "Yes, Richard, so I heard. As did the servants and, no doubt, the neighbors as well. It's comforting to find that some things never change."

Richard ignored her irony. "But some things must change. This family cannot continue to live in ease on the profits of the suffering of others. The needless suffering." He waved a large roll of paper in his left hand. "I have the plans of a model village for factory workers similar to the one Minton built—"

Lady Eccleson put her hand on his arm. "I shall be happy to look at them later, Richard. But I have a surprise for you." She signaled Jenny to come forward. There could be no shrinking back now.

Jennifer lifted her chin and stepped from the shadows of the curving staircase. "Hello, Richard."

His mouth twisted sharply as he checked the impulse to hold his hand out to her. Jennifer was sure she was the only one who saw the gesture, as she halted her own impulse to grasp his hand.

Richard all but clicked his heels as he drew himself upright and gave a stiff bow. "Miss Neville. What a charming surprise. Welcome to Greystoke Pitchers."

The momentary awkwardness was relieved by the entrance of Caroline Greyston urging everyone to come into the lounge for refreshment.

The next morning, after a troubled night, Jennifer allowed the maid Lady Eccleson had sent her to arrange her hair and help her into a freshly pressed morning dress of blue, green, and pink checkered cotton. The little maid fluttered like a hummingbird with bright, dark eyes as she fastened the agate stud buttons mounted on black velvet bows that adorned the front and wrists of the dress.

"There now, miss. You look lovely. Breakfast's laid out in the dining room." She bobbed in a curtsey.

"Thank you, Martha. Has the family eaten?"

"I think all have but Miss Livvy." Martha bobbed again.

That would do very well. Jenny had no wish to encounter the moods of Richard Greyston before breakfast.

The dining room was paneled shoulder-high with dark wood and hung with ornate gold-framed portraits, its parquet floor covered with thick carpet. Pale morning light filtered through the lace panels covering the tall square-paned windows. They looked out on a lawn now dotted with snowdrops and crocus under the oak and maple trees lining the garden. Jennifer had the room to herself as she filled her plate at the sideboard of covered dishes containing porridge, eggs, creamed kidneys, kedgeree, toast, and assorted preserves. She passed on the porridge and kidneys, but took a healthy serving of eggs and kedgeree and sat at the side of the table.

She was piling marmalade on her second piece of toast when Livvy came in and helped herself to a bowl of porridge. "I trust you slept well, Miss Neville."

Jennifer started to answer, then stopped. "No. I didn't." She looked at Livvy who had chosen a seat some distance from her. "I was troubled by your brother's reaction to my presence. And it seems you share his opinion. Must you call me Miss Neville now when we were on a first-name basis in London?"

Livvy ducked her head. "It—it is somewhat awkward to know what is proper. I shall be happy to call you Jenny. But you must allow Richard more time to adjust to the new circumstances."

"What new circumstances? Has something happened? You must tell me, Livvy. I am most concerned—"

She was interrupted by the entrance of the great-aunts, both dressed in proper black, with bonnets over their lace caps. Aunt Lavinia leaned on her walking stick, and Aunt Charlotte peered through her lorgnette. "There you are." Charlotte spoke first. "I cannot understand how the young can manage to lie abed half the morning. I breakfasted hours ago. Would you care to see Greystoke Pottery, Miss Neville? I have ordered the carriage."

"I should like that very much." Jennifer would like any activity that would take her away from the awkwardness she felt. And she was doubly pleased when Livvy agreed to accompany her. Whatever the problem was, Livvy apparently did not find her presence intolerable. And surely she could make an opportunity to find out what had happened.

But Jenny was surprised to discover that both of the older women intended to make the tour as well. "I have not been to Longton for years. At my age it is not wise to put off until tomorrow what one may do today. One cannot be assured there will be a tomorrow," Great-aunt Lavinia said as they settled into the well-sprung brougham. They took the hard-packed dirt road southeastward to Longton, one of the five towns that made up the great pottery-producing center of the Midlands. The trees lining both sides of the road were bare, and yet the countryside gave an impression of intense greenness.

As they drew nearer the factory site, however, the air darkened, and the February sun seemed dimmer, although the sky held no clouds. Then the carriage rolled up a small rise, and Jennifer saw the smokestacks of the potteries, each brick potbank belching a black cloud into the sky. She checked an impulse to raise a handkerchief to her nose. There would be no escaping the smoke. It was little wonder that the factory owners chose to live in Newcastle with its cleaner air and elegant walks.

The brougham passed through a wide gate in a high red brick wall. They came to a stop on a bricked courtyard before a building bearing an ornately lettered sign, "Greystoke Pottery, est. 1787."

"Jeremiah Greyston, my father's father, built this. Before that, pottery had been made at home. Potters as far back as Roman times, the Greystons were—as far as anybody knows.

And I intend to see that the tradition continues." Great-aunt Lavinia descended from the carriage with the help of two footmen.

Jenny turned to Livvy. "I don't understand. I thought she was your mother's aunt."

"Yes. But since Auntie GAL had no heirs, Father took Mother's name for the sake of the inheritance," Livvy explained.

Once outside the carriage, Jenny stood in amazement before the great bottle-shaped brick kiln across the courtyard. "I've never seen anything like it." Even at the far side of the yard, she could feel the heat radiating from the furnace. Behind that kiln rose the chimneys of three more. Then she saw the streams of small, ragged children, almost like rows of ants, carrying huge round clay containers on their heads, trudging toward the open doors of the far kiln. "What are those round things?" she asked.

"Saggars," Livvy said. "They fill them with the pottery and then stack them inside the kilns. Each oven holds about 2,000 saggars."

Jenny nodded and followed Livvy toward the main building. She had hoped to talk further with Livvy, but her friend seemed determined to keep to sightseeing. "Aunt Lavinia will want to see the color patterns and then spend her time poring over books in the office. I'll take you to the more interesting parts. When I was a child, I could stand and watch them throw pots all day. I always thought I'd grow up to be a potter, until George explained matters to me in no uncertain terms." She laughed and held her skirt away from the railing covered with a thick film of red clay dust as she went up the stairs. "Now I think it's most interesting to watch them shape the flowers."

The great-aunts moved ahead, and Jenny followed Livvy

into a side room where thin-shouldered, stooped women sat in rows at low tables, making delicately petaled flowers out of soft clay. Jenny watched in awe as the bony, nimble fingers of the woman in front of her formed a china rose by placing petal over petal. In a few moments the worker placed the finished rose on a tray in front of her.

In the same gesture she picked up another ball of clay, about the size of a walnut, and began working it to form petals. The tray was half full, but Jennifer could see that it soon would be covered with roses. Then the woman would turn to glazing another tray of flowers, and then there was a tray to be painted, Livvy explained. Fumes from lead paint filled the unventilated room. Jennifer shook her head. The woman was very skilled, but Jenny could not imagine doing such tedious work for fourteen hours a day, six days a week. And in a dim, damp room. Jenny looked at the woman's hollow cheeks and wondered if she had ever had a really full meal. And how many children did she have to care for at home?

Jenny turned away.

"Want to see the infamous jigger and jolley?" Livvy laughed and turned toward another room. Here an equally stoop-shouldered man stood over a wheel. He pressed a sheet of soft clay onto a mold and shaped the underside by holding a profile tool against it for a few turns of the wheel. Another man was making cups by pressing clay on a wheel in a hollow mold with a jolley. Both men were assisted by pale, hollow-cheeked children working as jigger-turners and mold-runners. "You can see how quickly the new equipment forms the pottery, but the workers will complain when someone loses a job." Livvy shrugged and moved on.

Jenny stood for a few minutes longer watching the skill of the men shaping the raw clay. Then she turned to follow her friend. Not wanting to get lost in the tangle of rooms, she hurried through the next doorway.

"Watch out!" The sharp male voice warned her too late. She felt the bump and heard the crash at the same time.

"Oh, I'm so sorry!" At her feet lay the broken pieces of what had been an elegant china figurine, apparently a shepherdess in a rose-draped pink dress and a shepherd boy playing a pipe.

She started to apologize again and then looked at the man she had cannoned into. "Richard. I didn't know you were here." The look on his face clearly said that he was not pleased to meet her and that she had made a bad situation worse by demonstrating his handicap.

Eighteen

"It was my fault," she cried and dropped to the floor to gather the broken pieces.

"It seems George was right about the competence of a blind man in a china factory." The bitterness in Richard's voice stung her as he took her arm and raised her to her feet.

"It was my fault, Richard. I wasn't watching where I was going." Suddenly there seemed nothing more to say. Or too much to say. She wanted to say so much that nothing would come out.

Richard broke the silence. "I assume you have come for a tour. I trust you are finding it instructive?"

"Yes. But this is only the third room I've seen."

"If you haven't been to the kilns yet, I would be happy to take you."

"Thank you." She hated the formality between them, but anything was preferable to silence. She took his arm.

Richard talked as they walked back through the building, down the outer stairs, and across the brick courtyard. "After the pottery is formed, it is allowed to dry. Then it is given a biscuit firing, which hardens the clay. The piece is then dipped in glaze and given a glost firing, which fuses the glaze with the body. After the decoration has been added, there is a final enamel firing, but that is done in a smaller kiln behind the yard."

They were now standing before one of the huge bottle-shaped brick structures that had captured her attention earlier. Richard was still being the perfect guide-host. "This outer bottle-shaped part is the hovel. It protects the inner kiln and creates a draft of air."

The door of the inner oven stood open, and Jennifer could see that it was half filled with wheel-shaped saggars full of pottery. The fireman stood on the top of a ladder, piling the cases to the height of three men. When the kiln was full to the door, he would brick up the door and begin the firing.

Jenny was fascinated. She had eaten on fine china all her life without giving a second thought to where it came from. Again she looked at the steady stream of children carrying their burdens to the kiln. Then Dick led her to another huge kiln where the firing was in process, radiating heat across the yard. Here the children were carrying, not the saggars of pottery, but scuttles of coal. Most of the urchins were as black as their burdens.

An equally blackened fireman tended the fire mouths at the base of the kiln. "It takes three days to raise the temperature sufficiently to bake the clay and then allow it to cool down again. Once the process starts, the fireman can't leave. Early in the morning you'll see him cooking his breakfast bacon on his shovel."

Just then a barefoot boy ran across the yard and handed a packet of sandwiches to the fireman. "Thank 'e, Tag. I'll just stoke this one more mouth, an' then us'll have our meal."

Richard nodded toward the fireman's voice. "Is that you, Thomas? I see your family is keeping you fed."

"Oh, aye, they're a right fine lot, they are. The missus is formin' flowers, and two o' the young 'uns carry saggars. Tag 'ere I'm trainin' to be a fireman. Even sleeps 'ere with 'is old da' when we're firin'. Don't ye, lad?"

Tag nodded his mop of streaky brown hair. "Tha's right. Warmer 'ere than it is at 'ome."

Dick and Jenny turned away. "It's fascinating, Richard. But the poor children."

"I know. So many grow up deformed from the weights they carry, and none receive an education. Come. Let me show you where they live."

A soft rain began to fall from the now-gray sky. Richard seemed to have little trouble making his way along the busy courtyard filled with people and carts and around buildings, which he pointed out as warehouses and workshops. They went out the wall behind the potbank. He stopped before a double row of buildings that seemed to Jenny to be as bad as anything she'd seen in a London slum. Only here the narrow passage that twisted between the terraces was mud rather than cobbles. The stench from the toilet at the bottom of the street mingled with the stink of pigs from the sty built against the wall of the building. Children tumbled with muddy animals in the confining alleyway, and laundry, streaked black with coal smoke, hung overhead between the buildings.

"I will leave it to your imagination what it's like inside the rooms," Dick said. "But perhaps I should point out that they sleep with their animals for warmth and that the damp carries the smell from the pigpen through the walls." He turned back toward the factory.

"And you have designed a model village to replace this?" Jenny asked.

"It's not my design; it's Thomas Minton's. He built one for the workers at his factory in Stoke-on-Trent. Rows of brick terraces, each house two up and two down, so the adults can sleep apart from the children. Every house has its own fireplace. And I would put a toilet in each house. Greystoke is one of the leading manufacturers of sanitaryware, yet few of the very people who make them have ever used such a convenience."

"Dick, it's a wonderful plan. You mustn't give up. Surely your father will see the right of it."

Dick shook his head. "I must get you back to Auntie GAL. I just realized no one knows where you are."

They found the aunts in the manager's office just beyond the laboratory where metals and minerals were mixed to make a wide range of brilliant colors. It was obvious Lavinia had been grilling the manager about every phase of the operation. "Yes, ma'am. We hold iron-clad to the original formula: six parts bone ash, four parts china stone, and three and a half parts china clay. It was good enough for your great-grandpa and mine, and it'll be good enough for our great-grandchildren, God grant them to us."

Lavinia thumped the brick floor with her stick. "See that you hold to it, Trenton. Too much letting down of the standard these days. I won't have it. Not at Greystoke." She turned to Jenny. "There you are, my girl. What do you mean, gallivanting off without a by-your-leave?"

"I do apologize, Miss Greyston. But Richard has been telling me about his ideas for the model village. They're wonderful. And I've seen how the workers are living now. The children—" Jenny rushed ahead until she was cut off by sharp raps of Aunt Lavinia's walking stick.

"What nonsense have you been filling her head with, Richard? It seems you're very free with other people's money. How would you propose to finance such a scheme, sir? From my pocket, I suppose?"

"Not at all, Aunt Lavinia. I have it all worked out. First, the buildings would be put up by small contractors on speculation, as they have done elsewhere. The workers would be encouraged to join a building club, which the pottery would form for them—I expect that would be your department, Trenton."

The manager snorted. "With respect, sir, they couldn't contribute more than a few pennies a quarter."

Dick nodded. "I realize that, especially those with irregular employment. But it's important that they contribute what they can so they'll feel the project is theirs. The major funding will come from increased profits of the pottery."

Lavinia scoffed. "And how do you propose we achieve that? I most distinctly heard you arguing for giving the workers shorter hours."

"I've studied Wedgewood's system. He's achieved great success with economy of labor by having his workers specialize. Instead of each worker making a pot from start to finish, one group does all the clay mixing, another all the forming, another specializes in glazing, another decoration —you see?" Dick spoke fast, his voice taking on a ring of assurance. "It'll take some retraining and reorganizing the factory, but I believe it can be done. I figure that in the output of ceramic tiles alone—"

"With respect, sir," Trenton cut in, his voice not sounding respectful at all, "the workers won't like it. You'll destroy their skill."

"No, that's just it. The plan doesn't destroy skill at all. It simply limits the workers' skill to a particular task so they can increase their proficiency by continued repetition."

"Aye, there's just the problem. You'll have inattention. No one can do the same job fourteen hours a day." The manager shook his head.

"But they won't need to. Wedgewood has found his specialized workers can achieve as much in ten hours of attentive labor, even eight hours—"

"Eight hours!" Lavinia's voice rose as if Richard had proposed an indecent act in the drawing room. "And what will they do with their spare time? They'll drink. You'll just be contributing to the immorality of the working class."

"No." Jenny could no longer restrain herself. "You can

start schools. Teach them to read the Bible. In London even adults come to the ragged schools."

"Wedgewood has developed a system of supervisors and managers to improve efficiency and quality. We could—"

"Wedgewood is a much larger and wealthier establishment than Greystoke. As is Minton. Wedgewood has his Jasperware, and Minton his Willow pattern. Our Royal Legend is a fine piece of artistry, but it has not built us a fortune the size of those you would compare us to."

"Yes, Aunt Lavinia, we are a smaller factory—therefore, we should be easier to reform and reorganize."

Lavinia looked him up and down sharply before replying. "You don't give up, do you, young man?"

Dick sketched a bow. "Forgive me if I have overstepped myself, Auntie GAL."

Lavinia sniffed, but Jenny thought she saw a twinkle in the ancient eyes. "We shall see about that. I have one more matter to discuss with Trenton." She dismissed Dick and Jenny with a wave of her hand and then stopped them again. "Richard, you may continue Miss Neville's instruction at your leisure. We shall not wait for her."

"Would you care to view the workings of the sliphouse, Miss Neville?" Richard offered his arm to Jenny, and once again they crossed the courtyard. Even before they entered the workshop, the noise of the great steam engine thundered at them. Inside, the room vibrated. Over the roar Dick pointed out the essentials of the process. "The raw materials are shoveled into that wooden bin we call a blunger. They are blunged with water for about a day to produce a creamy clay." He explained how the mixing continued and impurities were removed, but Jennifer was too chilled to follow the process closely.

She shivered and pulled her thick quilting-lined woollen

mantle close around her shoulders. At the same time she looked at the women passing magnets over the liquid clay to remove particles of iron. They were wearing thin, ragged cotton dresses and working with their hands in cold, wet clay. And she thought of Florence Nightingale confronted with freezing soldiers in the Crimea.

Jenny felt she could no more remain snuggled in her own cape and do nothing for those shivering around her than Florence Nightingale had been able to ignore the frostbitten soldiers. She tugged at Richard's arm and all but pulled him out of the sliphouse where they could talk away from the noise. "Richard, I have a little money of my own—not enough for any sort of reform, but . . ." She faltered. Would he think her pushy, interfering in his business? Would he resent her even further than he already seemed to do? A gust of cold wind blew down the courtyard, almost rocking some of the saggar-laden children off their feet. She had to go on, whatever Dick thought. "Dick, I'd like to buy warm cloaks for the women and children and shirts for the men." Dick was silent. "If you wouldn't mind, that is."

Richard's mouth twisted as it had when he was confronted with her arrival. Then he gave a curt nod. "That is very kind of you. As you see, the need is great."

"Yes. Could we do it now? Do you know where we could go?"

"The Northern Store in Newcastle, I should think. They're the largest dry goods mercantile. If you'll be so good as to wait here, I'll just step across the way and tell Kirkham to bring the Victoria." He turned so quickly he almost bumped into a child carrying a hod of clay.

Jenny bit her lip. She knew how he hated bumping into things. Her day had been such a failure, and it seemed that the harder she tried, the worse it got. She had failed to find out what was bothering Livvy. She had made matters worse between Richard and his great-aunt Lavinia with her interfering. And everything she did seemed to increase the distance between herself and Richard. Her only hope was that at least she might accomplish something for the workers.

Kirkham put up the calash top of the carriage and climbed onto the driver's seat in front. Richard sat beside her in silence as the fine pair of matched bays trotted smartly toward Newcastle. Jenny made another attempt. "Richard, I know you're discouraged, but you mustn't give up. Your plans for the village and the pottery are excellent."

"Yes, they are. I thought I had really found my calling—something I could do. But it appears that I was wrong. Again."

"No, you aren't wrong. There must be a way." Then she had a new idea. "Perhaps Arthur would know of something! You traveled north together, didn't you? Did you discuss your plans with him?"

"No. It was he who discussed his plans with me."

"Yes, that's what I mean. Arthur knows so much of reform and has so many excellent undertakings. We must see what he can do."

But again Jennifer's attempt to be helpful had failed. The silence in the carriage was heavier than before.

The wheels of the Victoria clattered over the cobbles of Newcastle's High Street, and Richard pointed out some of the landmarks. "That's Kendrick's Store. Auntie GAL won't have her provisions from any other grocer. And there's City Hall." The traffic became more congested with carts and wagons of every description, and people crowded the pavement along the street.

"What is it? Is this market day?" Jenny leaned forward to see better.

"The Stones," Dick replied. "Open air market every day. Some have stalls." He waved toward the ones they were now passing. "Most just sell right from their carts."

"Oh, markets are such fun. Let's look here. Might there be shawls and mantles for sale?"

Dick shrugged. "I expect they have about everything."

Kirkham stopped to let them off and then went to find a place to park the carriage away from the tangle of market traffic. Under the guise of seeking warmth, Jennifer held tightly to Richard's arm. She wanted to protect him from any more awkward accidents this day. Whatever the barrier between her and Dick, it was high enough already.

She was soon captivated by the atmosphere of the market as sellers everywhere called their wares, housewives haggled loudly over prices, and children and dogs chased in and out among the stalls and shoppers. A cart piled high with hand-loomed rugs attracted Jenny with their bright colors and patterns, as did the next stall of fine embroidered table linens. Several wagons offered eggs and cheese, jams and preserves, and rutabagas, turnips, and carrots.

Jennifer began to fear that Dick had been overly optimistic about the market having everything. Just then a small boy skipped by munching an apple. Jennifer blinked. Was it possible? Perhaps all tow-headed urchins looked alike. Yet that head of strawlike thatch was so distinctive. "Josh!" she cried.

The boy stopped and turned. His blue-brown eyes turned saucer-round, and his mouth dropped open mid-bite. "Miss, is that you?"

"It certainly is, Josh. I remember you said your new employer was taking you north, but I had no idea I'd see you here."

"Then you ain't forgot me?"

"Certainly not. And I hope you haven't forgotten your alphabet."

"No, miss. Not quite, I 'aven't. Not as I 'ave much time for learnin', wot with the market an' the 'orses. But I can write my name fine."

"Does your employer have a stall here, Josh?"

" 'im as I'm helping fer the guv does. Right over 'ere. Army blankets." He puffed out his chest. Jennifer could see he had grown considerably. It appeared his employer fed him well. "British army 'as the best in the world."

"That's true—when they can get them." Jenny's reply held a note of irony that was lost on Josh but not on Dick. "Let's see your cart, Josh."

"This way." He darted off through the crowd and stopped at a cart parked before a distinctive black and white building. Josh saw her looking at the building. "Market Inn. Fair posh it is—that's where the guv stops when 'e comes up." He pointed to a shiny black gig with red wheels. "That there's 'is carriage, too." He turned back to his market wares. "There's blankets, miss."

Jenny looked at the wooden cart piled high with heavy woollen goods. She ran her hand over one of the thick gray blankets. "What we could have done with these at the hospital." Her reference to their shared experiences seemed to lessen the distance Richard had placed between them. She put a blanket in his hands and reached for a shirt from the stack.

"Sometimes we even 'as medicines." Josh grinned at them in his best salesman manner.

Jenny turned to Richard. "Dick, these are just what we want for your workers. The women can use the blankets for mantles and put them on their beds at night, and the men can wear the shirts. But something's wrong here."

He nodded. "I know. At least these will be going for a good cause now, but they should have been used in the Crimea. I know a lot of the supply problems were from stupidity and red tape, but how did these get here? And medicines?"

"Of course we heard rumors of graft—accusations even." Jennifer groped for the memory. "I recall hearing an argument about it in the hospital. It was that Dr. Gavin who came out with the commission."

"The one who was shot?"

"Yes. The night before he was shot—that's why I remember it—I heard him and Dr. Pannier arguing about someone holding back the supplies. . . . You don't suppose Gavin was shot because he was involved in graft?"

"Or maybe—," Dick began.

"Miss, do you want to buy summat?"

"Yes, Josh, I do. I'd like to make a special offer for your whole cartload."

Josh's eyes got big again. "Whoosht! That'd be right fine! Then I could get back to the stable. I got extra chores 'cause tomorrow's a meet." He started to dash toward the Market Inn, then turned back. "I'll get Mr. Coke. Don't go away."

Jenny turned at the sound of a brisk stride and palms rubbing together. "So, young Joshua tells me you fine people are interested in purchasing some woollens. I don't need to tell people of your discriminating taste that these are the very best quality—finest British made." His smile emphasized the frequency and brightness of his freckles.

"Yes, I was thinking—," Jenny began, but Dick stepped forward.

"Coke! Jamie Coke, hardest riding sergeant in the Lancers. It's you."

There was a pause while the busker switched roles. Then he drew himself up and sketched a salute. "Lt. Greyston, sir."

"Good to see you survived, Coke. You appear to be doing well."

"Yes. Yes, fine. That is, this is just a sideline. Do this for a friend really. I'm in the sporting business. Have my own stable." He suddenly seemed confused, as if he didn't know what to say next.

Jennifer saw her chance and made an offer for the blankets and shirts well below their value, expecting a counter-offer. To her amazement, Jamie Coke made no effort to haggle. Dick said he would send a servant with the money to pick the purchases up, and the matter was concluded.

Jennifer gasped as they walked back to the carriage. "Something was not right there."

Dick nodded. "He wanted to get rid of us, didn't he?"

"Do you suppose they are army contraband, and he was afraid we'd know it?"

"That doesn't make sense. That would be all the more reason to drive a hard bargain—even try to keep us from getting the goods if he feared we might file a complaint against him."

"Hmm. I'm delighted to have those shirts and blankets. But I certainly would like to know what's going on. Oh, Dick, I didn't tell you what I discovered just before leaving London either."

She related how the mission had been replaced by a brothel and that the Health Department seemed powerless against the landlord.

Dick listened attentively, and her spirits rose. Working together on this had brought them closer again. Perhaps everything would be all right. She went on with her story. "Arthur was out of town, and I didn't know who to turn to, so I went to Lady Eccleson."

Richard pulled himself up stiffly. "I'm certain that as soon as Mr. Merriott has his seat in Parliament, he will be able to put all such matters to right."

They rode back to Greystoke Pitchers in silence, Jennifer feeling more confused than ever. What had she done wrong now?

Nineteen

"Thank you, but I think I won't go to the races tomorrow." Jennifer placed her knife and fork vertically across her plate, a signal to the footman to remove them.

"That is most wise of you. A day in bed would do you a world of good." Lady Eccleson peered at her through her lorgnette. "Your color has not improved at all. As a matter of fact, you appear to be more moped than you were in London."

"Nonsense, Charlotte. The girl needs more fresh air. Go to the races, Miss Neville." Jenny forced a smile at Great-aunt Lavinia and heartily wished someone would change the subject. She certainly was more dispirited than she had been in London, but fresh air or the lack of it was hardly the problem.

"I had decided not to go myself. I don't care much for horse racing—great crushing crowds all yelling and stamping for three minutes and then long periods of standing about in the damp with nothing to amuse one." Livvy pushed a brussels sprout about her plate with the back of her fork. "But I'm certain Miss Neville would prefer to be hostess to Mr. Merriott tomorrow, so perhaps I will go with you, Dick." The sharpness was back in Livvy's voice.

"Mr. Merriott? Arthur is returning tomorrow?" Jennifer's head jerked up.

"It was his plan to have his work in Sheffield completed by today. He said he would pay us a visit on his return south. I believe he is to inspect a factory at Stafford and then return to

London." Livvy gave her a keen look. "But I expect you know all that."

"No. I really know very little of Arthur's plans." The footman set a tall crystal dish holding a scoop of lemon sorbet garnished with a mint leaf before Jennifer, but she did not reach for her spoon. Arthur was coming tomorrow and going on to London. This was her chance to escape the uncomfortable situation with Richard here. She had thought she would be obliged to wait until Lady Eccleson returned to London, but if Lady Eccleson could spare Martha for a few days, she could travel with a maid under Arthur's protection.

She looked at Richard sitting between his mother and sister, his blond hair gleaming in the gentle gas light, the shadows of his sharp features emphasized by the whiteness of his stiff collar. Tomorrow would be her last chance to reach him. If she were to leave and never see him again, she wanted one more chance to learn what had gone wrong in the friendship she held so dear. "If you really don't care for racing, Livvy, perhaps you would be willing to greet Mr. Merriott. I believe I will be guided by your Great-aunt Lavinia's advice."

Later, in her room Jenny knelt down for her evening prayers. She found her attempt to reach God as futile as her attempt to reach Richard. She tried to pray for her friends. She tried to pray for her country, as she had ever since the earl had opened her eyes to the need for the land to see a great revival, for the Lord to raise up a torchbearer who would light spiritual fires in all the languishing, barren places. But tonight all the windows of heaven were shut. She fell into her childhood pattern of asking a rote blessing on all her family, ending with "and God save the queen." She slipped between her covers. In spite of the thickness of the featherbed, however, she shivered long in the darkness.

★ ★ ★ ★ ★

The next morning, though, she was determined to be her brightest. She opened the door of her room just enough to bring in her shoes, freshly polished by Cory the boot boy the night before. If this was to be her last day with Richard, she would do her best to make it a good one, no matter what his restraint. She would wear her brown velvet suit with the white silk blouse. It was from the House of Creed and was the most elegantly tailored garment she had ever owned. The fitted jacket, ornamented only with a row of gold buttons, flared wide over the fullness of her skirt, and the sleeves had wide cuffs over the gathered silk at her wrists. She had Martha arrange her hair, which just matched the deep chestnut fabric, with extra smoothness. This would offset the stylish brimmed hat with its curling feather plume, which was certain to outshine all the ordinary bonnets around.

It seemed that Richard had set himself to be a good host that day as well. As the coachman Hexam drove the Victoria at a brisk pace the twenty miles southeast to Rugeley, he told her something of the history of the area and its landmarks, instructing Kirkham to point out various parks, churches, and stately homes as they passed them.

They took luncheon at the Rugeley Arms Inn, which seethed with the enthusiasm of the race-course crowd: stable owners, moneylenders, professional bettors, hangers-on. Richard requested a private parlor, but the best the host could offer him was a private table in the back dining room, which was already filled nearly to capacity. Even this room rang with arguments over which horses were surest to win and boastings of the great fortunes that well-placed bets would bring.

"I am sorry, Jenny. I shouldn't have brought you here. I hadn't realized it would be quite so raucous." Richard leaned across the table to speak to her.

Jenny's heart leaped. It was the first time he had called her Jenny since her coming north. But this was hardly the place to discuss their relationship or the deeper questions that had filled her thoughts since she had spoken to Shaftesbury. This place was entirely given over to racing fever, and there could be no fighting it. Richard's hand rested on the table. She touched it lightly. "It is very stimulating, Dick. Don't worry. After all, there is little left to shock one who has nursed soldiers."

A serving girl brought their steak pie and vegetables. Since Kirkham was eating in the public room, Jenny wondered whether she should offer to help Richard. But then she saw that he was doing very well—surely far better than a few months ago. Did he really see better, or was he simply becoming more accustomed to not seeing?

As if in reply to her thoughts, Dick smiled at her. "If you would consider a compliment from a blind man, I should tell you that I think your suit is very elegant. The velvet feels exquisite."

"Thank you. That is a compliment I value." Her immense pleasure rang in her voice. Perhaps she could approach deeper subjects even here. Had she only imagined the barrier between them?

But then a deep, raspy voice at the next table took her attention. "Well, gentlemen, I assume you have all placed your money on Windflyer. I can tell you my horse won't let you down. Your fortunes shall be made."

"Your horse? Coke says the animal's his."

"Yes, yes. My partner is a bit inclined to overspeak himself, but he's a fine hand with horses. Can't complain about the work at his stable, so I let him take his share of the credit and beyond."

Then Jenny recognized the voice. "Dick, that's Dr. Pannier. We should say hello." She turned, then cried out in surprise as a familiar tow-headed figure darted across the busy room, dodging waiters, dogs, and gesticulating diners. "Josh, you do show up in the most surprising places!" she cried.

"'ullo, miss. Got to find the guv. Coke's sick." He swiveled his head, looking every direction until he saw the table behind Jenny. "Oh, Guv'nor!" He darted to Pannier. "Coke's powerful sick. It's the indigestion again. 'e's upstairs on 'is bed. 'e needs more of 'is medicine."

"In bed?" Pannier sent his chair crashing backwards as he jumped up. "He should be at the track! Thank goodness I brought my medicines. Don't worry, gentlemen, Windflyer will run. And he will win. Your money rides safe on him," Pannier announced to the table as he hurried out behind Josh.

"So Dr. Pannier is Josh's employer!" Jenny watched the departing figures.

"And Coke's friend," Dick added. "Interesting."

They were still digesting this revelation when Kirkham entered to suggest that they get on to the track. And, indeed, they started none too early, for all the way was heavily congested.

The race course just outside of town was more crowded and noisier than the inn. Country squires, punters, touts, and tic-tac men crowded the wooden rail lining the track. At the end near the finish line, however, a small covered stand offered seats for the gentry. Dick and Jenny left Kirkham standing at the rail and found a place in the stands. Uncertain how much Dick saw of the proceedings, Jenny kept up a lively narrative of the first two races, caught up herself in the excitement of the cheering and the sense of power and speed as the horses swept by. "Oh, Dick, they're beautiful!" She grabbed his arm. "The winner was named Jigger. He must be a potter's horse."

A fresh group of horses paraded past the stands on their way to the starting gate, the announcer calling their names. "Oh, there's Windflyer. Number six." Jenny pointed. "Dick, he's beautiful. Taller than all the others. Black with one white forefoot and a star on his forehead." She grabbed her companion's arm. "Dick, can you see him at all? He's absolutely magnificent."

Dick didn't answer her, but he turned to follow the direction of the parade. In a few minutes the horses were behind their gates, under starter's orders. Jennifer held her breath. The gun fired. Windflyer took the lead immediately, a full jump ahead of the other horses. The field streaked down the track.

"Windflyer!"

"Come on, boy!"

"Go, go!"

The stands roared and shook with the shouts of the crowd and the pounding of the horses' hooves. Windflyer held his lead, his proud head stretched forward, his long legs outstripping all contenders.

"Windflyer!" "Windflyer!" It seemed that everyone at the race had money riding on that starred head.

Windflyer crossed the line a full length ahead of the nearest contender. Jennifer grabbed Richard. "Dick, it was wonderful! I've never seen such an animal."

But it was Kirkham, grabbing his other arm, that Dick turned to. "Did you see 'im, sir? I mean, even from here, could you tell? It's 'im. I'm sure."

Dick was very quiet in the tumultuous crowd as he asked, "Who?"

"Legend. Sure as I know my own face in the mirror. Windflyer is Legend."

"Are you certain? I had an impression, but I couldn't be sure. It's been more than a year, Kirkham."

"Come on. Touch him. You'll know. And so will he."

Kirkham urged them toward the winner's circle where the horse was already encircled by officials and jubilant supporters.

They were almost to the circle when the sound of a hunting horn made every head turn toward the official booth. The announcer's voice rang out over the suddenly quiet crowd. Officials of the Jockey Club had ruled. Windflyer had jumped the gun. He was disqualified. Darrow's Pride, the second-place horse, was declared winner.

An angry roar grew around them until Jennifer feared the mob might begin throwing something heavier than their torn-up betting stubs. But Richard paid no attention to the crowd as Kirkham cut a way to the now-displaced horse.

A larger crowd milled around the disbarred winner than around Darrow's Pride. The jockey in his green and purple silks stood beside the tall black horse. All around them people shouted and gestured angrily.

Dick stopped and gave a whistle that cut through the roar. "Legend. Is that you, boy? Come on."

The sharp black ears pricked forward. The starred head rose. The horse gave a soft whinny. Ignoring the jockey holding him on a loose rein, Legend moved forward and nuzzled Dick's palm.

Jennifer's vision blurred with tears as she watched Dick stroke the long, powerful neck and run his hand down the glossy mane. She couldn't hear the words, but she could hear Dick's voice murmuring softly.

"Here, now. What's the meaning of this? What are you doing to my horse, sir?" Pannier's voice growled over all the other noise.

"Your horse, Dr. Pannier? I think not. But I should be most interested in hearing how he came into your possession." Richard turned to face Pannier, but he did not take his hand from Legend's bridle.

Pannier opened his mouth to answer, but just then Josh came tearing through the crowd, literally shoving at the legs of people in his way. "Guv'nor, Guv'nor, come quick! Coke's took that bad." He grabbed Pannier's well-tailored coattails. " 'urry, or it may be too late."

"Richard, I should go with them. They may need a nurse." Richard started to protest, but Jennifer darted after the doctor.

Josh led them through a maze of carriages and wagons to the stables behind the racetrack. Before they were halfway along the row, Jenny could hear sharp cries and groans from one of the middle stalls. Coke lay huddled on the straw, a pool of his own vomit beside him. "Bring fresh straw, Josh," Jenny ordered.

With a renewed cry Coke clutched at his stomach as if he would tear out his own bowels. Pannier knelt beside him. "I left my bag in the gig. There is nothing I can do."

"Chalk or magnesia mixed into a cream with a little water." Jennifer's reply came as a rote response. But where were they to get magnesia at a racetrack? Even as she watched, the victim was gripped by a violent spasm, arching his body backward. In all her nursing experience Jennifer had never seen such severe rigidity of muscles. "Warm water, Josh. And blankets. It is the best we can do."

Josh dashed off to grab a horse blanket from the next stall. Before he could return, another seizure gripped Coke's body, pulling his carrot-red head backward almost to his heels.

Coke fought for a breath that shook his whole frame. His body spasmed. Then he lay silent. Even in death his body retained the shape of a bow.

Josh handed the blanket to Pannier, who covered his former partner. The doctor shook his head. "I could do nothing."

An elderly local physician whom someone had fetched from the stands came forward. "May I be of service? I am a doctor."

"As I am." Pannier stood to shake hands with him. "You are too late, Doctor, but you could have done nothing. My friend died of apoplexy."

Leaning on his stick, the white-haired doctor peered at the contorted body through rheumy eyes and nodded. "Ah, yes. A sad affair, indeed. Apoplexy, you say? I shall so certify. Yes, very sad."

Pannier pumped his hand vigorously. "Yes. Yes, you do that. We must leave it in the hands of the officials now. Yes, apoplexy." Pannier suddenly seemed in a hurry to leave. "Josh! Where are you, boy? Come."

Josh stood unmoving, staring at the body. "I give 'im the medicine like you said, Guv. Honest, it weren't my fault!"

"Come along, Josh." Pannier grabbed his hand and pulled him roughly away.

Jennifer couldn't believe what she had just seen and heard. She had observed only two cases of death by apoplexy in the Crimea, but neither of them looked the least like this. It looked much more like the poisonings she had witnessed. Most had been from bad food, but there had been more than one case of strychnia poisoning among the Turks when careless workers ingested rat poison. She didn't understand how an experienced doctor could make such a mistake. She must speak to him about it. "Dr. Pannier—"

But he had disappeared in the crowd, dragging Josh behind him.

"Dr. Pannier!" She looked to her right and left, undecided as to which way to go.

"Here, Miss Jennifer—this way!" Ahead of her Kirkham motioned toward a line at the betting windows. "He went to that window. Come on, I must talk to him about Legend."

They pushed through the crowd until they reached the window just behind Pannier. Jennifer blinked in amazement as she saw him turn in his tickets. This man claimed ownership of the horse he called Windflyer. She had heard him urge all in the inn to place their money on Windflyer. And yet he had bet on Darrow's Pride, which had paid off at tremendous odds. Pannier left the window with his breast pocket bulging.

Jennifer drew back, trying to make sense out of what she had seen, but Kirkham challenged him.

"Here now, what's this? You had your money on Darrow?"

Pannier pulled himself up and gave Kirkham a supercilious look. "I always hedge my bets. Any experienced punter will tell you it's a wise policy—as you can see. This way I more than made up for my losses on Windflyer." Pannier pushed away from them with Josh in tow.

Jennifer and Kirkham found Richard outside the winner's circle still holding Legend over the protests of Coke's stable lad. Jenny ran to him. "Richard, we must talk."

"Stay with Legend," Dick ordered Kirkham. He offered his arm to Jenny, and they went back to the privacy of the Victoria.

"I don't understand—Pannier was so clearly touting Windflyer in the inn. And yet he had his own money on Darrow's Pride." Jenny pressed her hand to her forehead as she told Dick what they had seen at the betting window and what Pannier had said to Kirkham.

Dick nodded. "That's easy enough—he drove the odds

down on his own horse and drove them up on the horse he meant to bet on."

"Yes, but that would only work to his advantage if he knew Windflyer would lose."

"Or that the horse would be disqualified, which is somewhat easier to arrange. For example, by instructing the jockey to jump the gun." Suddenly Dick's frown broke into the broadest smile Jennifer had ever seen on his face. "Yes! And when the Jockey Club hears about that and the fact that Legend was confiscated from the Crimea, they'll certainly affirm my ownership."

"But how could Pannier have taken him from the battlefield? He was working in the hospital on the other side of the Black Sea."

"He didn't. Coke did. He was right beside me in the charge."

Jenny thought for a moment. "Yes, that makes sense. But the 'surplus' supplies at the market—Pannier must have been the one to get his hands on those somehow."

Dick nodded. "He probably bribed an official. I believe that's what you heard him and Gavin fighting about just before Gavin was shot."

Jenny grabbed her companion's arm. "Dick, you don't think Pannier . . ."

Dick shrugged. "It seems possible—even likely. But it could never be proved."

Jenny paced a few steps. "It just doesn't seem possible. Pannier is so respectable. A doctor. The hardest-working member of the Health Department. I've seen him myself treating cholera in the slums, inspecting brothels . . ." She stopped suddenly. Or was he? "Richard, I've heard that much of the worst slum property is owned by wealthy citizens who profit from the sweatshops and worse."

"Yes. I take your meaning. Few landlords would be so brazen as to show their faces to collect their own rents, but Pannier had a perfect excuse as Public Health Department doctor." Dick thought for a moment. "That's something that *could* be proven."

"Yes, and it would cause him embarrassment. But it's not illegal to own slum property."

"No, but we might at least get a few brothels closed and the mission and Brigade Home reopened."

Jennifer grabbed Dick's hand. "Yes! We must go to London. Tell Shaftesbury everything. He'll know what to do." Then she realized she had yet to tell the most startling revelation of all. "But, Dick, that's not all. You stayed with Legend. You don't know about Coke." She recounted the scene in the stable.

Dick put both hands on her shoulders and seemed to peer at her as intently through his dark glasses as if he could see her clearly. "Pannier gave Coke medicine at the inn. Coke died a few hours later in the stable. And you're certain it wasn't apoplexy?"

"I'm certain."

"Then we must find a policeman."

"Yes, we must. Dick, I'm worried about Josh. He's seen everything, even if he doesn't understand it. Pannier will realize he can't allow the boy to be questioned." Jenny saw again Pannier's viselike grip on the thin wrist as he dragged the boy through the crowd. A heavy coldness grew in her throat. "Dick, Josh is in danger."

She struggled to think clearly, her mind in a whirl. Where would they have gone? Back to the Rugeley Arms? Surely not to London. Then she remembered. "Josh said Pannier was staying at the Market Inn." She looked around for help. "Dick, what shall we do? I can't drive."

"I can, Jenny." He took off his dark glasses and blinked at the grayness of the cloudy late afternoon. "On gloomy days, I seem to need these less and less."

Then he reached to unhitch the quiet-standing bays.

"Dick?" Jenny put a hand on his arm.

"Do you trust me, Jenny?"

"Yes." She would have said more, but the lump in her throat stopped her. She took his hand, and he pulled her on to the driver's seat beside him.

Twenty

Pannier had a considerable head start, but traffic on the New-castle road was thinner now that most of the racing crowd had left. Also, the strips of fog that swirled up from the River Trent and the evening dimness closing in would not be the disadvantage to Dick that it was to drivers who relied less on senses other than sight.

Jenny was amazed at his skill as he kept the pair's speed steady, although the horses were so well trained they could have probably made their way on their own. As they sped along the road, Jenny kept careful watch for any place Pannier could have turned out or stopped at an inn, though that seemed unlikely. With every cart and wagon they overtook, she looked carefully at driver and passengers. Pannier, though, would certainly be driving the smart gig she had seen in Newcastle, and they encountered no such vehicle.

Jennifer could see the intensity of Richard's concentration and did not want to distract him with conversation. So she prayed.

It was dark by the time they reached the Market Inn. The wheels of the carriage rang hollowly on the empty cobbled street. Patches of gold shone through the fog from the gas lights lining the now-deserted Stones. The parlor of the inn was vacant. A bored-looking young man came in from the dining room when Jenny rang the bell on the counter. "You have a doctor staying here? I need to see him." Jennifer ran her hand over her forehead as if she were feeling faint.

"Room five. Top of the stairs, hall to the right." The youth turned back to his serving.

Hand-in-hand, Jenny and Dick ran up the stairs. They paused in the narrow hall outside the dark door with a white number five on it. Small whimpering sounds came from the room.

"It's Josh," Jenny whispered.

"Drink it, boy." Pannier's gravelly voice was distinct.

"No!" Josh's whimpers turned to an alarmed cry. "It's wot you give Coke. I saw what 'appened to 'im."

The smacking sound of a hard slap was followed by a sharp cry.

Jenny beat on the locked door. "Josh!"

Richard pushed her out of the way and shoved his shoulder against the door. It didn't give. He stood on the other side of the narrow hall with his back against the wall and kicked at the door with well-aimed blows of his boot. The lock burst on his third strike.

They rushed into the room. It was empty. Lace curtains blew at the open shutters. Jenny ran to the window and leaned out. She heard the clatter of feet jumping from the iron stairway to the cobbles below.

Dick put a hand on her shoulder and pulled her back. "Get a constable, Jenny. I'll follow them." He stepped through the window.

She stood for a second. *Go for a constable? Where?* And how would she find Dick if she did locate an officer?

She heard the clatter of boots on the fire escape. She didn't care what Dick told her to do. Everything within her screamed to be with him.

Jenny gathered her skirt and all but plunged through the window. "Dick! I'm coming!"

The fog swirled heavily around the fire escape, making the steps wet and slick. Jenny grabbed the rail and clattered down. Her heart was beating so loudly she could hardly hear Dick's feet just ahead of her in the night.

As she ran, she wasn't certain whether she was hearing Dick or Pannier. Occasionally a cry from Josh assured her that Pannier had not escaped altogether. But most of the time Jennifer felt she was rushing headlong into thick, damp nothingness.

At last a breeze swirled the fog aside. She saw Richard a few yards ahead of her. "Dick!" She plunged ahead and caught his arm.

"Jenny, I told you to stay back." Even as he protested, he thrust ahead in the blackness.

"I don't want to lose you." She held on tightly. As the fog closed in again, her only contact with reality was the warmth and firmness of Dick's hand.

The velvet skirt of her suit became heavy with damp. She clutched at a handful of the thick fabric and held it high, wishing she could take it off. Her foot struck an uneven paving stone, and she lurched against Dick. He reached to steady her with his other hand, but he never broke his steady, long-legged stride.

Once again Josh cried in the blanketed night ahead of them. The smack of a sharp blow followed. At least they hadn't lost their quarry. But they seemed no closer.

What if they passed them in the dark? What if they reached them too late? Where was Pannier going? She knew nothing about the lay-out of Newcastle. But Dick did. And in the dark a man used to relying on feel and hearing rather than on sight was at an advantage. All she could do was rely on him. And God. She tried to pray, but her thoughts made little sense.

Suddenly Dick stopped. Had he lost them? She had heard nothing for several moments—or for much longer. "Dick?"

"Listen," he whispered back urgently.

She could hear nothing. Then she heard. A soft lapping of water. "The river?"

She sensed, rather than saw, Dick shake his head. "Longport Canal. There would be no better place to dispose of a body. I think we're on the bridge." Jennifer held her hand out as they inched forward. The stone capping the brick wall was cold and wet when she found the edge. And her heart was as cold and heavy. She knew what Pannier planned. And if anyone ever found the body, who could prove it wasn't an accident? There would be no eyewitnesses. She could only be a few yards from Pannier, and yet she could see nothing.

It was just the tiniest scrabbling sound. Jennifer would never have heard it had Dick not tensed. She followed him to her left, edging along the waist-high wall. They had gone some distance when Dick stopped. She, too, felt something was wrong. Surely they had gone too far. Had they passed Pannier in the dark? Dick took her elbow and led her across the bridge. They had been searching the wrong side.

Just as they reached the far wall, a flutter of breeze shifted the fog. A dark shape loomed in front of them. Solid and stocky, a figure in a dark cape struggled to lift a small wriggling, flailing form over the wall.

As if they had planned it, Jennifer flung herself forward and reached for the boy at the same moment Dick lunged at Pannier. Jennifer felt her hands close on Josh's arm and shirt. She clutched the small boy to her as the men struggled on the bricks at her feet.

"Another spoonful, young man. No arguing."

"Auntie GAL," Richard protested, but in the end he lapped every drop of tonic from her spoon.

"And you're next, young lady." Jenny knew better than to argue. "As one of Miss Nightingale's nurses, you don't need anyone to assure you of the efficacy of sulphur and molasses."

"Yes, Miss Greyston." Jennifer closed her eyes and swallowed the foul-smelling, bitter-tasting black liquid.

"What the pair of you meant, getting soaked and chilled to the bone, I can't think."

"They was rescuin' me. Coo—you should 'a been there. I thought I was a goner." Even wrapped in a thick blanket, Josh's teeth still chattered.

"Hold still, young man." Josh held a hand to his mouth as Great-aunt Lavinia's spoon descended toward him, but there was no defense. "Cannock, you may take him to Martha. Tell her to bathe him with hot water and my best lye soap."

Josh made protesting noises as the butler pulled him to his feet, but at the doorway he called over his shoulder. "It were a right fair scrapple, eh wot?"

"Well, now." Great-aunt Lavinia turned back to Richard and Jennifer. "So after all that chasing, you turned this murderer, kidnapper, and what all else he may be over to the constable and came back to Greystoke Pitchers like two drowned rats."

"That's about the size of it, Auntie GAL." Dick grinned at her.

"Well, don't let your success in rescuing that boy put you above yourself. You still have a great deal to answer for, young man. In my day gentlemen did not involve young ladies in a ruckus like this."

"I'm afraid I involved myself, Miss Greyston."

A sharp rap of the walking stick told Jenny she had made a mistake in calling Great-aunt Lavinia's attention to herself. "Nor did young ladies of good repute attend horse races."

Jenny's jaw dropped.

"Be fair, Vina." From the other side of the drawing room Charlotte Eccleson raised her lorgnette at her elder sister.

"You're the one who told the girl to go to the races."

"Of course I was. Always wanted to go when I was her age, but Mama wouldn't let me. You have spunk, girl. I like you. But as for you, young man—"

As she turned back to Richard, the door slammed loudly, followed by the clump of boots on the tile floor of the hall and a sharp bark.

"George, we can smell that animal before we see him. And your boots are muddy."

George ignored the matriarch of the Greyston family as he flung himself into a chair. "Beastly day. Thought I'd never get away from the pottery. What in the world did you say to Trenton, Richard? He was bombasting me with facts and figures about improved paint formulas and increased production. Since when is the factory any business of yours? Almost made me miss the race. Just got there in time to see my horse lose. Had a bundle on Windflyer. What a pretty mess." Bennett growled at Dick from under his master's legs as if the disaster at the race track had been Richard's fault.

But Great-aunt Lavinia did not mean to be disregarded. "George, I am most obliged to you for mentioning the matter of the pottery. I have an item of business I wish to discuss with Richard. As you do not care to hear it, I advise you to make a polite excuse for removing yourself, your muddy boots, and your smelly dog from the drawing room." Lavinia pointed toward the door with her walking stick. George obeyed.

Richard came to his feet as well. "Auntie GAL, I realize that my coming to Greystoke has caused nothing but trouble. I apologize—"

"Sit down, Richard," Lavinia ordered. Richard sat.

Jenny had a sudden thought. "Legend. George has been betting on Windflyer for months. Why didn't he recognize him?"

"Because George has the imagination of an unglazed teapot," Lavinia snapped. "It is for precisely that reason, Richard, that I have changed my will."

"Auntie GAL—"

"If George had been running the pottery in my papa's day, we would still be a domestic affair with the kiln behind the coalmaster's house. That's why I changed my will today. You shall be the one to inherit Greystoke Pottery, Richard. George is much better suited to running his wife's estate in Yorkshire."

The coal shifting on the grate was the only sound to follow Lavinia Greyston's stunning announcement. "Don't bother thanking me, young man. This is purely a business decision. Don't think I haven't been listening to everything that's been said here in the past week. Your father has done a tolerable job running the factory for me, but it is time for new blood."

Jenny pulled herself to her feet as if fighting her way from a confusing dream. Events had moved too fast. She didn't understand all the family connections, and her velvet suit was still wet in spite of the blazing fire. "That sounds like wonderful news, Miss Greyston. Richard, I congratulate you. But I know you have family business to discuss. Would you please excuse me to change my dress?"

She was halfway across the room when the door burst open and Livvy flew in. "Dick, there's a horse in the stable—it looks like Legend!"

Jennifer took one look at the stolid, familiar form behind Livvy and caught her breath. "Arthur. Hello. I had forgotten . . ." She made a groping motion with her hand. "Please excuse me. I must change." She fled from the room.

Jenny was immensely grateful to find Martha on the upstairs landing, just returned from installing a well-scrubbed Josh in bed in the bootboy's room. "Help me change,

Martha." Jenny felt unable to cope with even such a simple task as undoing the buttons of her jacket.

Jennifer had intended to put on something like her green merino and go back downstairs. It wasn't until Martha slipped her flannel nightgown over her head and tucked her shawl around her shoulders that Jenny realized the maid had prepared her for bed. "There now, miss. You just sit by the fire while I warm your bed for you." Martha pulled the bell and instructed the upstairs maid to bring a supper tray to Miss Neville. Then she turned to shovel some glowing coals into the long-handled brass bed warmer. Jenny suddenly realized how lovely it would be not to have to cope with anything else.

Thoughts of Richard and Arthur, of chasing Pannier and of going back to London all blurred in her mind as she sank against the warmed cushions and closed her eyes. There was still so much that had to be sorted out.

Twenty-one

"Good morning, miss." Jennifer blinked when Martha placed a tray on the bed. She had said morning, but surely this was her supper tray. Then the maid pulled the curtain, and the pale sunshine of a winter morning lit the room.

"What time is it, Martha?"

"Ten o'clock, miss. I hope you don't mind my waking you, but Lady Eccleson said it would be best, considering—"

"Ten o'clock? Oh, no. Has Mr. Merriott left yet?" Jennifer sat upright as quickly as she could without spilling her tea.

"Yes, miss, about two hours ago." Martha turned to lay out Jenny's lilac and beige cotton day dress trimmed with white-work embroidery.

Jenny groaned and leaned back against her pillows. Now how was she to get to London? She thought of yesterday's adventures with Richard—of the closeness of thought and action they had shared. If he returned to being distant again today, it would be all the harder to bear after such accord.

But staying in her room would solve nothing. She could not hide forever. After eating the soft-boiled egg and a bit of toast, she washed in the warm water Martha had brought and dressed quickly. She was hurrying down the hall toward the stairs when Dick stepped out of the library. The door had been standing open as if he were waiting for her. "Jenny, I must speak to you." He paused uncertainly. "Did you sleep well?"

"Yes, I did." Richard was dressed carefully, and his heavy blue glasses shaded his eyes, but Jenny had the impression that he had had none too much sleep.

"You have no ill effects from last night?"

She tried to cover her impatience. "Richard, I'm fine. What is it? You haven't been waiting here just to inquire about my health."

"Yes, I have. In a way, that is. I wanted to be the one to tell you." His voice was gentle. He stepped aside, ushering her into the still-curtained room. "Sit down, Jenny."

"Richard, I am fine. What would you tell me?"

"Jenny, please." He took her hands, led her to the sofa, and sat beside her. "It is Livvy." He paused. "I don't know how to tell you. That my own sister should be the one . . ."

"The one to what?"

"Jenny, Arthur and Livvy are married."

Jennifer stared. "Married? How is it possible?"

"I don't know. I cannot imagine how Arthur could have done such a thing to you, how Livvy—fully knowing of your attachment . . . She was very unhappy when I told her of your engagement, but I had no idea—"

"What are you saying? My attachment . . . What engagement?"

"Yours and Arthur's. How he could be so dishonorable? How you must be feeling—"

Jenny choked. For a moment she felt almost strangled. Then the joy rose in her throat. A gurgle of laughter surged out as she formed a picture of what must have happened. "Do you mean to say that Arthur and Livvy went all the way to Gretna Green and back on the train yesterday? That the stuffy Arthur Nigel Merriott *eloped* with your sister?"

"Yes, and after he told me only a few days ago that he was engaged to you."

Jenny wiped the tears of merriment streaming from her eyes. "I was most certainly never engaged to Arthur. Richard, what exactly did he say? Could you possibly have misunderstood?"

"You weren't engaged?" Dick thought for a moment. "It was on the train. He told me clearly he was engaged to be married and quite soon. Then he would stand for Parliament at the next election."

"But did he say he was engaged to me?"

Dick stumbled to his feet. "Oh, what a fool I've been. I was thinking of you, so when he said . . . Now I'm not sure what he said." He ran his hands through his pale curls. "What a mess I made of things."

"On the contrary, apparently you didn't make a mess at all. I'm sure Livvy and Arthur are very happy. Thinking she had a rival for Arthur's affections must have been just the thing to convince Livvy to elope." She paused to think. "Yes. They should do very well together. His seriousness and her lightness should be just the right balance." Then she giggled. "Have they gone to inspect a factory on their honeymoon?"

Dick, however, did not share her levity. "But, Jenny, your feelings . . ."

"My feelings are engaged elsewhere, sir."

Richard sat down again and took her hands. "Oh, Jenny, may I hope? You saved my life twice, you know, once at Scutari and again when you burst into my existence in London. But now—"

He dropped her hands and stood abruptly. "Jenny, I have no right to ask this—bumbling and scarred as I am. I have no assurance my sight will ever be anywhere near normal. I may spend the rest of my life stumbling around and hiding behind these odious dark glasses. It's no life I should ask you to share. But, Jenny, the truth of the matter is, I can't help myself. I don't want to spend the rest of my life groping in the dark without you." He sat beside her once again.

"We all see indistinctly in so many ways—and you have been so much clearer-sighted than I was about so many things." Jenny reached up and took his glasses off. She ran her fingers gently over his scarred forehead and around his eyes. "The future is a clouded mirror for everyone. But anything with you would be far better than living in the complete darkness of a world without you, Richard."

He took her hand in his and kissed her fingertips. Then he found his way to her lips.

That was the moment Aunt Lavinia chose to push open the double doors of the library. She stood regarding them, tapping her walking stick as they pulled apart slowly and smiled at her. She gave a satisfied nod. "About time too, I must say. I have never known you to be so slow before, Richard." She started to go, then stopped. "I thought you would like to know that I have engaged the services of a new bootboy."

"What about Cory?" Dick asked.

"It was past time he be moved up to footman. Besides, Josh puts a much better shine on my shoes than Cory ever did." She closed the door behind her.

But with the reminder of Josh and the world from which he had come, Jenny's bubble of euphoria burst. She sighed and leaned back on the sofa.

"Jenny, what is it? If you want more time to think—"

"No!" She sat upright and grabbed Richard's arm as if clutching a lifeline. "Oh, Dick, it's the dark I spoke of earlier. I've wanted to talk to you about it ever since that night at the concert, but there was never time. And now, when I should be so happy, when everything should seem so perfect—"

"Can you explain?"

Jenny took a deep breath and ordered her thoughts. "We have had such a victory, Richard. We put one criminal out of business; we paved the way to close a few brothels and rees-tablish a ragged school and mission; we—you—did the groundwork to reform one pottery and build model housing for forty-some workers and maybe half that many children. . . . But I've never felt more discouraged. Such victories show me the futility of our efforts. It was all we could do far more than we could hope to accomplish, and yet it is so little. The dirt, the vice, the evil is so overwhelming."

"But, Jenny, if everyone—"

"Oh, I know, that's what people always say—if everyone did their part—but, Richard, that's not the answer. We can never work hard enough."

Richard nodded. "You're right; we can't overcome evil with hard work. Love, joy, and peace are our only weapons against evil. But the results of evil—the dirt, the disease, the poverty—we can fight with food baskets, model housing, and parliamentary commissioning."

Jenny gave a weak little half smile. "It's just like all our scrubbing floors in Scutari—when the real problem was the rotting sewers under the floors. No scrub brushes in the world can rout out the heart of darkness—only the light of goodness can do that. I understand—but that's what's so dis-couraging. The Earl of Shaftesbury told me that night at the *Elijah* that we must wait for God to send the torchbearers. But waiting is so much harder work than scrubbing."

Dick, who knew something about waiting, had no answer for that, so he just held her in his arms.

Twenty-two

Jennifer and Richard had been back in London for more than two months. The glow of their successful adventures had lingered awhile in the city's gray fog, but the happy conclusion she expected to their mutual declaration of love had not developed. At times Jenny could recreate in her mind the closeness, the delight, the triumph of that night. But then the memory would fade.

She knew Richard was busy arranging legal affairs and, with Kirkham's aid, poring over yet more parliamentary reports preparatory to taking over the reform of Greystoke Pottery, but still she had expected him to renew talk of their future together.

And now matters had gone on so long that a certain awkwardness had set in. She could not initiate discussion of marriage plans without seeming unmaidenly, and she worried that Richard might be having second thoughts about his proposal when his eyesight was still precarious. It even seemed of late that he had been avoiding her.

If there was no talk of marriage plans, however, plenty of other discussion surrounded Jennifer. All England was abuzz with the revelations made almost daily in the *Times* and various broadsheets of the affairs of Dr. William Pannier. It seemed that in spite of all his financial shenanigans, he was deeply in debt. He had bet on many losing horses; his stable was mortgaged; he had borrowed more than £12,000 from moneylenders, who were pressing him for payment; he had even forged his mother's signature on certain papers designed to placate his creditors. And apparently he had purchased brothels with profit from graft he had committed in the Crimea.

The subjects of feeding and clothing the poor took second place even at Lady Eccleson's committee meeting as the latest revelations were analyzed over teacups. Jenny, however, shifted on her velvet chair. At last she and Richard were to go out today. The mission was to be rededicated. And she and Richard would attend. Alone. Perhaps today he would bring up the topic she so longed to discuss.

She took a sip from her gold-bordered cup and looked at the door for at least the tenth time in as many minutes. Where was Richard? He had been very specific. He had an early afternoon appointment but should be back shortly after the committee meeting convened. It had seemed a good idea to meet at Lady Eccleson's, but now Jenny fretted. Had her hopes for the day been only wishful thinking? Or perhaps she had been right in supposing Richard planned for them to have an important discussion but now had changed his mind. Where could he be?

"Blink again."

But Dick did not need to be told to blink. As Dr. Halston turned up the gas lamp, Dick's eyes flicked shut.

"Yes, the affection is still attended with photophobic pain about the orbit and sclerotic injection."

Dick made an impatient sound. Couldn't the man speak English? If one couldn't see, one could at least hope to hear something sensible.

Halston cleared his throat. "That is, light-induced pain in the sclerotic membrane, which is the hard outer case of the globe, and the sclerotic tunic—which you would call the white of the eye—causes the lids to close spasmodically. Perhaps we should give it a little longer. After this period of time, however, I had hoped—"

"Yes, Doctor, I had hoped as well." Richard thrust on his thick bottle-bottom glasses and tall black hat with equal impatience and strode from the room, not even pausing when his hasty exit sent a small table crashing. He had no desire to hear whatever milksop comfort Halston might offer.

A number of cabs stood at the covered stand at the corner of Harley Street and Marylebone Road, but Richard was too agitated to ride. He must think. He hesitated. He should turn toward Portland Place where Jennifer was waiting for him at Aunt Charlotte's. But that was only a few streets away. He needed more time.

He had been so determined. He knew the procedure well enough. Halston had done it many times in the past eighteen months. Dick had made up his mind. He would *not* cry out when the light flared up before his eyes. He *would* hold his eyes open against the glowing mantle of the lamp. Well, he had made no sound. One could control that. But the reflex of his eyelids was beyond his mastery.

Richard turned his back on Portland Place. Regent's Park. One might wander there for hours on its broad walks and circles. He had sensed Jennifer's impatience when he did not again take up the matter of their marriage. He should have spoken weeks ago, at least to warn her that all might not be the fairy tale ending they both desired. He should have told her of his fears. But it was easier to remain silent and hope.

Hope and plan for this day—the day when Halston would proclaim miraculous progress, when he and Jenny would rejoice together in the reopening of the mission. The day when— A hoop rolled by a small boy careened in front of him. He tangled in it and all but fell.

"What's the matter, Guv'nor? You blind?"

★ ★ ★ ★ ★

Jennifer shook her head at Branman's offer to refill her teacup. Richard would come soon. Surely.

Col. Biggar harumphed and twitched his curling moustache. "The *Times* said this morning they've granted that Pannier fellow a change of venue—whatever that is. Newfangled nonsense. Seems feeling in Staffordshire is running so high against the scoundrel he can't get a fair trial there. Moving it to the Old Bailey."

Miss Joye Bales nodded her blonde curls. "Yes, Papa read us the account this morning. It does seem strange though that none of the experts can decide what that poor Mr. Coke died of. Self-generating tetanus does sound like such an odd notion, don't you think?"

Her sister Grace stirred another spoonful of sugar into her cup. "What do you think, Miss Neville? You've had medical experience. Some have suggested epilepsy or angina pectoris. Does the matter sound like one of those to you? Surely it wasn't strychnia poisoning. Oh, do say."

"What?" Jenny started at hearing her name. "Poison? Oh—"

"No, no. Arachnitis—inflammation of the spinal membrane, the *Times* said," Col. Biggar interrupted. "One can always rely on the *Times*."

"Well, it's certainly a scandal, whatever the cause. Public Health official profiting off slum property. Not at all the thing." Lord Selbourne spoke from the other side of the room. "And the brouhaha over the evidence—unthinkable that such things could happen in England."

"I suppose they just meant to be considerate to the fellow —professional courtesy, innocent until proven guilty and all that." The colonel paused to clear his throat. "But allowing the accused to participate in the autopsy does seem to be going beyond the bounds of fair play."

"Someone certainly went beyond fair play," Mrs. Biggar murmured from her corner.

"Quite right, quite right, my dear. Tampering with the evidence—not at all the thing to do." Col. Biggar picked up his wife's thought and ran with it. "Jostling the doctors who were extracting organs, breaking the seals on the specimen bottles, bribing the post boy to upset the fly carrying the evidence to the London train—not at all what one expects of British justice. We would have never borne with it when I was out in India. Did I tell ever you about the Ghurka uprising in '32?"

"Yes, dear, I believe you did." But Mrs. Biggar was drowned out by Lady Eccleson calling the meeting to order. Jennifer was glad for an end to the discussion of Dr. Pannier. She could not think of him without recalling the suffering this one man had caused.

If one person totally sold out to evil could do so much harm, surely one sold out to truth could accomplish even greater good. She thought of the earl—certainly an example. Once again she glanced toward the door. They would miss the earl's speech if Richard didn't come soon.

Around her flowed a lively debate as to whether to open a home for fallen women in the Limehouse district or to promote the work of the existing Society to Return Girls to Their Homes in the Country. But Jennifer did not follow it closely. Such good works were desperately needed, but what about the wider, more desperate need for all society to be renewed?

She recalled the Scripture Charles Spurgeon had quoted —the promise that had given her so much hope. Like Jennifer, the prophet had cried out, "How long, O Lord, how long?" And the answer had come: "The vision is yet for an appointed time . . . though it tarry, wait for it; because it will surely come; it will not tarry."

Jennifer set her teacup aside with a clatter. She would not tarry either. If Richard Greyston did not appear to escort her, she would go alone.

"Please secure me a cab, Branman."

She was descending the stairs when a tall, lanky figure with military bearing rounded the corner. She opened her mouth to upbraid him for his tardiness but stopped when she saw the tight set of his mouth. She had not known Richard to withhold that much tension and pain since Scutari.

She ran forward and grabbed his hand. "Come. I have a cab. We'll be late."

Richard started to resist. He had been certain he had delayed long enough. He was sure she would be gone by now. This ceremony was so important to her, and she hated being late. Why was she still here? He tried to withdraw his hand but felt himself being propelled forward. And even as he contended against the feeling, he was glad she was here. Glad to be in the cab with Jennifer.

The vehicle lurched and swayed as Jenny urged the cabby to hurry. The rattle and clatter of London's traffic and the calls of street vendors made conversation difficult. Richard was thankful, for he did not want to speak yet. He must tell Jennifer the decision he had reached. But not yet. He would not spoil the occasion for her. She was an amazing woman. She had not uttered one word of reproach for his lateness. But he could take advantage of her good nature no longer. He would speak this evening. He must. Explain all his hopes and their extinguishing. Then he would make a clean break and return to Newcastle for good after the meeting.

Jenny kept her eyes peeled as the cab jostled its way down Tothill Road. She was so anxious for her first sight of the evidence of their success. The cab lurched around a corner, and she grabbed Richard's arm. "Oh, there it is! It's grand."

The mission sign, larger than the one that had been taken down to make way for Pannier's brothel, welcomed them with gleaming white letters. Mrs. Watson bustled out breathlessly, exuding cheerful energy as she hurried them in. ". . . and sakes alive, the ragged school enrollment has nearly doubled in just these few days—and us not even officially opened yet. Come on in, you two. I've saved you seats down front, but it wasn't easy, what with everyone wantin' to get close to the earl as they do."

Jennifer and Richard slipped onto a narrow wooden bench while the congregation concluded the opening hymn led by Mr. Walker. Applause echoed in the room when the Earl of Shaftesbury rose. "My friends, you have done well; you have done excellently well in the work here. God has blessed you and those you minister to, and He will continue to do so."

Applause again. It was a triumphant occasion. Only Jenny and the man seated so close to her knew the true scope of the victory that brought them to this moment. And yet as the earl continued, with every word he spoke, the weight of discouragement that she had felt for so many weeks, even months now, increased. It even overrode her concern for Richard. Almost. Something was very wrong, she knew. He had spoken barely more than five words.

But now Shaftesbury recaptured her attention. "It is because of your very accomplishments that I feel constrained to warn you: Doing good isn't the most important thing—loving God and accepting His love is the heart of the matter. Then we can do good to others as a means of showing His love. That's the only way we will really accomplish anything. Building model housing and lecturing people on cleanliness is only washing the outside of the cup and leaving the inside dirty."

Shaftesbury looked directly at her. "Our need—England's need—is for national revival. We must work for the poor, but pray for the Spirit. Our efforts will never win. We cannot overcome evil in our strength, but the Lord can. Be steadfast and persevering, fully engaged in the work of the Lord. Your toil is not in vain when it is done in the Lord.

"God speaks to us today as He did to Moses: 'Before all thy people I will do marvels such as have not been done in all the earth, nor in any nation; and all the people among which thou art shall see the work of the Lord.' That is God's promise, and your part is to obey."

Jennifer nodded at the speaker's words. Yes, obey. Take the next step in faith—as Richard must take each step in faith, seeing through a glass darkly. And the time would come. A lightness flooded her. And yet at the same time, she felt the weight of longing more than ever before.

After the earl's closing prayer, everyone in the room began moving and talking, greeting old friends, rejoicing in the reopening of the Lord's work in a spot so nearly lost to the devil. But Jenny sat, still wondering how much longer they could hold out if God didn't send His torchbearer soon. The earl had told her long ago that they must go on stacking brushwood to be ready for the great fire the Spirit would light. But how long must they wait?

"Jennifer!" She turned at the sound of the sweetly musical voice.

"Oh, Miss Thompson, er, I mean, Mrs. Spurgeon." She laughed and embraced her friend. "I had not heard that you were returned from your wedding trip."

"Oh, yes, for quite ages and ages. We are the old married couple now."

But not so old that the bride had quit blushing, Jennifer noted.

"And your work at the chapel is going well?"

"Oh, you cannot imagine. We had already rebuilt the church once to accommodate the crowds that come to hear Charles preach, but every Sunday hundreds are turned away." She gave a small giggle. "My dear Charles says containing our congregation in New Park Street Chapel resembles attempting to put to sea in a teapot."

"It's no wonder. Your Charles is a fine preacher."

"Oh, yes. And you must come Saturday week to the Crystal Palace. Charles is preaching for the day of national fasting."

"I would like to very much. All London is talking about it. But I . . ." She glanced toward Richard. He stood aloof from the milling crowd. Waiting and silent. "I shall have to see."

She turned to Richard, her heart in her throat. The time had come. So many considerations had crowded her mind, but now her whole attention was his.

The sweet April evening greeted them as they stepped out of the mission. Jennifer was glad there were no cabs in sight. "The daffodils are in bloom in St. James's Park. Shall we walk there?"

St. James's was the oldest royal park in London and one of the most attractive, especially now that the trees lining the lake were so delicately frosted with spring green. They arrived at the bridge spanning the center of the lake just as the keeper began feeding the large array of ornamental waterfowl that lived there. Two gawky, long-beaked pelicans swooped low over their heads. Jenny jumped. "Oh, what alarming creatures. They say they are descended from those placed here by Charles II at his restoration."

Richard made no reply. And Jennifer remained silent. It was for Richard to initiate the topic so dear to her heart. They strolled on, by unspoken consent moving away from the sound of the band playing a lively march. Jennifer did not feel lively. And when Richard finally spoke, his words bore no animation. "Jennifer, I cannot tell you what pain it gives me to inform you that I shall be going forthwith to Newcastle. I do not intend to return anytime soon."

Jennifer felt only one piercing stab of pain. Then her own hurt was overcome by the agony in his voice as he continued. "I had hoped . . . I had believed . . ." He struggled for breath. "I called in Harley Street today. It seems that the intentions I declared in such haste at Greystoke are not to see fulfillment."

Jennifer started to protest. A resounding *no* rose inside her. She had waited so long for this conversation, but this was not what she wanted to hear. She clenched her fists to control her impulse to tremble. She would *not* cry.

A pelican plopped to a perch behind them. It sounded for all the world like a rat falling off a wall. She stiffened her spine and raised her chin. "I see, sir. You are informing me that your affections were not engaged as you led me to believe?"

"It's not a matter of my affections. It is a matter of my expectations. Dr. Halston was very apologetic."

So he had been with Dr. Halston. And the news had not been good. She caught her breath. He did so well, went about all his work with such confidence, needing so little help, that one forgot how severe his disability was, how he hated wearing the conspicuous blue lenses. And he had seemed improved. Perhaps it had been a matter of adaptation, not improvement. Perhaps his vision was worse. But in that case, he would need her all the more.

And she needed him for something far greater than seeing. She needed Richard for her very breath.

Across the park the band struck up the "March Militaire." Richard stood, as he had throughout the conversation, so stiffly she expected him to salute at any moment. It was a situation that called for giving orders. "Well, I am exceedingly disappointed to hear that you feel no warmth for me, Lt. Greyston. But the fact of the matter is that *my* affections were very *deeply engaged.* As an officer and a gentleman, you made certain commitments from which I cannot see my way clear to release you at the moment."

"Jennifer, you don't understand."

"On the contrary, I understand only too well. You think that because the announcement of our engagement has not yet appeared in the *Times*, it will be a small matter for you to cry off. You are very wrong in that. It is a matter of great significance to me."

But she miscalculated in bringing up how important Richard was to her. The stiff resolution that had carried her through so far began to slip away. She had no anger left to hold on to. She feared her knees would give way.

Fortunately, a sharp breeze blew across the lake at that moment, whipping the fringe of her mantle. "I am cold. I cannot discuss this further. You will please take me home."

Inside the cab it was all she could do to keep from flinging herself into his arms and sobbing. She longed to plead with him, to try to make him understand how little other considerations mattered next to their being together. She managed to avoid that. Just. But her voice was soft as she clasped his hands at the door. "Richard, do not go north yet. Please." She would have implored harder, but she sensed his weakening resolve. "The day of national fasting is Saturday. Please."

"Very well. We shall go to that together, Jennifer. But I would not have you take false hope. It will be best to make a clean end of things."

She started to protest, but he silenced her with a finger on her lips. "Jenny, I cannot marry you as I am."

And then she understood. The stone wall he had once spoken of—the one he felt he had ridden into at a full gallop, the one that had been so long in coming down but that they both thought breached with his pottery reform. The wall was back up. Rebuilt thicker and higher for its having so nearly come down.

Twenty-three

When Saturday arrived, Jennifer knew that her reprieve had ended. She had come to realize that because Richard was an officer and a gentleman, she might inveigle him to marry her by pleading or ordering. But by doing so, she would destroy the qualities she held most dear. If he were to come to her at all, it must be freely on his own terms.

The only way to approach the day was as if that evening in St. James's Park had not occurred. Nor those wonderful moments in the library at Greystoke Pitchers. She and Richard Greyston were friends. Very dear friends. They were attending a day of national importance together. A happy memory of their last time together might be the best she could ask for. She would do her best to make it so.

But once she put considerations for her own happiness behind her, she found other reasons for concern. Primarily Dick's comfort. Even his safety. What would the Crystal Palace with all its panes of glass be to a man with photophobia? What if the morning's gentle clouds should disappear, and it should turn out to be a brilliant day? Richard had explained nothing to her. Was he in danger of severe pain? Of increased damage to his eyes? Did this excursion contain a potential threat to any hope of restoring his vision or their relationship?

But as Lady Eccleson's smart carriage rolled across Tower Bridge and on south of London, Richard seemed to share Jennifer's intention that their last day together be pleasant. He filled the time by recounting his having heard Spurgeon preach years before when he was a gownsman at Cambridge.

"Word of the boy preacher had reached our skeptical ears at university. I was less than enthusiastic about going, but it was a bright spring morning, and it was a pleasant ride along a country road to the village of Waterbeach." He smiled at the memory. "The lad in the pulpit was no more than eighteen, as verdant green a bumpkin as one could hope to see. The chapel, a former barn with whitewashed walls and thatched roof, was filled to overflowing. And when he began preaching, it was easy to understand why . . ."

Richard continued, and Jennifer smiled and murmured responses, but she was not listening. She was worrying. Her brow furrowed, she took frequent furtive glances upward. The sky hung a pale blue-gray, giving hope that it would darken. But what if it didn't? What if the clouds cleared instead?

And it did seem to be growing brighter by the time they reached Sydenham in South London. All eyes lifted to the gigantic glass and steel structure that had been built for the Great Exhibition and reassembled here in 1852. Then they alighted from the carriage, and Jenny held tightly to Dick's arm as they moved through the vast throng. He advanced confidently, but she was determined to be close by should he need to close his eyes against a sudden burst of sunlight.

They had no sooner found seats in the vast crowd than the powerful organ made the vaulted roof vibrate with "A Mighty Fortress Is Our God." But Jennifer did not sing with the throng. Instead, she listened to the words of the great hymn: "Our Helper He, amid the flood of mortal ills prevailing . . ." And she realized how, in the pain and confusion of the past days, she had failed to turn to that Helper, either for herself or for Dick.

"Did we in our own strength confide, our striving would

be losing . . ." Jenny closed her eyes in silent prayer.

Now she realized how she had lost sight of the larger picture—of her place in God's work on earth, in London, in Tothill. Her heart had looked for too much from Richard. She might never have him back. But she could go on as long as she did not lose that most vital of all relationships. "The Spirit and the gifts are ours thro' Him who with us sideth . . ."

She opened her eyes and looked around at the ardent faces. The longing she had felt so intensely for the welfare of her country and the poor returned also. Now her desire to see a spiritual awakening returned also. And here were thousands of others who had gathered under this great crystal dome for the same goal. They needed a miracle. Surely it would not be much longer. *Please, God.*

The preacher took his place on the platform erected at the far end of the transept. He looked much as Jenny remembered him—rather stout, a round beardless face, dark straight hair framing his boyish countenance. His manner appeared plain, perhaps even a little awkward. And his high black satin stock was decidedly unfashionable. In spite of his great success at the Park Street Chapel and his marriage to the accomplished Susannah Thompson, this was still the boy preacher of the fens, the young man who had filled the Sunday schools of Cambridgeshire villages with such enthusiasm that he attracted the attention of a London congregation.

When Charles Spurgeon began preaching, however, in that rich, powerful voice, all awkwardness disappeared. Jenny forgot everything else and fell as fully under his spell as the other 23,000 listeners. "We are gathered here in this great Palace built to symbolize the achievement of our age—the success of industrialization, the wealth and power of our nation. What better place to declare to you that we are also a nation of sinners? All around us we see people acquiescing to the faith. But that is the problem—such is not faith at all. It is mere assent.

"Assent is not saving faith. It will not save souls. It will not save our nation. All around us are unbelieving minds that have been blinded by the god of worldly success so that they do not see the splendor of the Gospel that shows forth the glory of Christ."

Jennifer gripped her hands so tightly her fingers ached. She wanted to pray, but the strength of her feeling blotted out any words her mind might form.

"I say to you that the time has come, the time for the kindling of true faith in the hearts of the people. It is time for those who have blinded themselves to the light of Christ to open their eyes. Christ must be our sun. Christ must be the center of our lives."

Please, God, a miracle.

"Let the name of the Lord be declared in Zion, for He will arise and have mercy on England. The appointed time has come."

Yes. Yes, so be it.

The service ended, but Jennifer sat, coming back as if from a long distance. Gradually the words of those around her penetrated her consciousness.

"Mr. Spurgeon was only ten years old when a godly man prophesied that he would preach the Gospel to thousands in Rowland Hill's Surrey Chapel. I understand he has done that." Lady Eccleson, who was sitting behind them, spoke to a gentleman Jennifer did not know.

Jennifer's mother joined in. "I have even heard Spurgeon called the Modern Whitefield."

"Comparisons to Whitefield and Hill are all very well," Lady Eccleson's friend said, "but I should style him the greatest preacher since the days of Saint Paul."

Jennifer couldn't believe what she was hearing. The great preacher that their day so needed, the voice crying in the wilderness that had not yet come to her own generation, the preacher like those of the past for whom she had prayed—God *had* sent His torchbearer.

The crowd moved on, but Jennifer's amazement held her. She had been so blind. God was working all the time, preparing the way, but she had seen only the problems, only the smallness of her own efforts. Her stumbling block had been her own lack of vision.

She turned to Richard, still sitting beside her in the emptying hall, waiting patiently behind his dark glasses. "Oh, Dick!" She grabbed his arm. "Wasn't it wonderful?"

As she spoke, the last cloud scudded away, and the sun shone in an aureole of light through the thousands of glass panes forming the building. Jenny gasped at the brightness and jumped to her feet. "Come. We must get you to a darker place."

Still holding his arm, she moved in front of him toward the aisle. Her one thought was to get Richard out of this shrieking, springing light.

Her very concern brought the disaster. As Richard rose, the fringe of her cloak caught on his glasses. Jenny pushed ahead, and her mantle ripped the protecting shades from his eyes. Jennifer gave a cry of alarm as they crashed to the floor. "Oh, no. No!"

For an instant she was back in Scutari as the final bandage dropped from Dr. Menzie's fingers. She saw the bright rays piercing the blue-gray eyes. She heard again Richard's cry.

She thrust her hands out to cover his eyes.

But he caught her wrists.

"Richard, what is it?"

He blinked and squinted against the light. His eyes watered. But he did not cry out in pain. He did not close his eyes.

Jennifer held her breath as Richard let go of her wrists and gently cupped her face in his hands. "Jenny, my dear Jenny. You are beautiful."

She smiled her joy. But her own eyes were too blurred with tears to see him clearly.

All around them the shimmering building vibrated as the organ pealed forth the postlude: "Arise, shine, for thy light is come, and the glory of the Lord is risen upon thee."

Afterword

Dr. Pannier's crimes are modeled on the celebrated case of Dr. William Palmer (who did not serve in the Crimea as far as I know). The Palmer trial was the first in history to be granted a change of venue. Palmer was hung at Stafford on June 14, 1856. At the sale of his stable one of his horses was purchased by Prince Albert.

Spurgeon's sermon at the Crystal Palace was actually delivered on October 7, 1857 (about a year and a half later than I have portrayed it). Not all the words I gave him here are taken from that sermon but are much in the spirit of his preaching.

New Park Street Chapel was empty when Charles Spurgeon began preaching there. Within a few months such crowds gathered to hear the twenty-year-old country lad preach that the chapel was enlarged. The remodeled chapel instantly proved too small. While his great tabernacle was being built, Spurgeon preached regularly to a congregation of 10,000 meeting in a music hall. In 1861 the Metropolitan Tabernacle was opened. Spurgeon preached there until his death, filling its 6,000 seats several times a week. The church also sponsored a pastors' college, an orphanage, and other charities, some of which continue to this day. More than 2,500 of Spurgeon's sermons were published, and many are considered classics of the faith. He and Susannah had twin sons, Charles and Thomas.

While the sweeping revival Jennifer envisioned had to wait another generation, the ministry of Charles Haddon

Spurgeon is often cited as part of the groundwork for the great reawakening that swept England and America in the late nineteenth century.

I have been a friend of All Souls for many years. Their vibrant work continues today in the heart of London and around the world.

—*DFC*

References

Altick, Richard D. *Victorian Studies in Scarlet.* (New York: W. W. Norton & Co., 1970).

Beeton, Isabella. *Mrs. Beeton's Book of Household Management.* (1861.) First edition facsimile (New York: Exeter Books, 1986). A treasury of remedies and recipes. Almost all medicines referred to in this book are based on Mrs. Beeton's suggestions.

Cook, Sir Edward. *The Life of Florence Nightingale.* 2 vol. (London: Macmillan and Co., 1914). Copious direct quotations from newspapers and letters.

Cook, Richard Briscoe. *The Wit and Wisdom of Rev. Charles H. Spurgeon.* (Baltimore: R. H. Woodward & Co., 1891).

Hodder, Edwin. *The Life and Work of the Seventh Earl of Shaftesbury, K.G.* 3 vols. (London: Cassell & Co., 1886). The authorized biography. Very complete.

Pollock, John. Shaftesbury, *The Poor Man's Earl.* (London: Hodder and Stoughton, 1985). Excellent. Most of my quotations of the earl's own words, especially in chapters 7 and 10, are taken from this source.

Selby, John. *Balaclava: Gentlemen's Battle.* (New York: Atheneum, 1970). Particularly helpful maps and pictures.

Spurgeon, Charles H. *All of Grace.* (Grand Rapids: Baker Book House, 1976). A collection of his sermons.

Woodham-Smith, Cecil. *The Reason Why.* (New York: E. P. Dutton, 1960). Gripping account of the charge of the Light Brigade.

_____. *Florence Nightingale.* (New York: McGraw-Hill, 1951). The definitive biography.